THE OFFICIAL

Tower of God

COLORING BOOK

S.I.U.

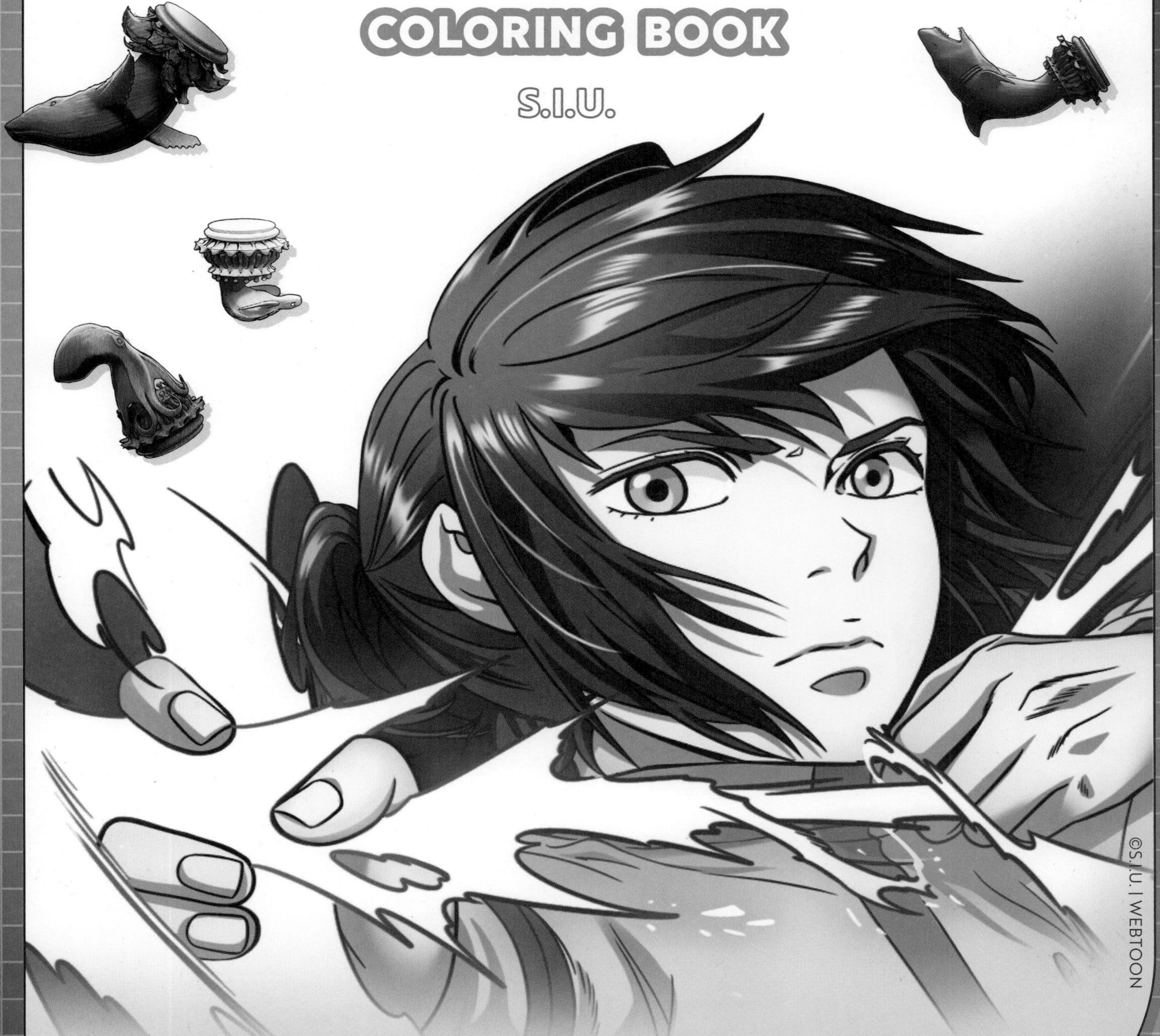
©S.I.U. | WEBTOON

Walter Foster

INTRODUCTION

Follow Twenty-Fifth Bam into the seemingly impenetrable Tower of God.

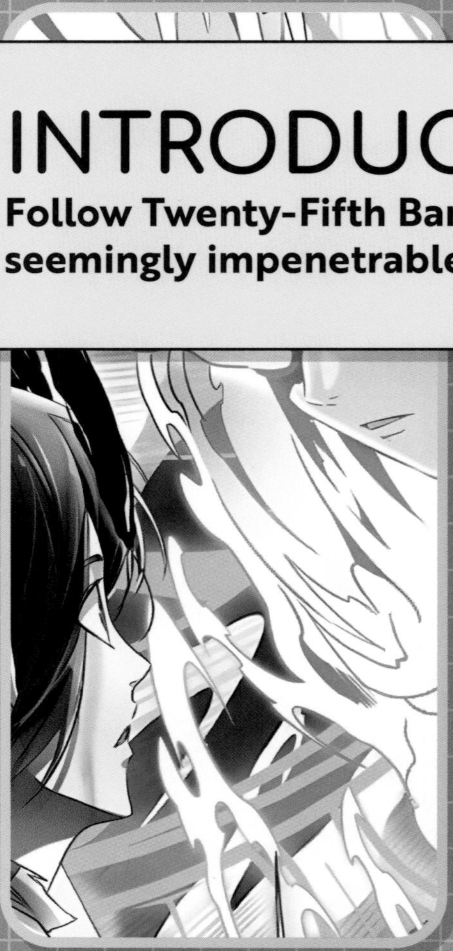

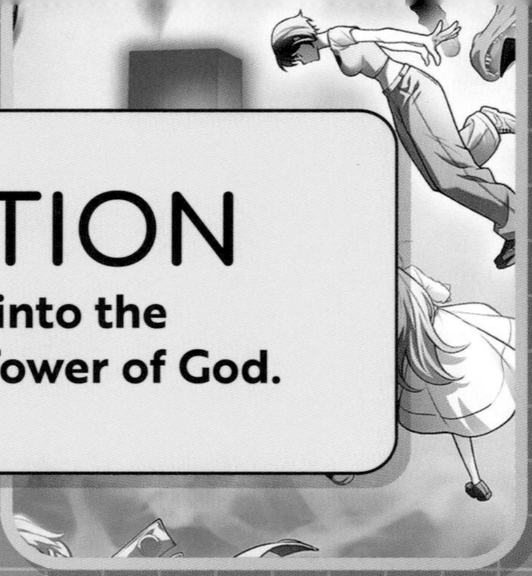

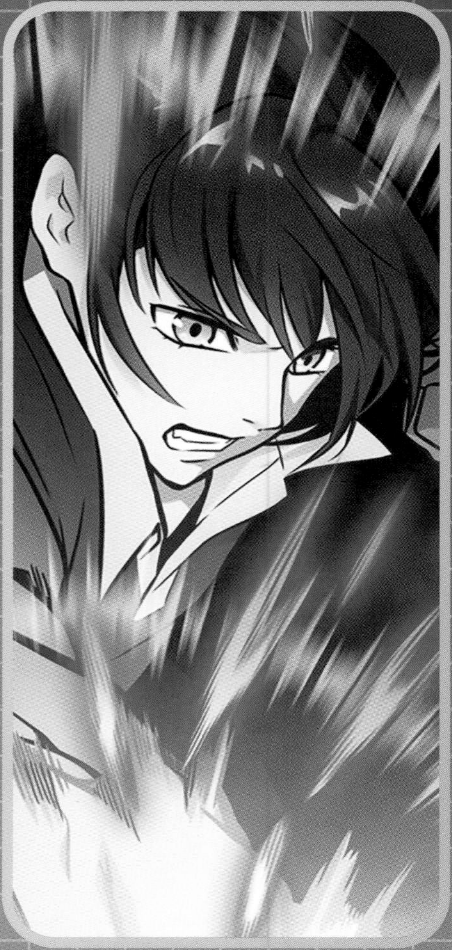

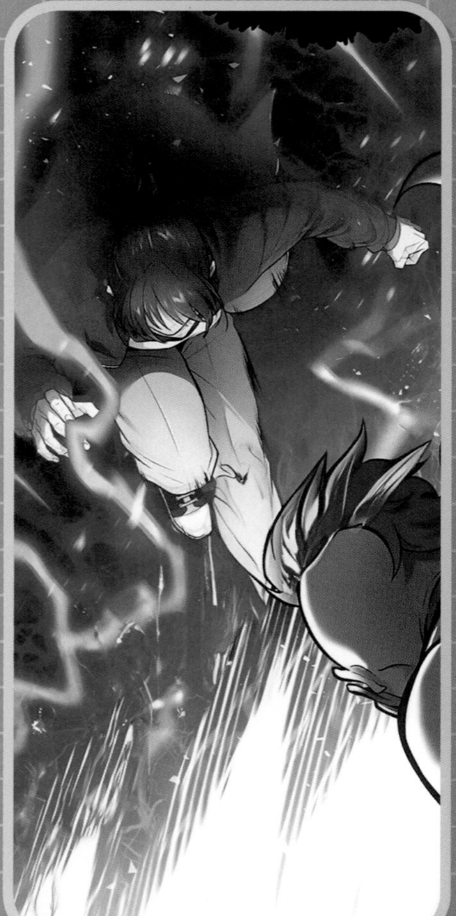

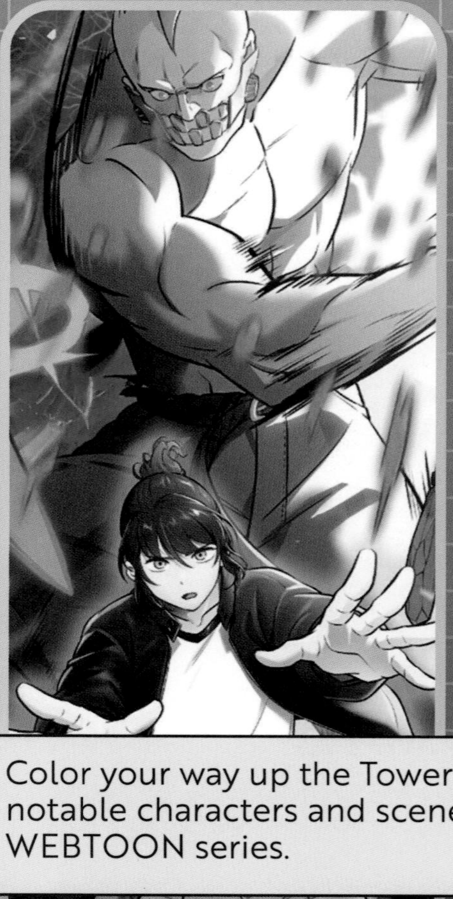

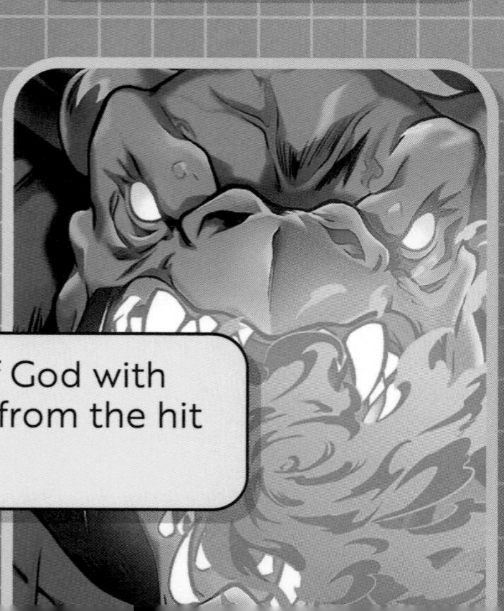

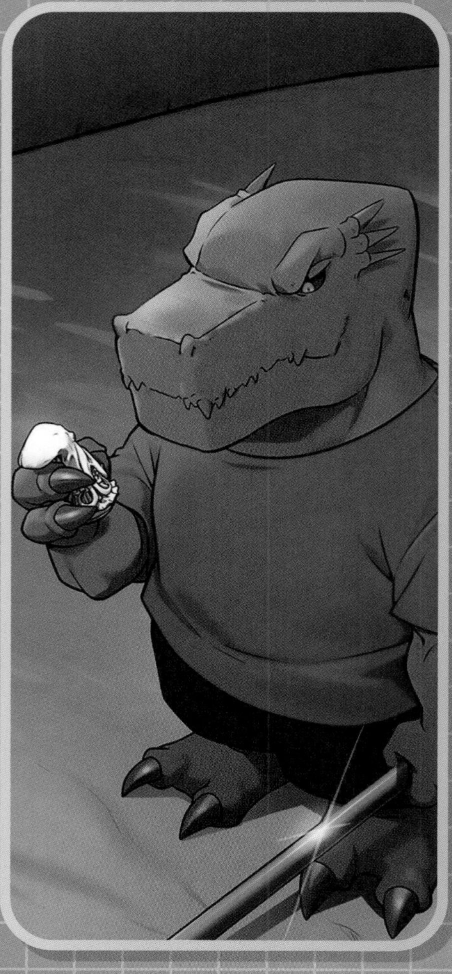

Color your way up the Tower of God with notable characters and scenes from the hit WEBTOON series.

What Is Tower of God?

With 1.2 billion readers and 3.6 million followers on WEBTOON, plus more than 85,000 followers on its official Instagram account, Tower of God is one of WEBTOON Original's leading webcomics. Follow the fast-paced adventures of Twenty-Fifth Bam, Rachel, and the other Irregulars, Regulars, Rankers, and Great Warriors working their way up the Tower of God, which has been adapted for television on the streaming service Crunchyroll.

Check out the latest episode of the hit WEBTOON series.

SYNOPSIS

Twenty-Fifth Bam has lived his whole life in a world of darkness. His only comfort has been the companionship of his best friend, Rachel. When Rachel advises him to forget her and then mysteriously vanishes through the doors of the seemingly impenetrable Tower of God—right before his eyes—Twenty-Fifth Bam vows to find a way inside the enigmatic otherworld. Thus begins his epic journey of ascension to the top of the Tower. With the tests of will, wits, and strength that lie ahead, as well as unforeseen danger lurking around every corner, Twenty-Fifth Bam will be pushed to his limits in the quest to find his friend. But will their reunion be a happy one, or will revelations about Rachel uncover a web of secrets that could change their friendship forever?

About WEBTOON

WEBTOON is the world's largest digital comics platform, home to some of the biggest artists, IP, and fandoms in comics. As the global leader and pioneer of the mobile webcomic format, WEBTOON has revolutionized the comics industry for comic fans and creators. Today, a diverse new generation of international comic artists have found a home on WEBTOON, where the company's storytelling technology allows anyone to become a creator and build a global audience for their stories. The WEBTOON app is free to download on Android and iOS devices.

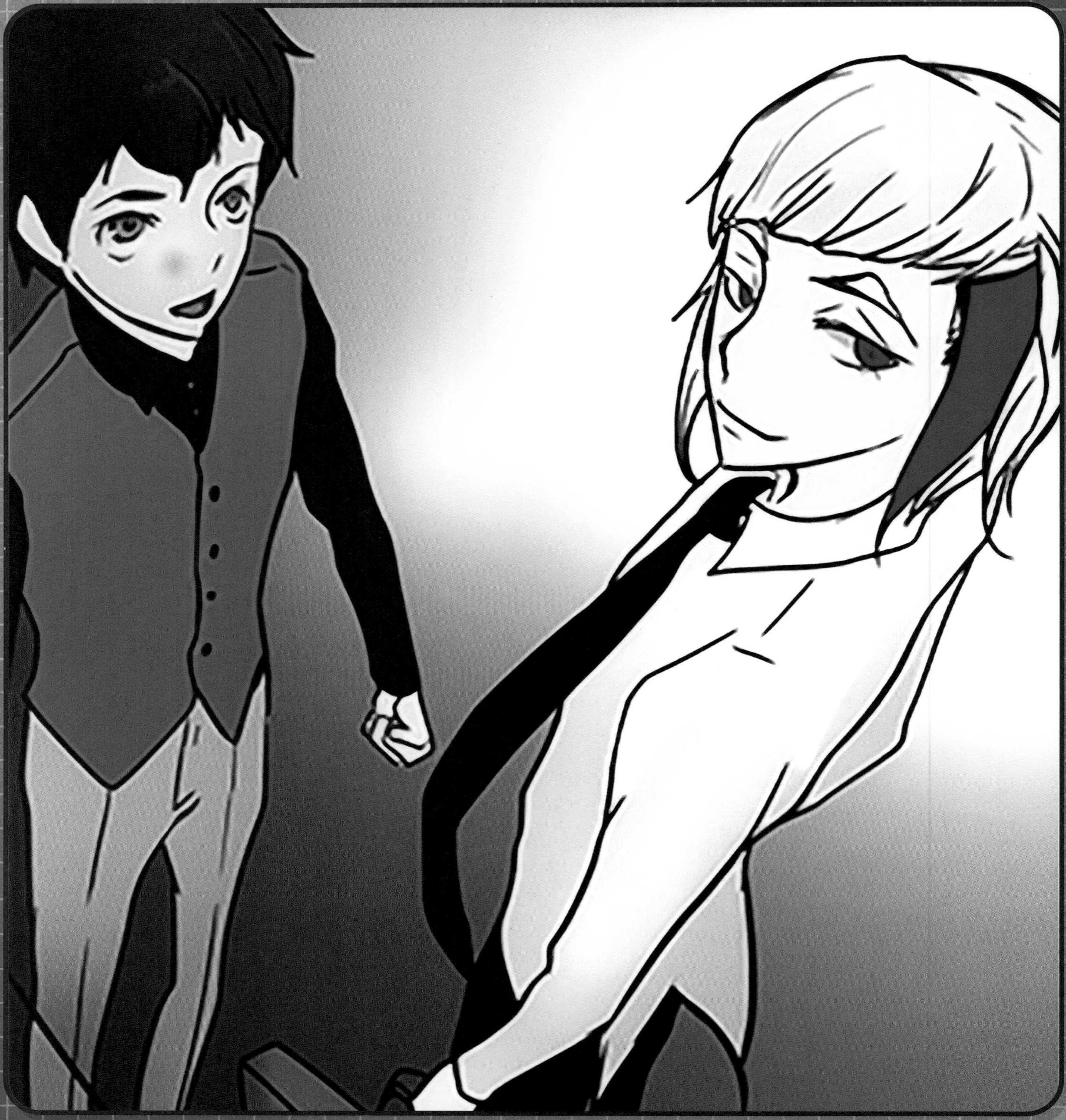

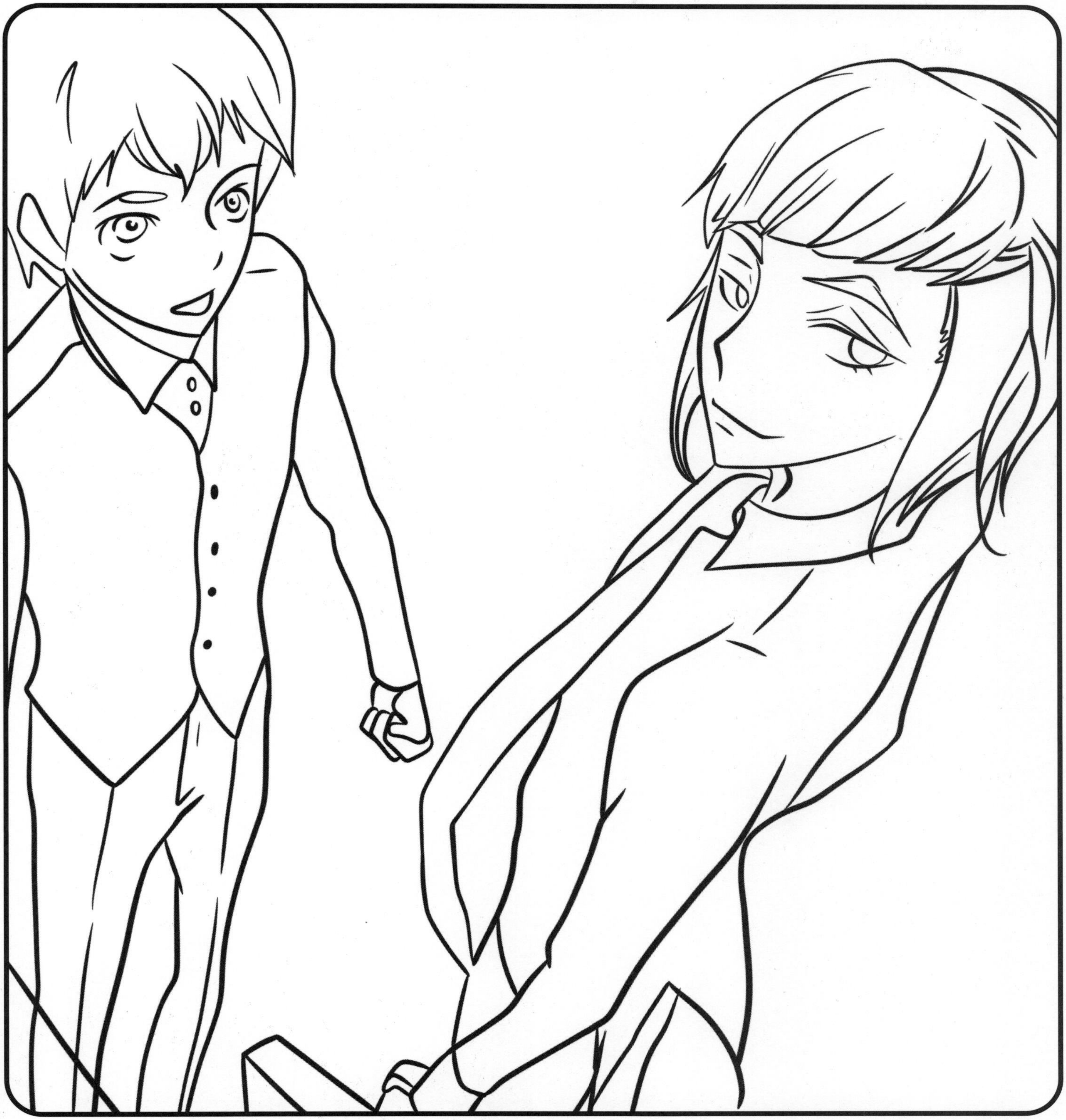

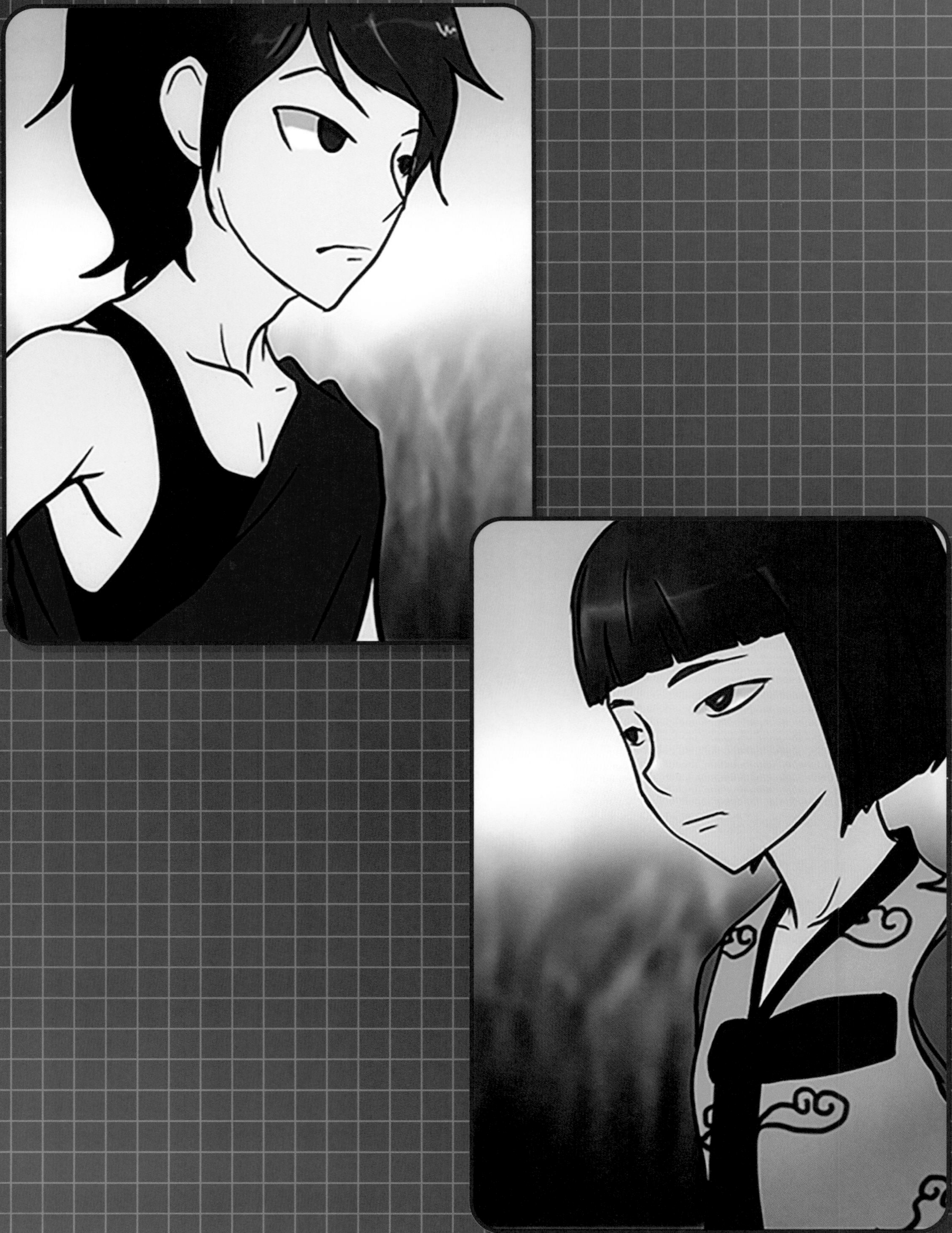

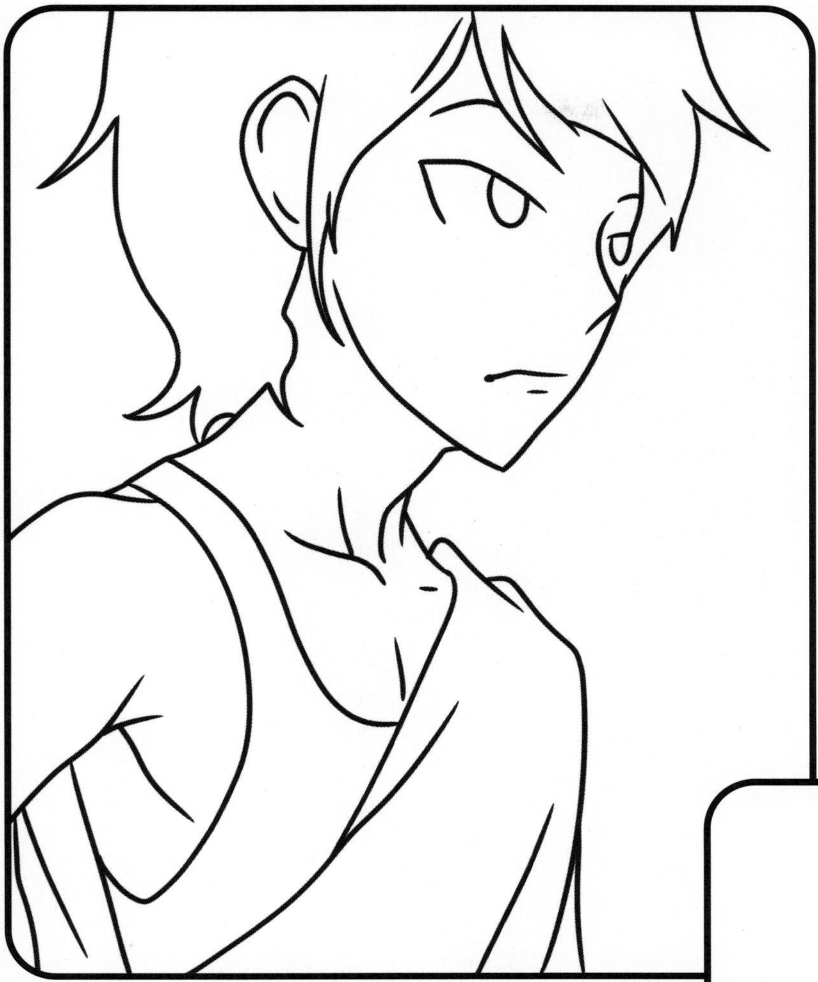

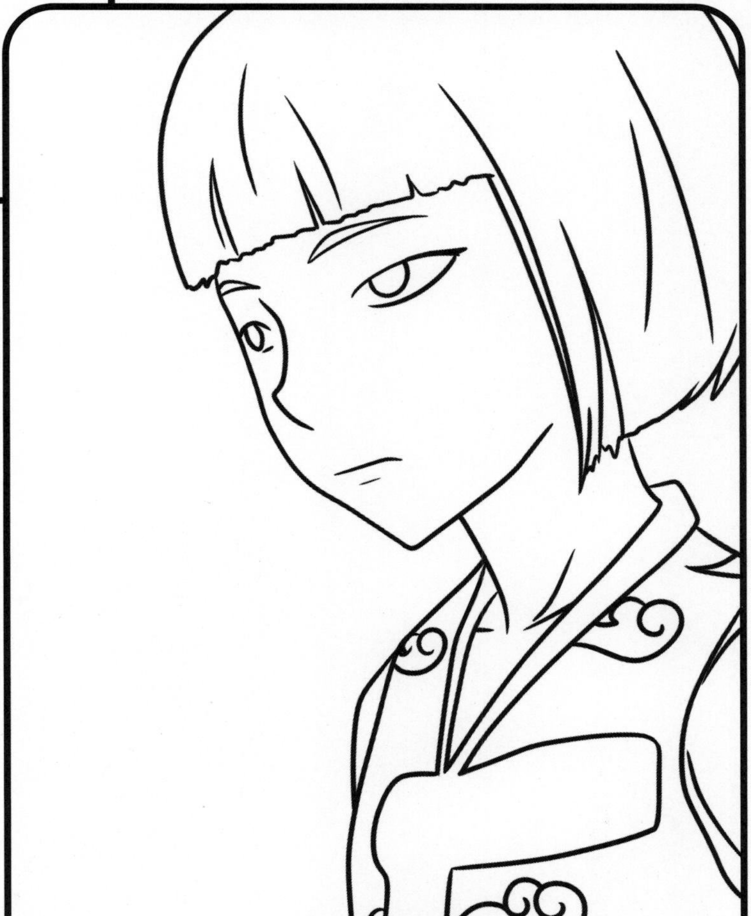

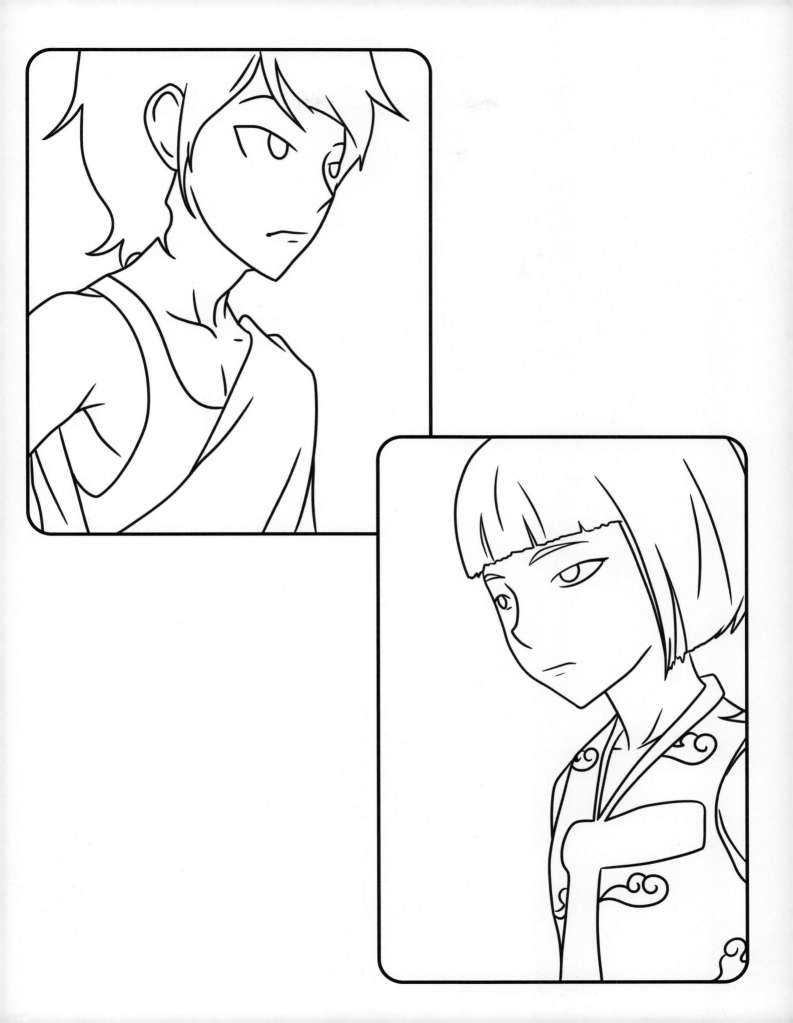

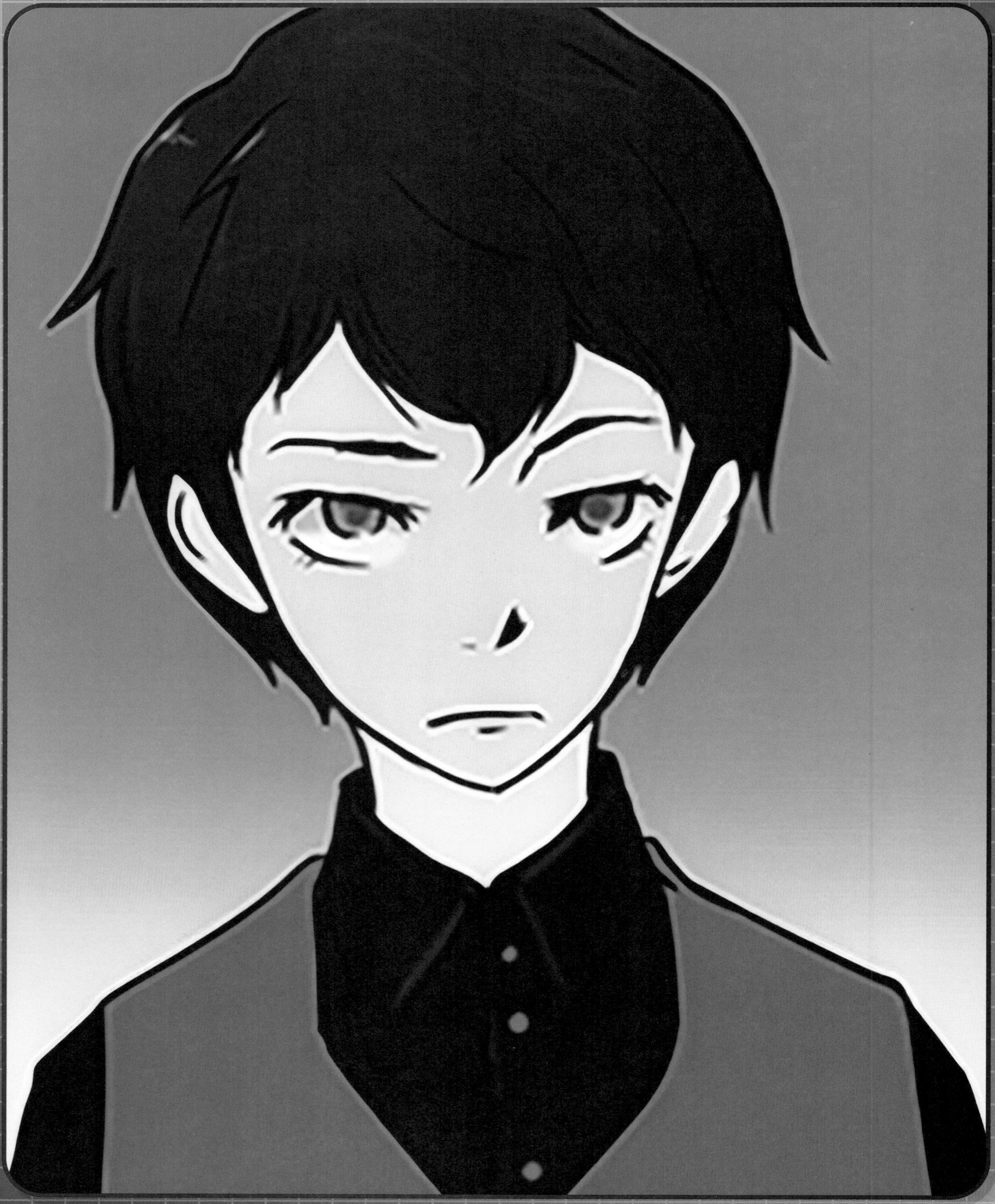

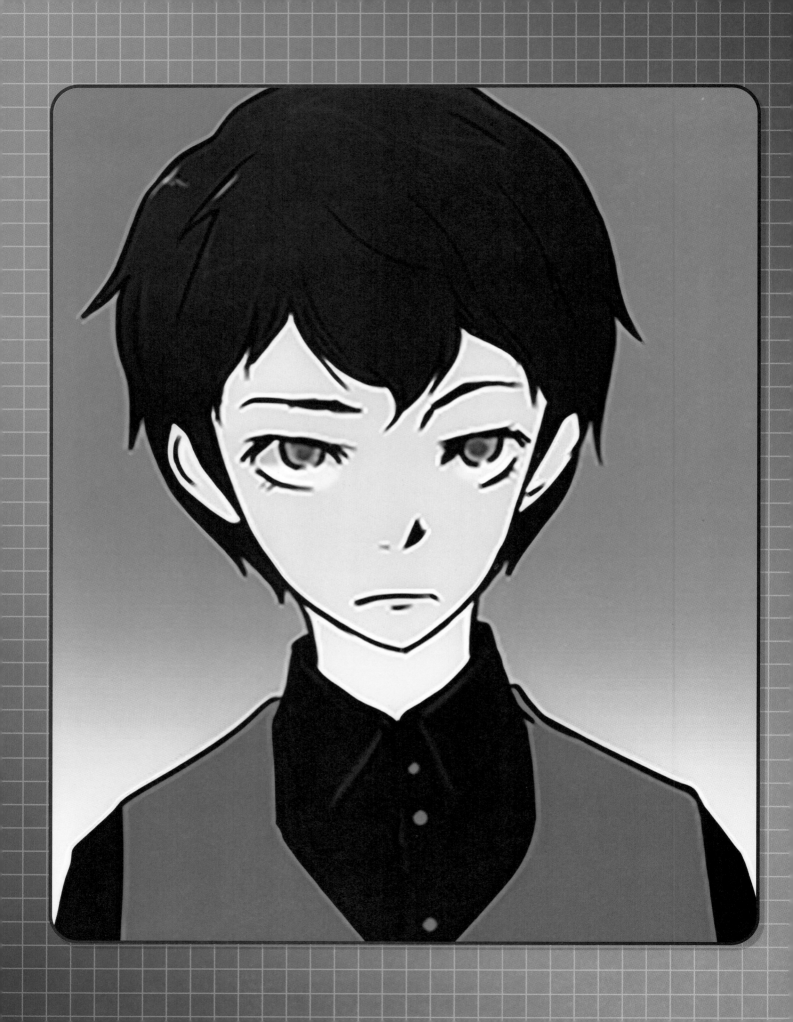

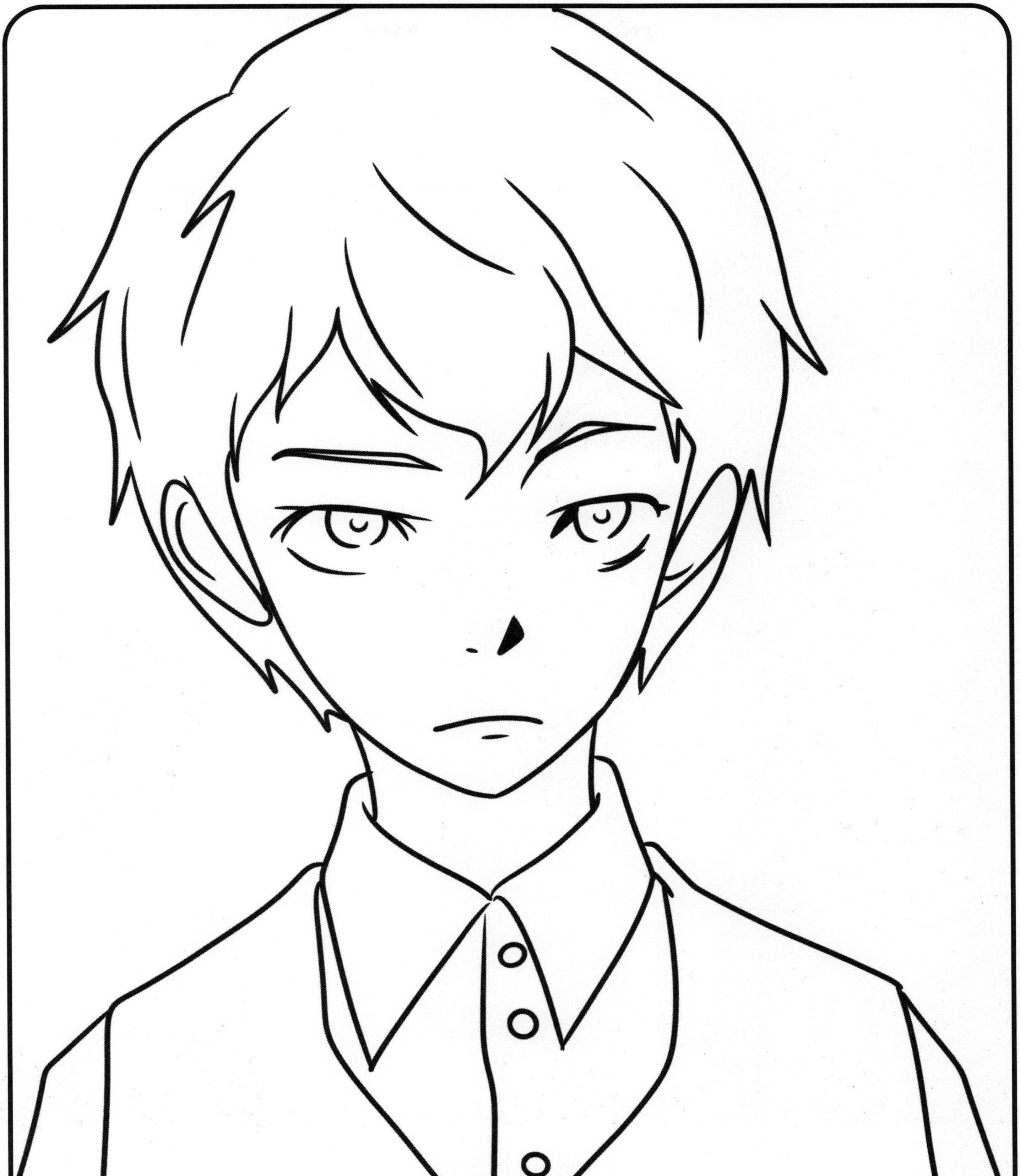

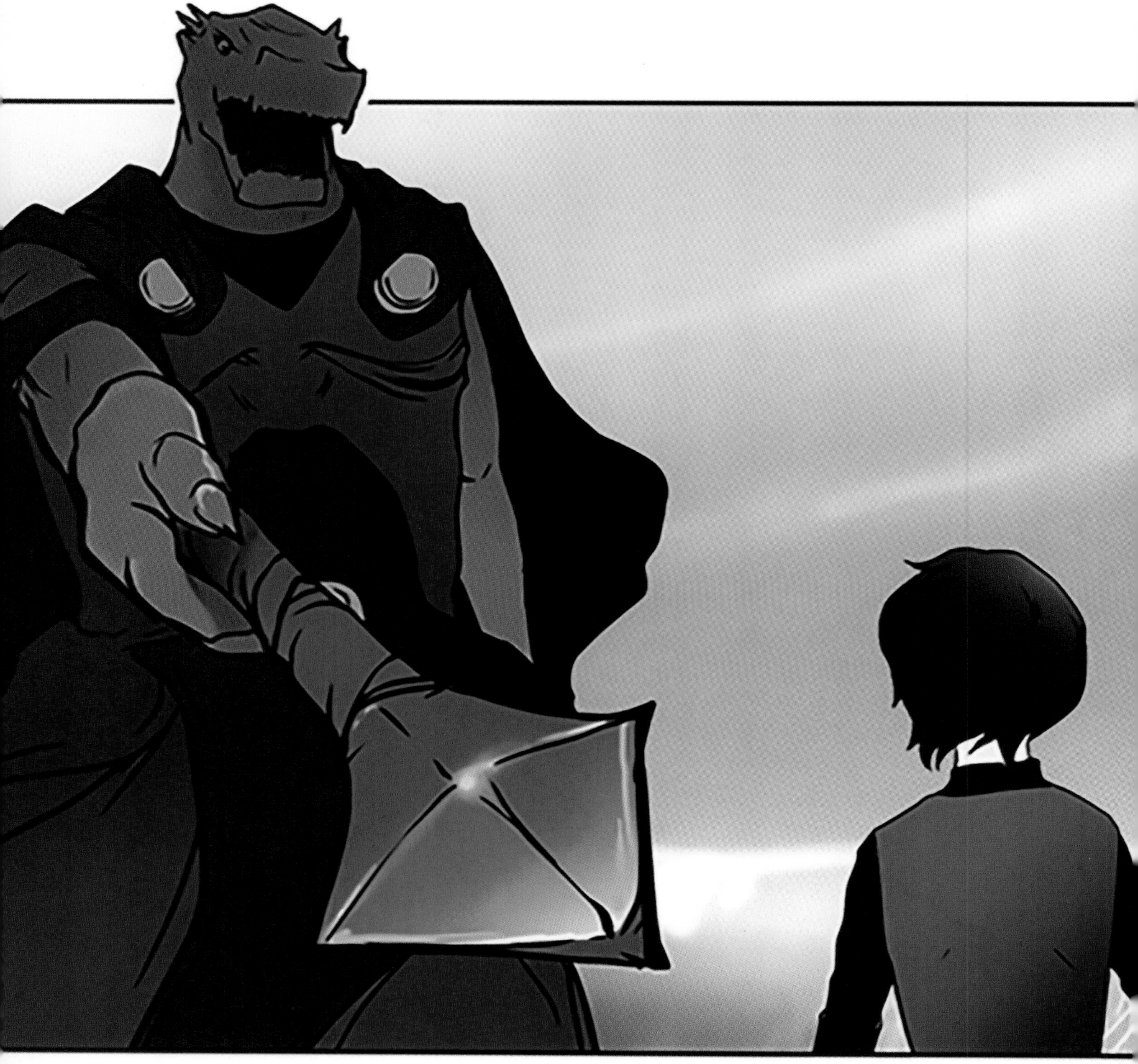

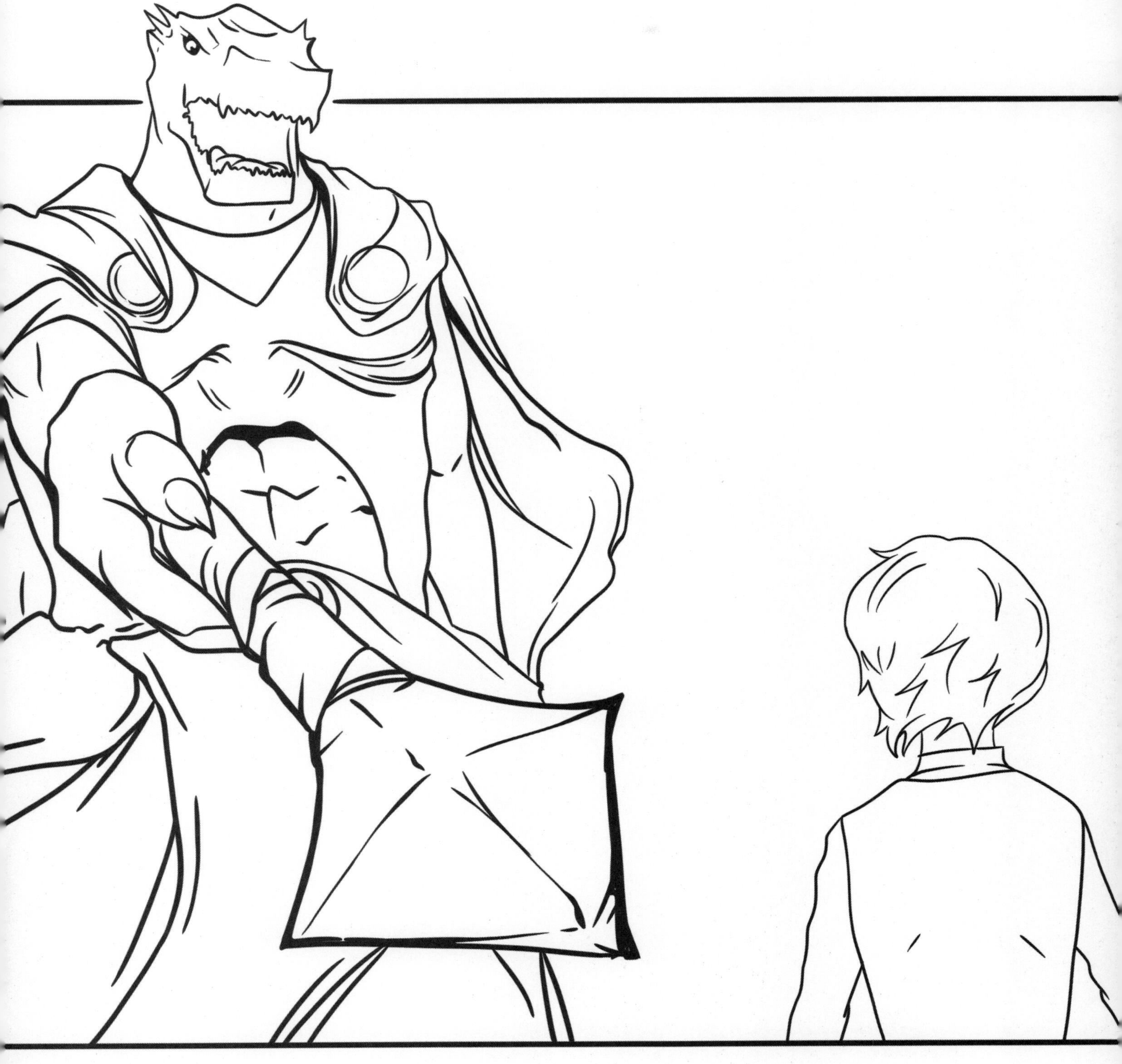

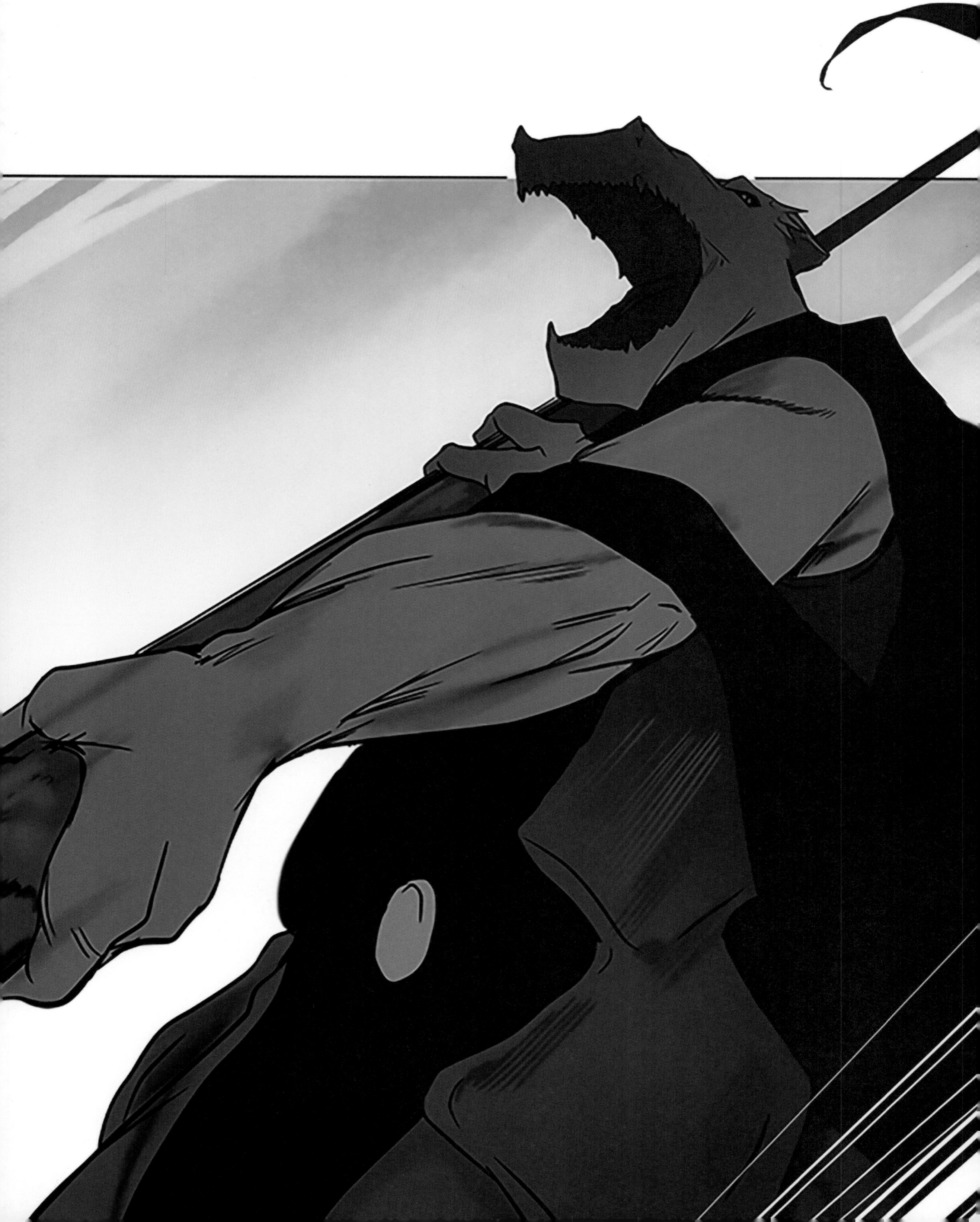

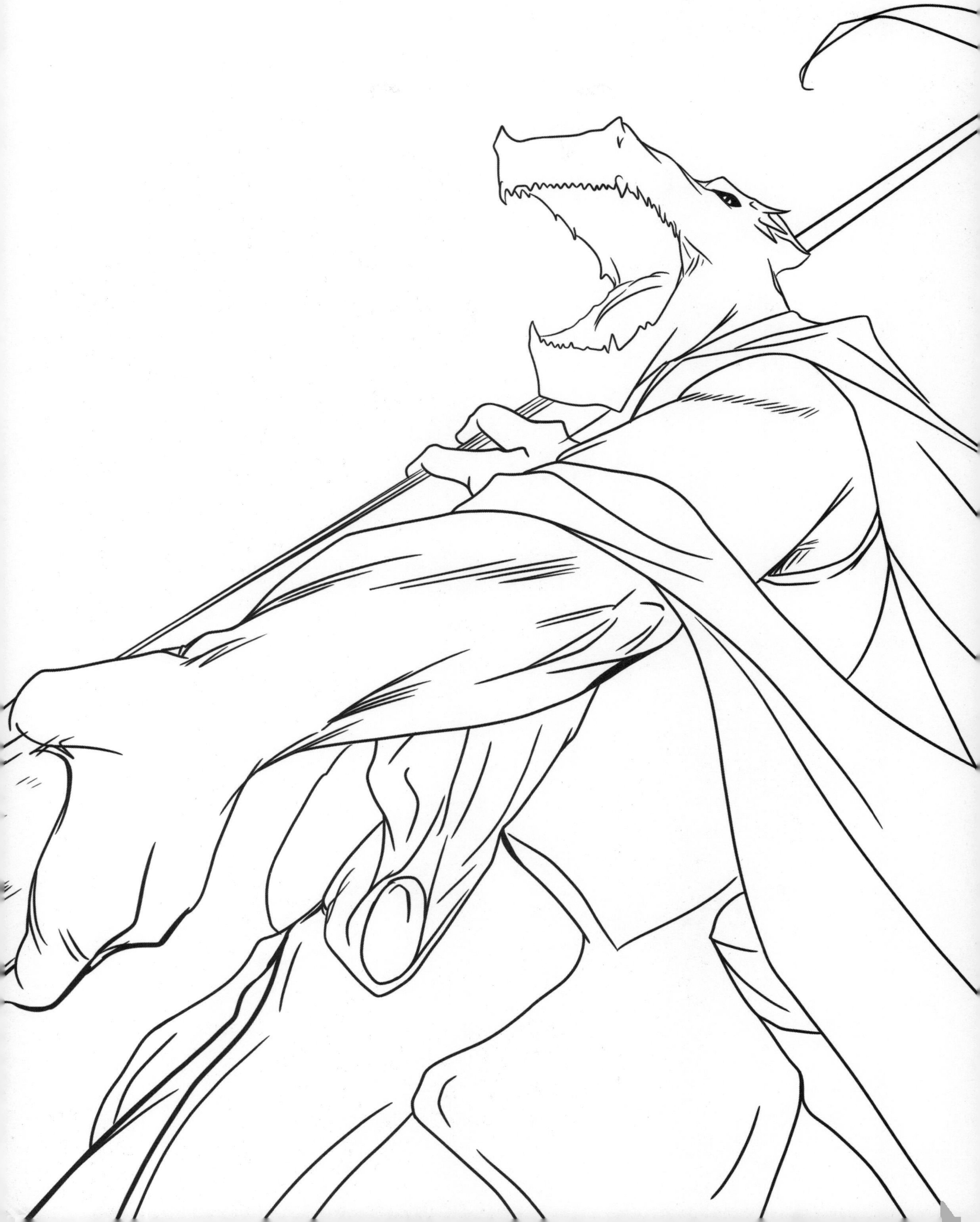

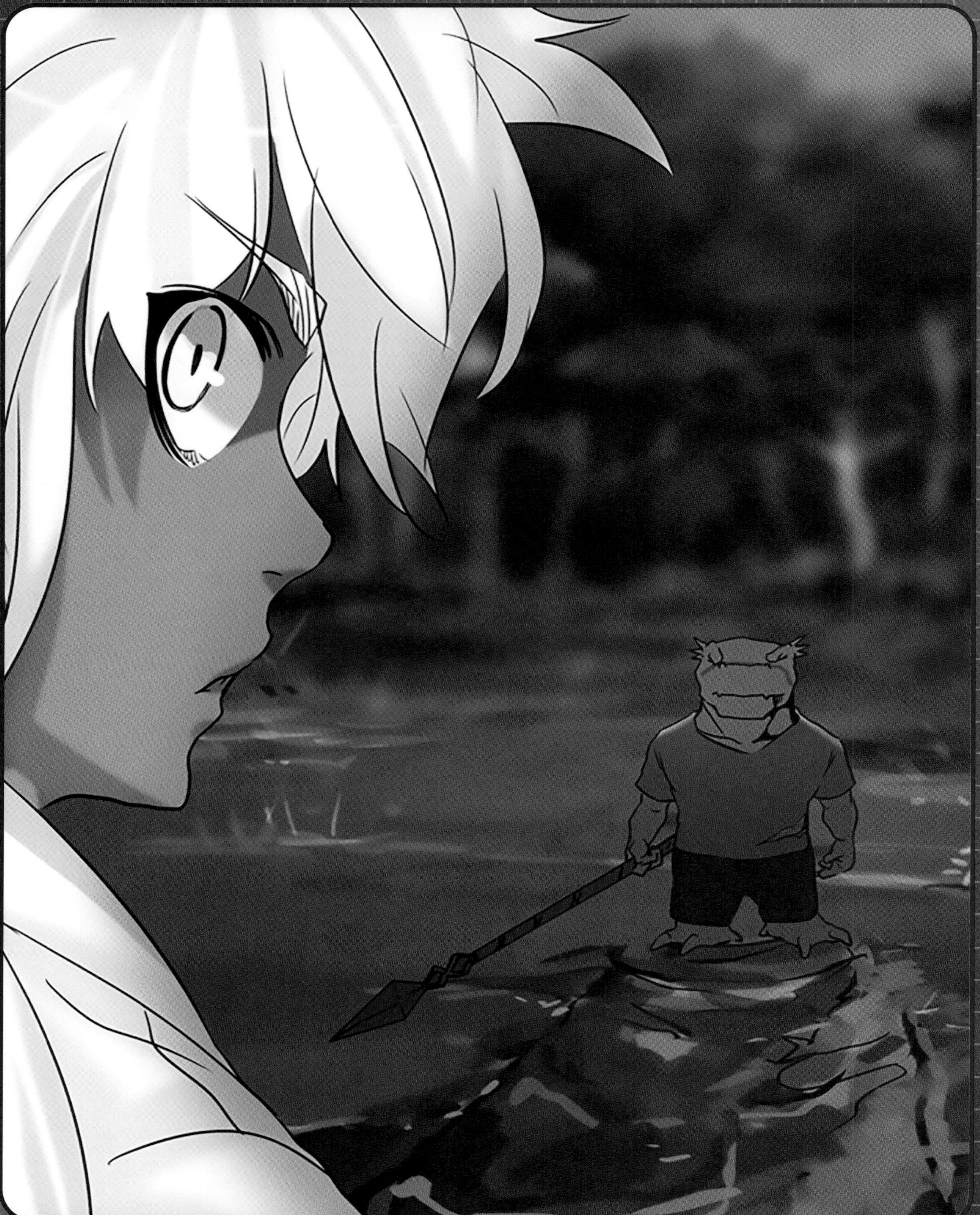

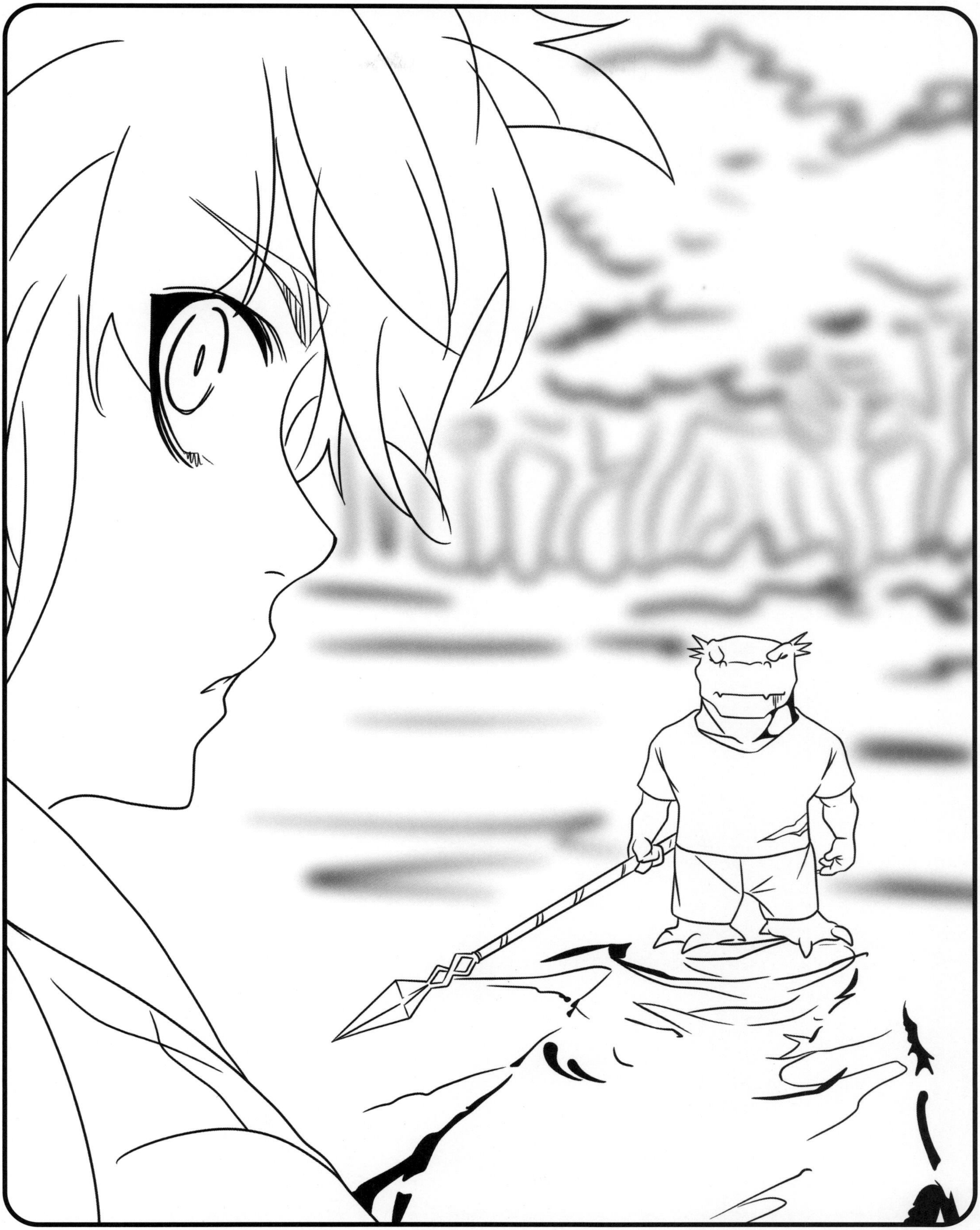

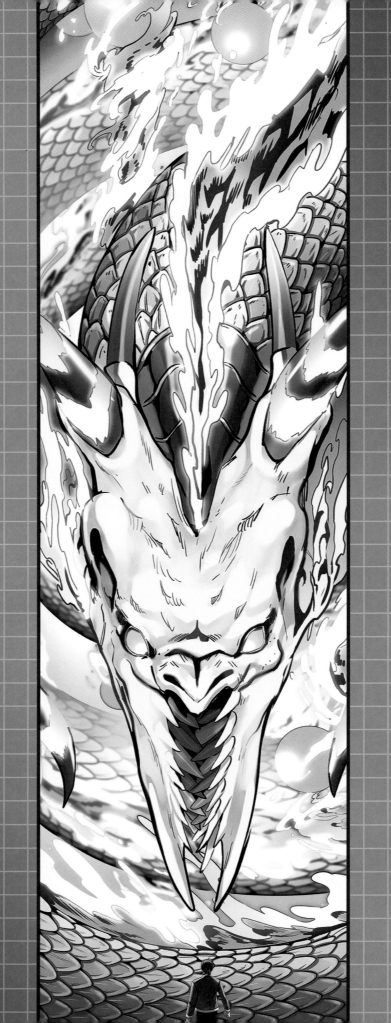

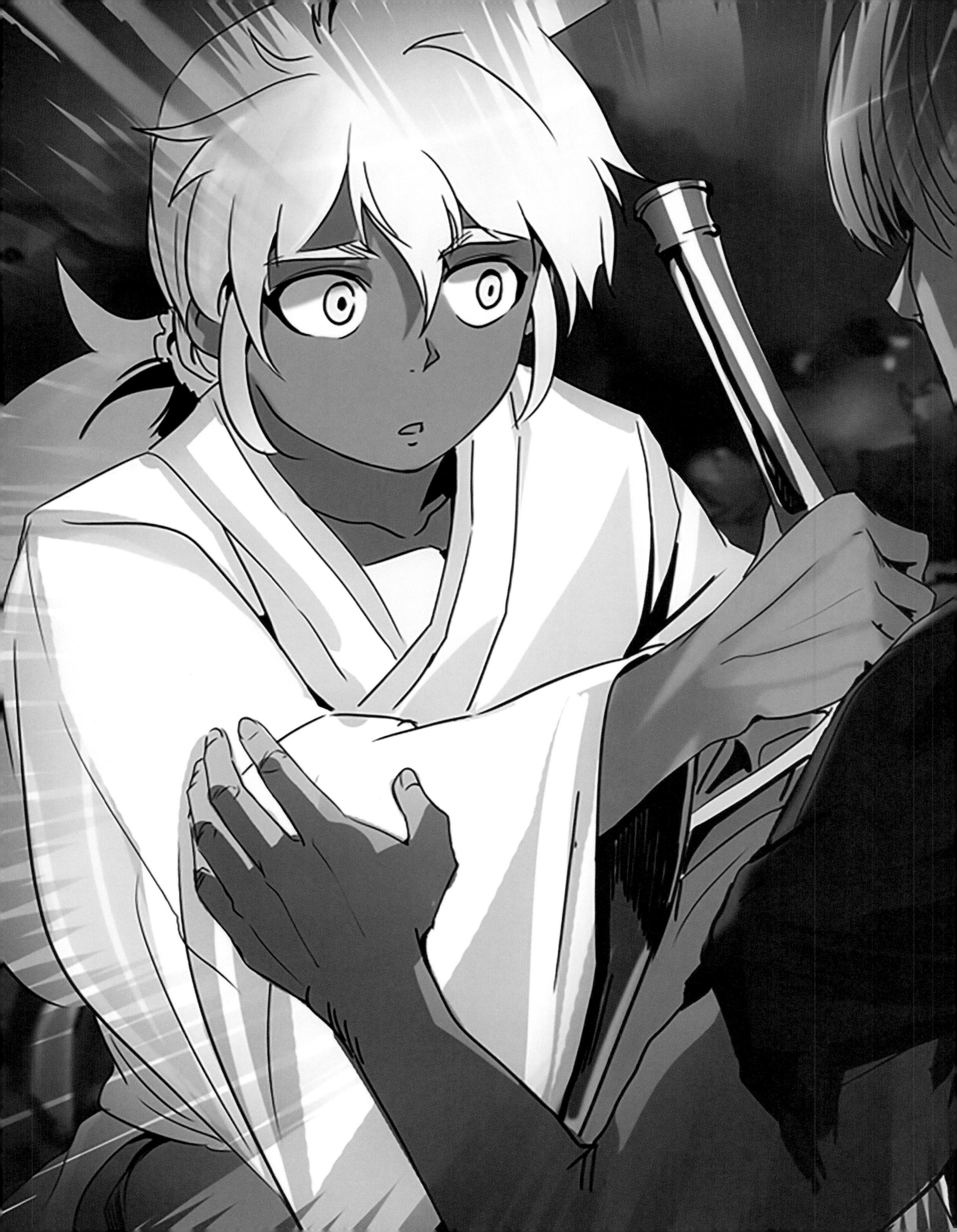

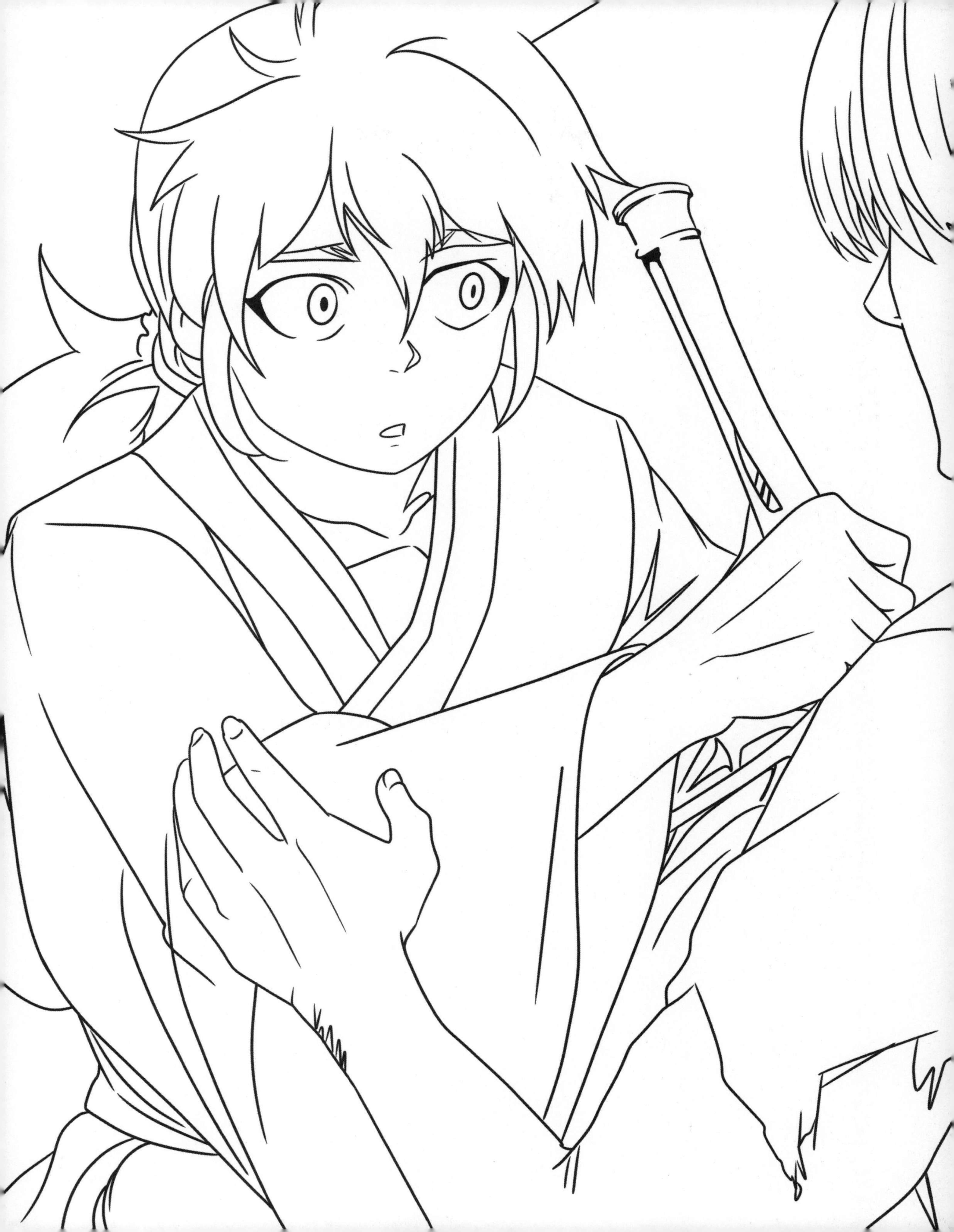

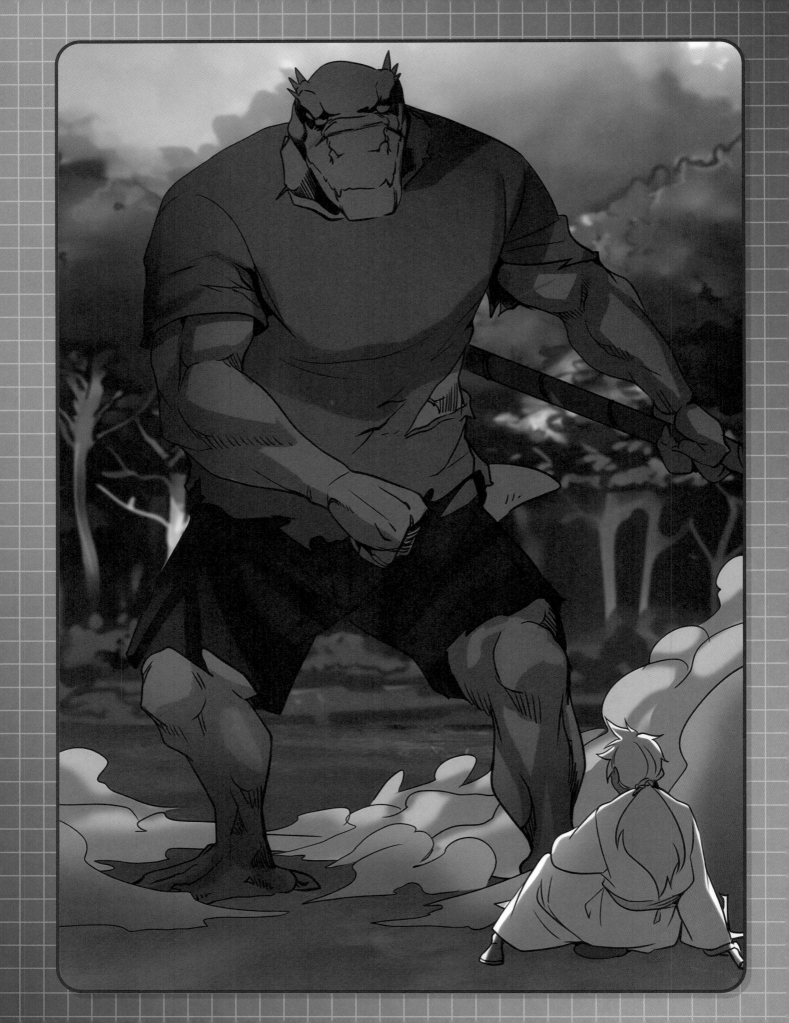

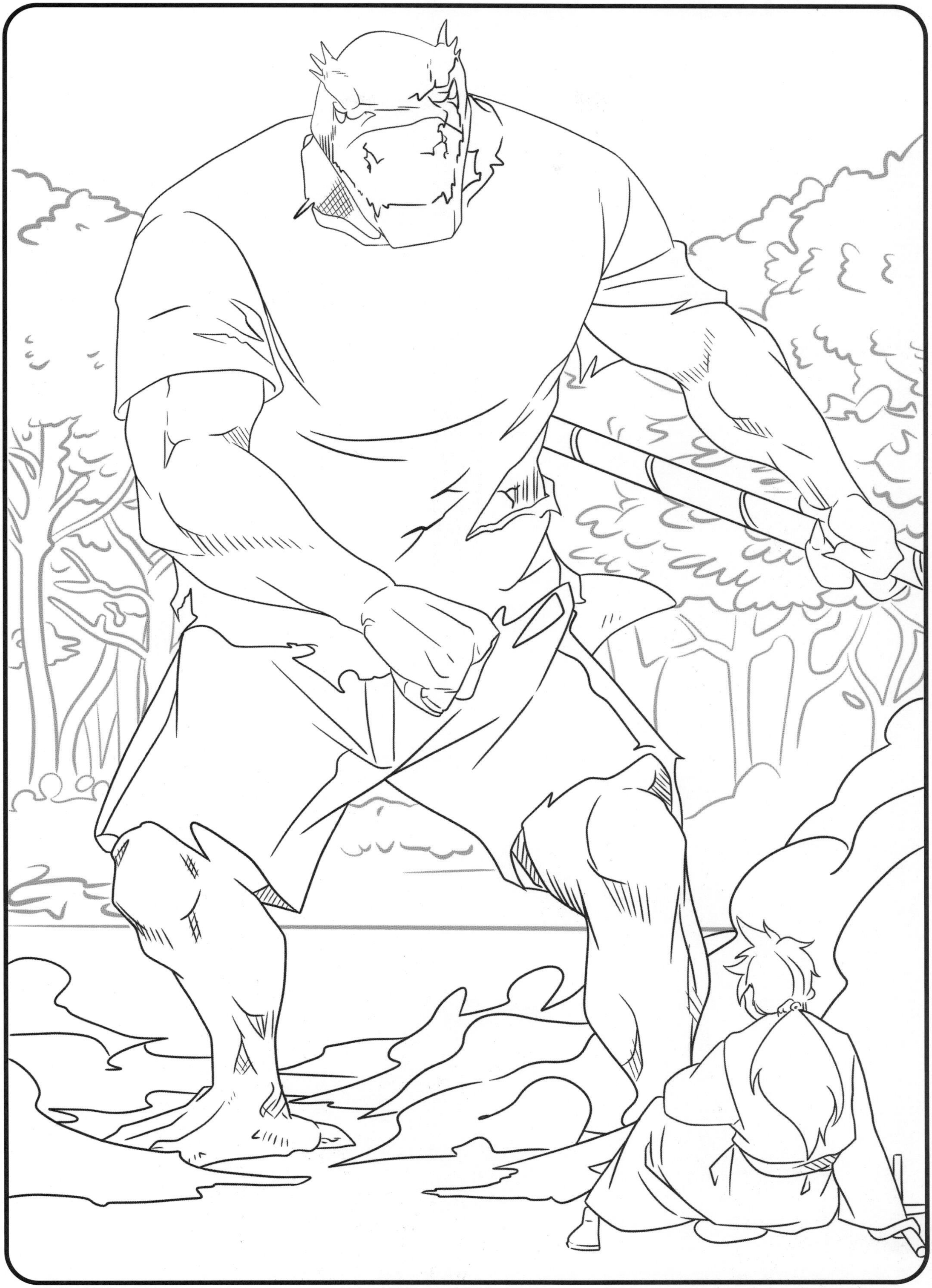

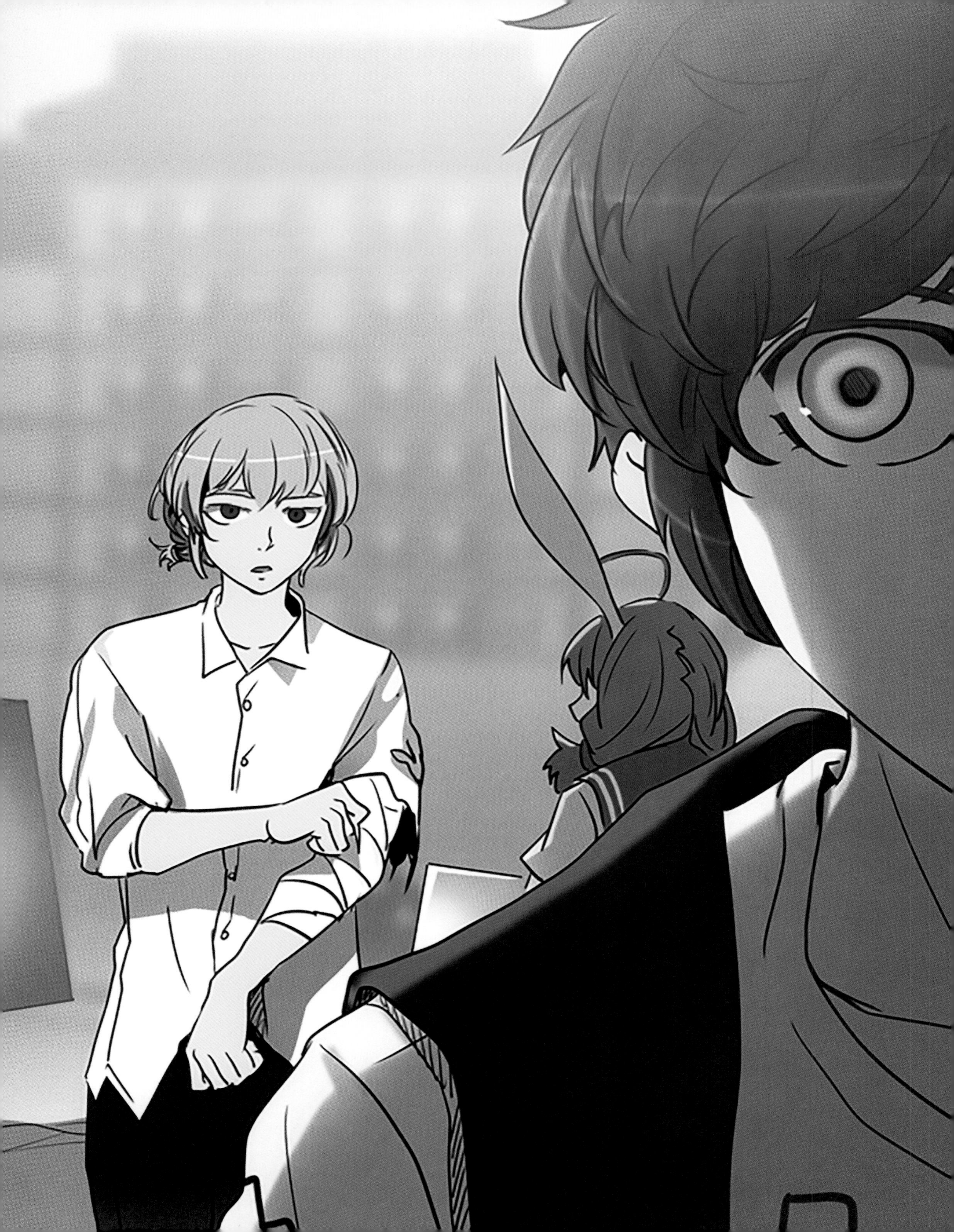

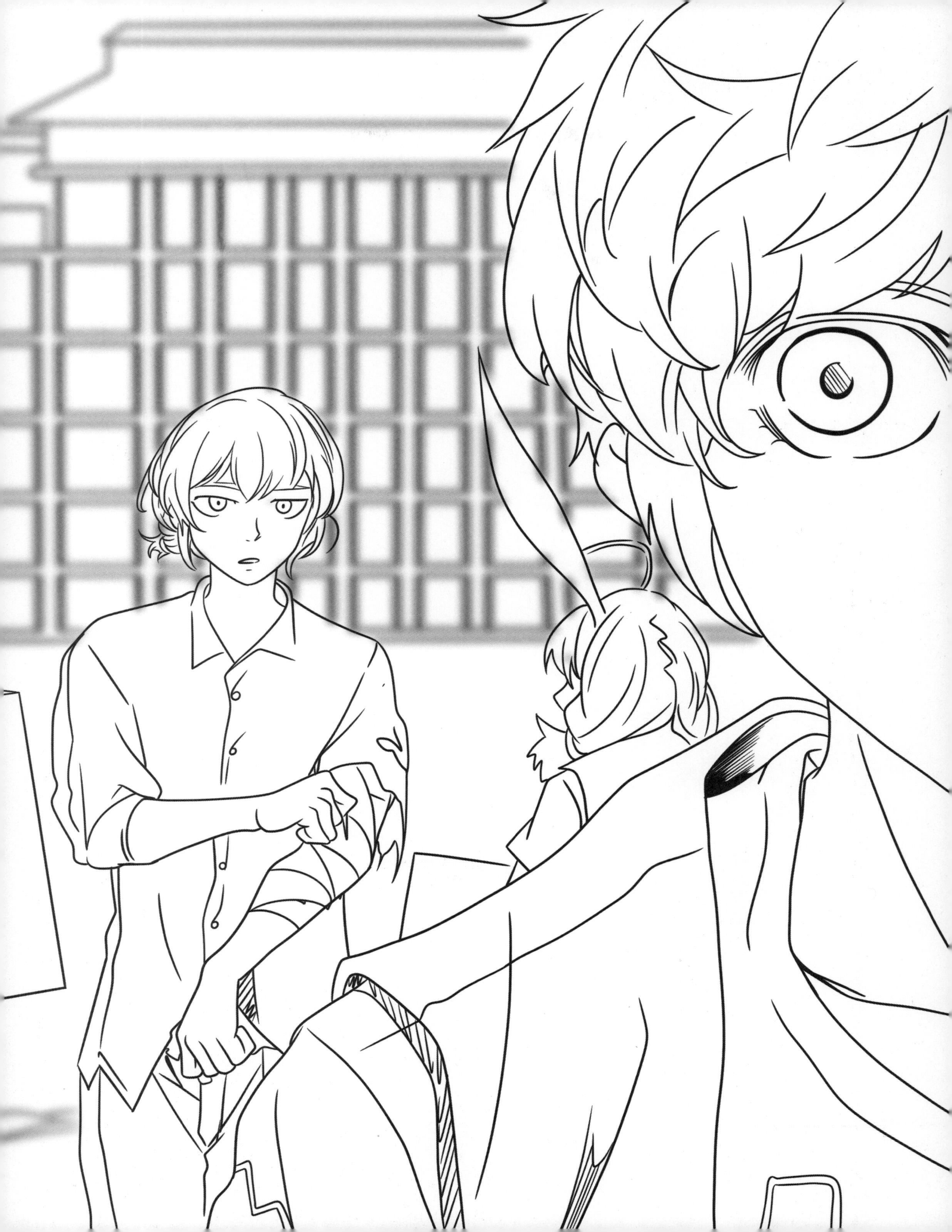

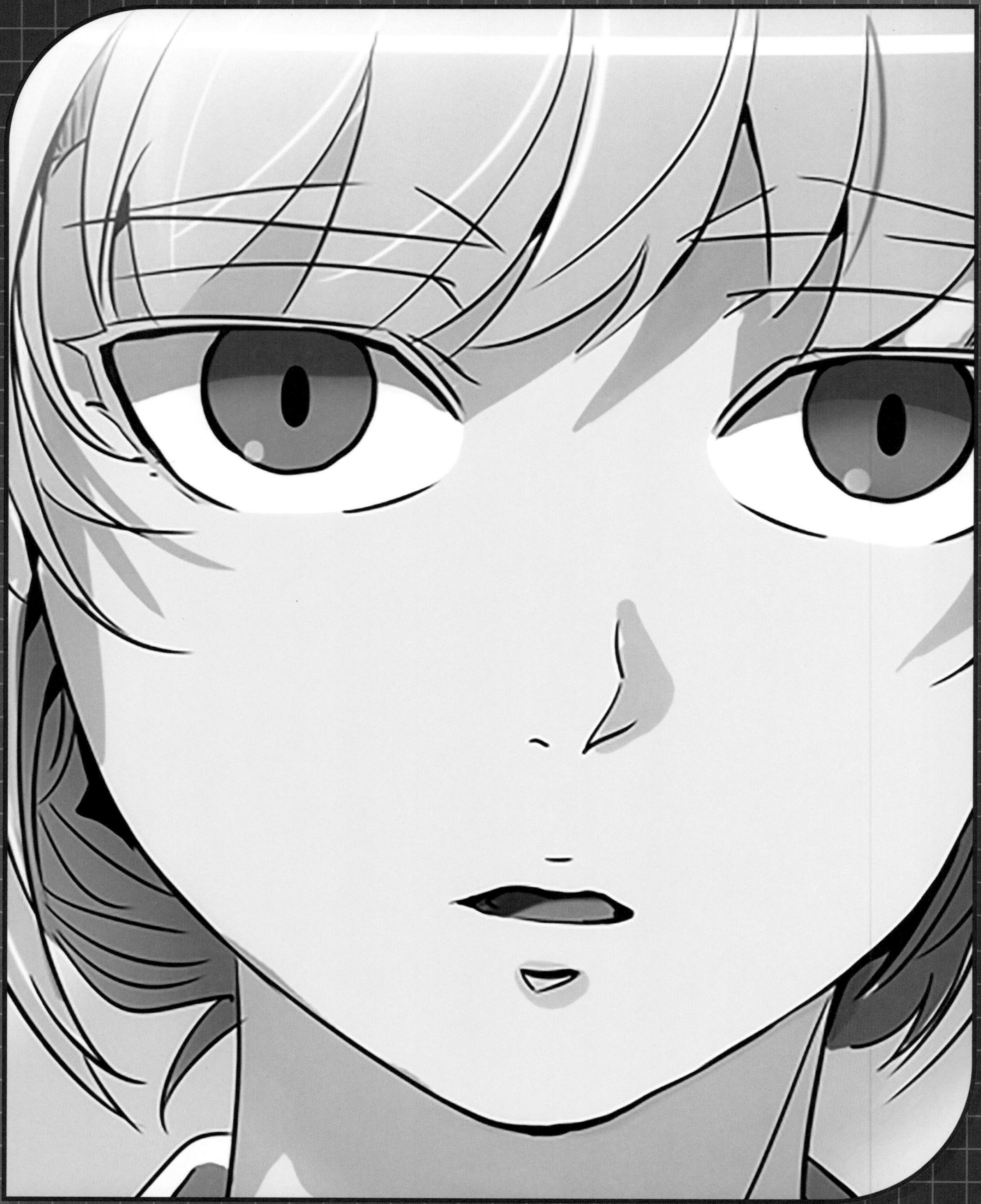

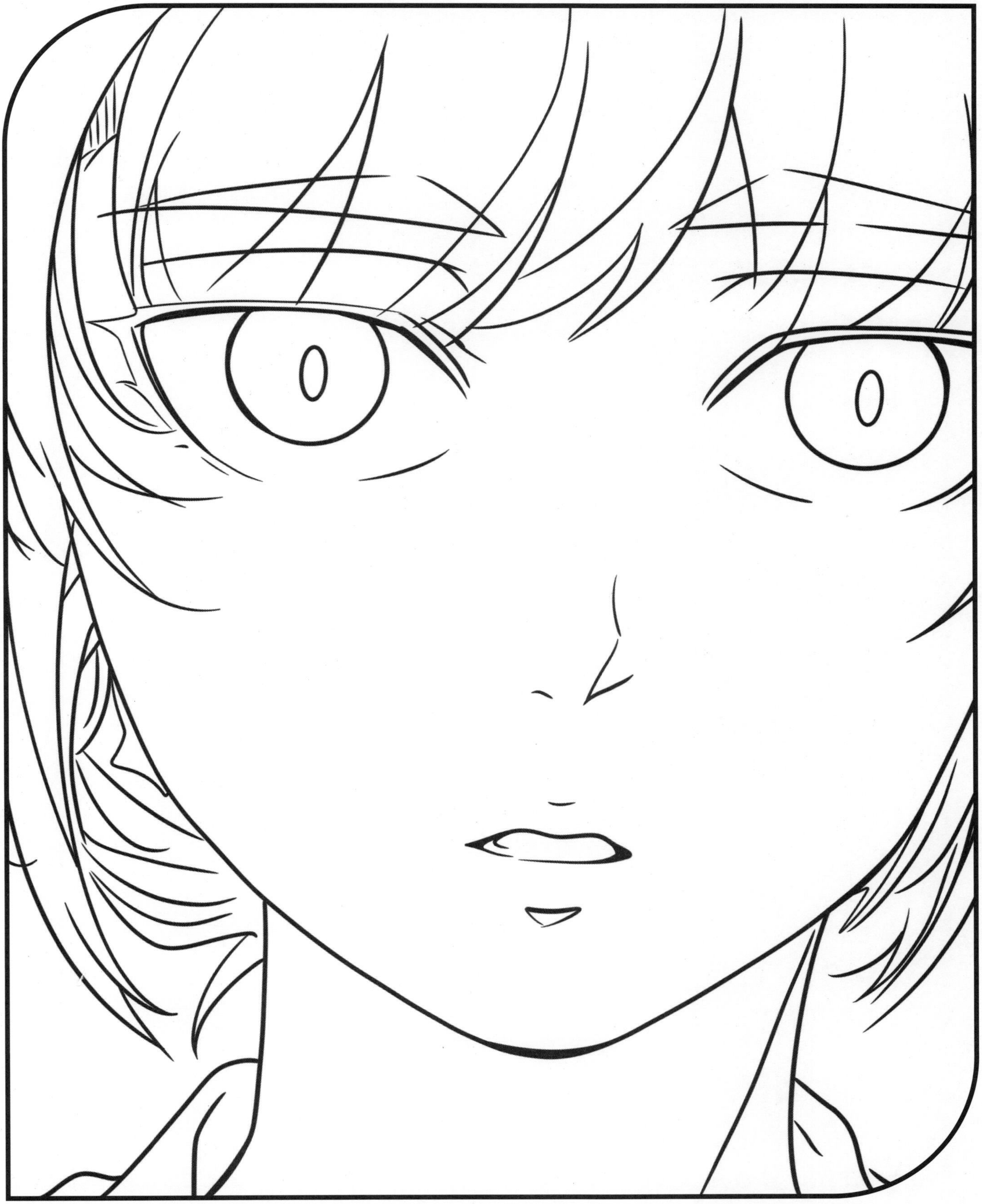

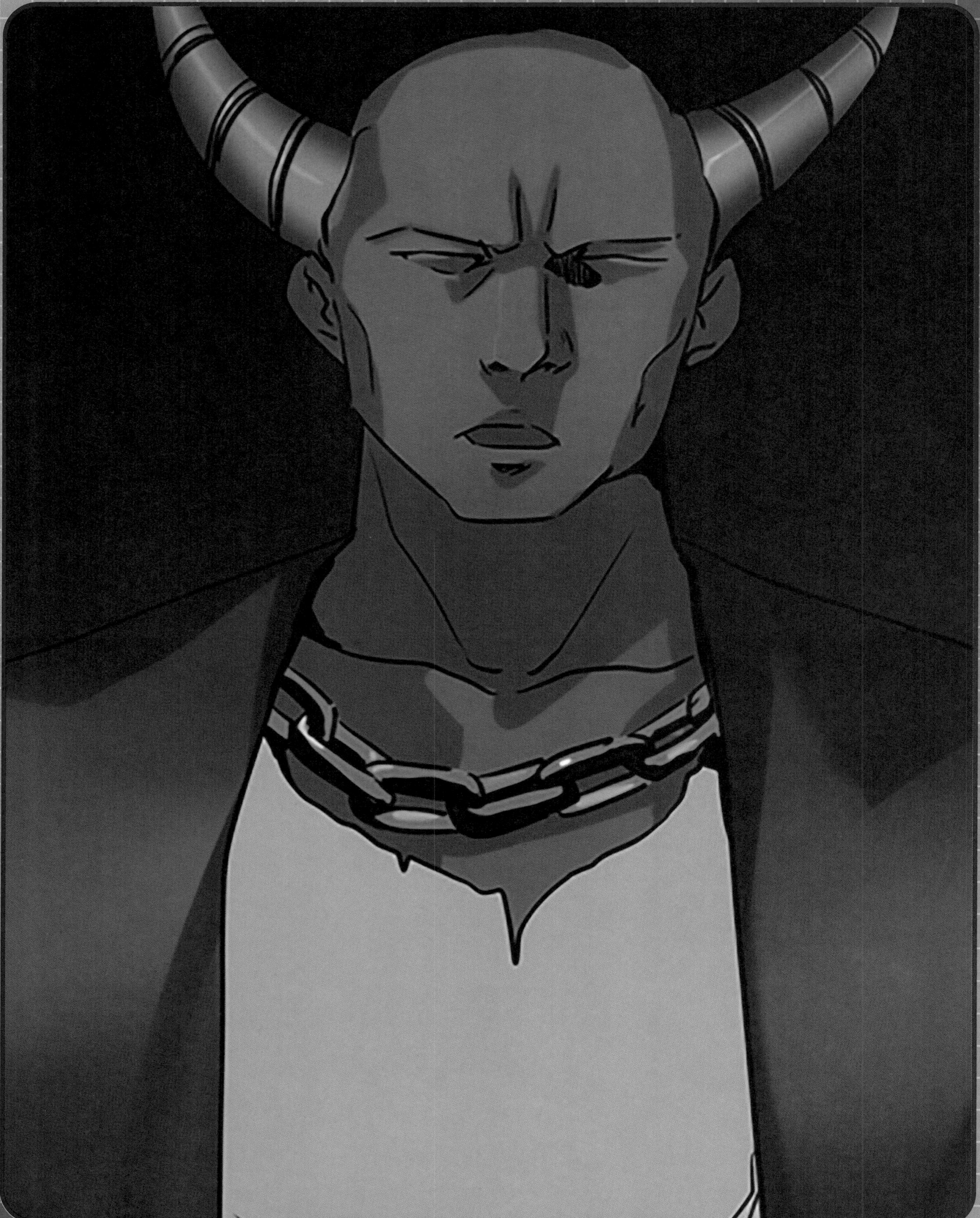

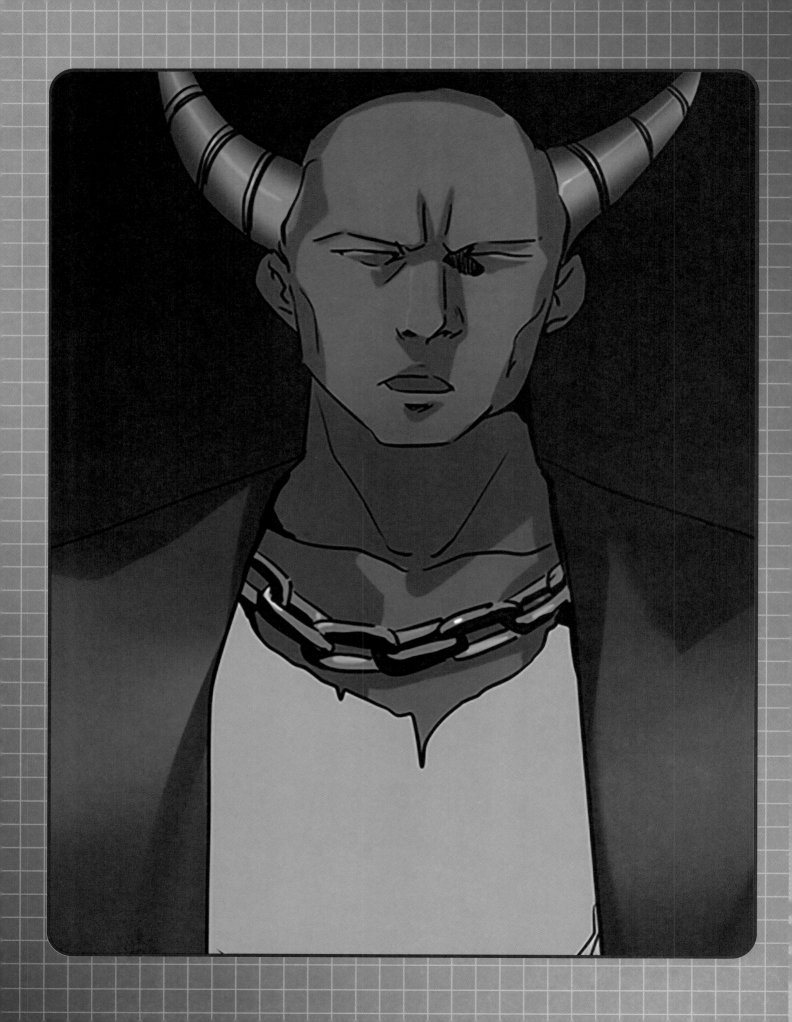

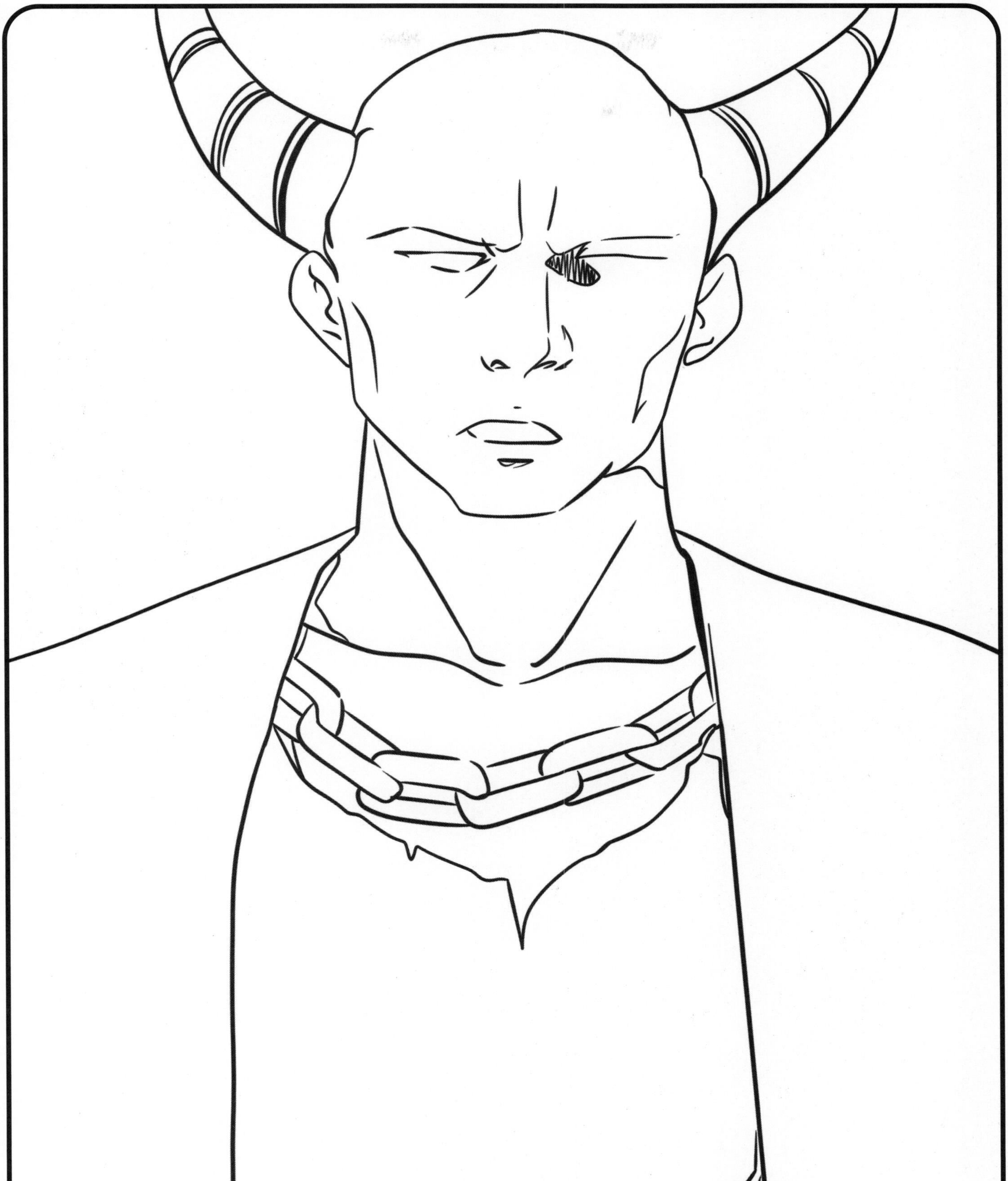

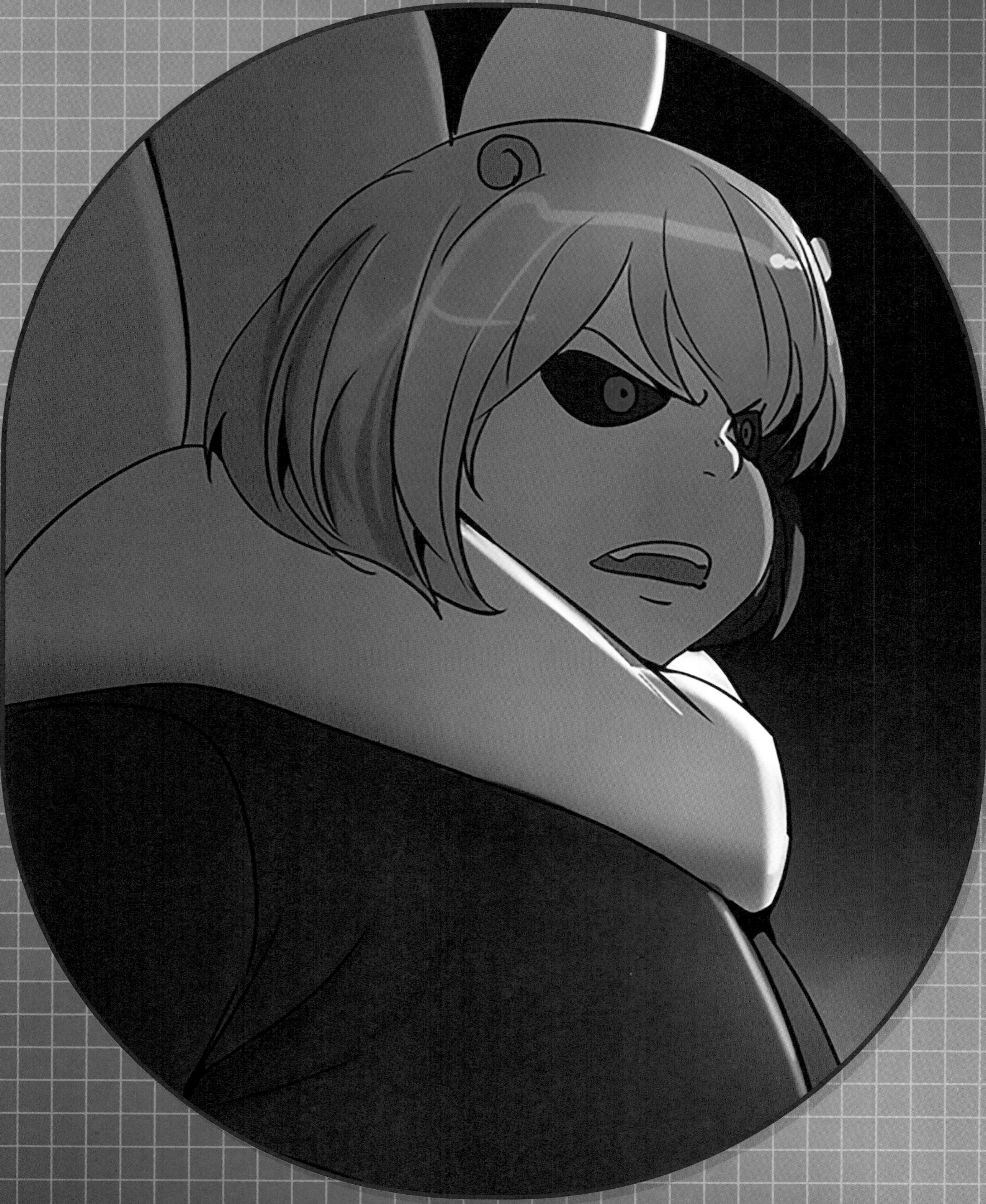

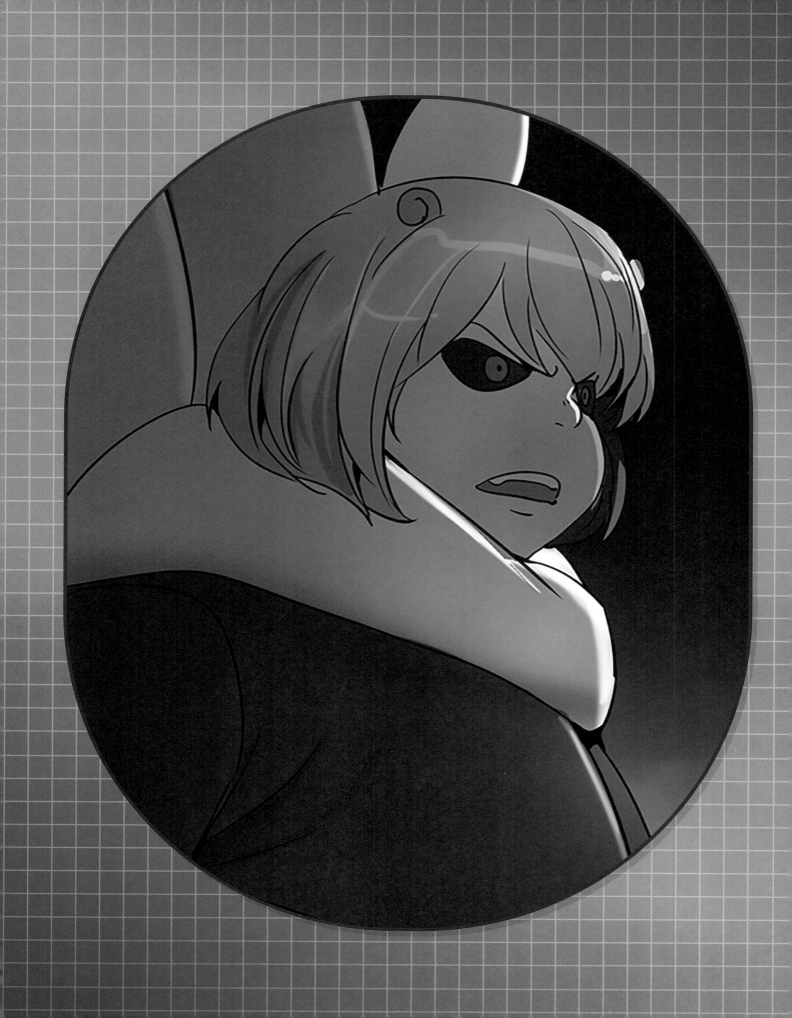

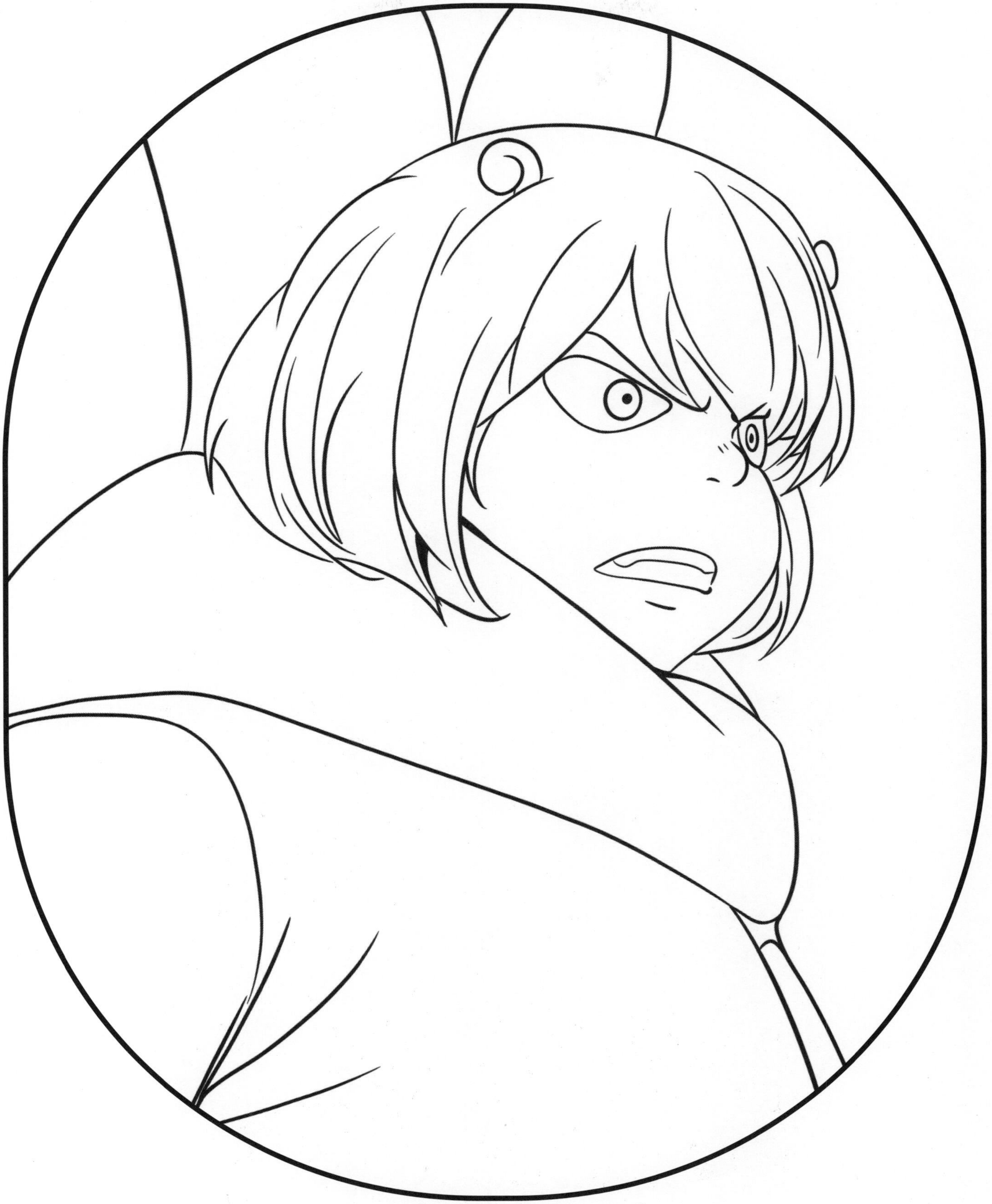

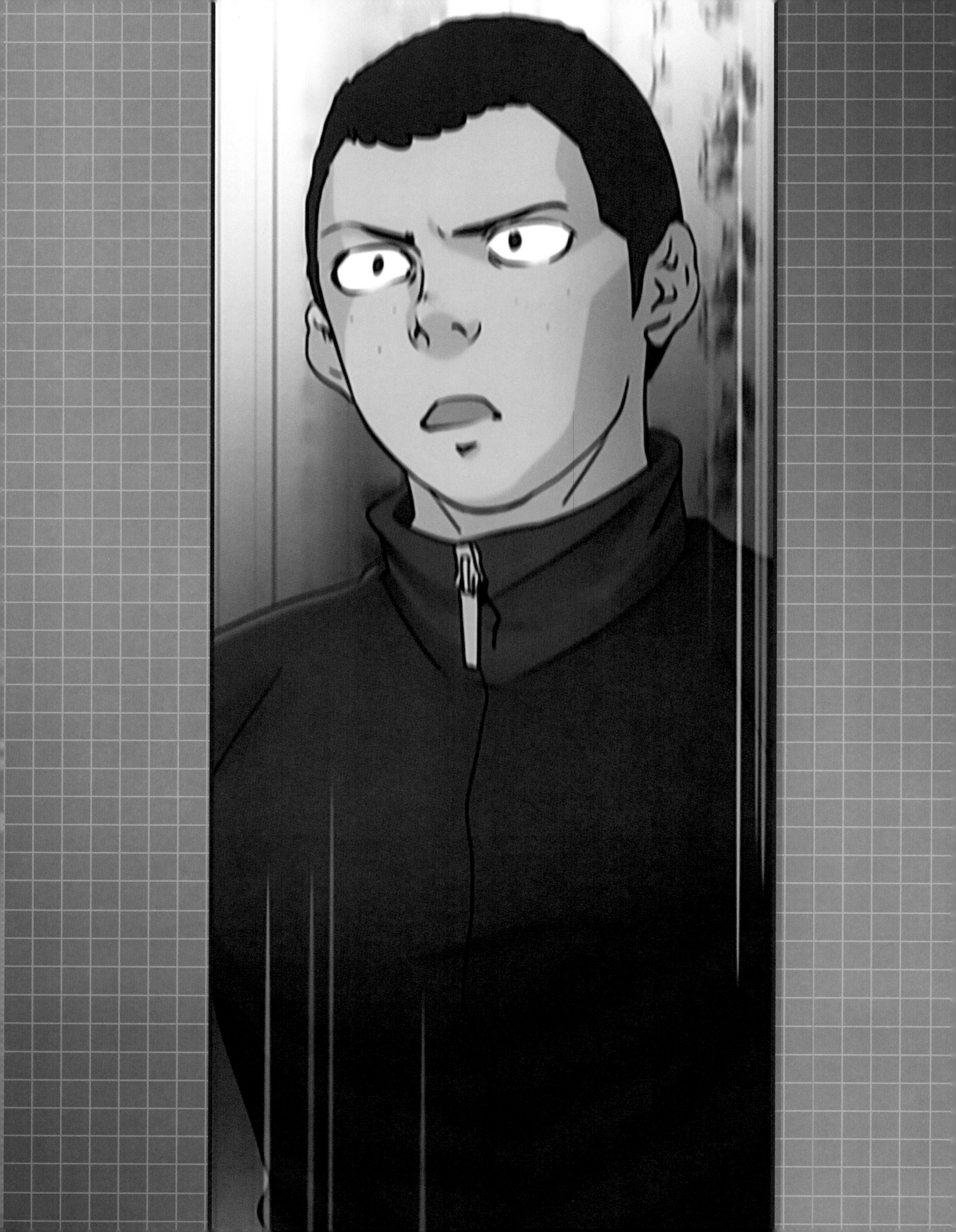

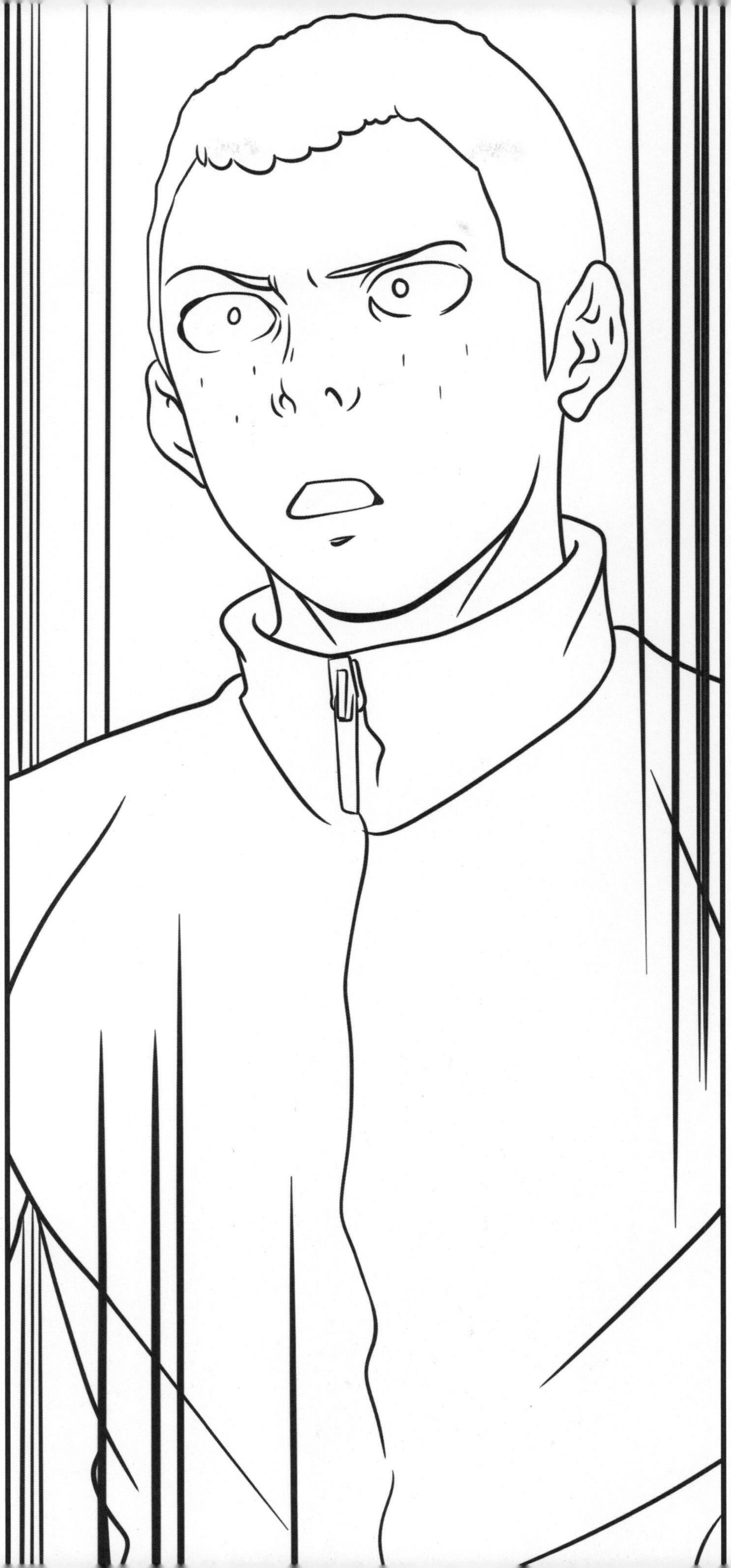

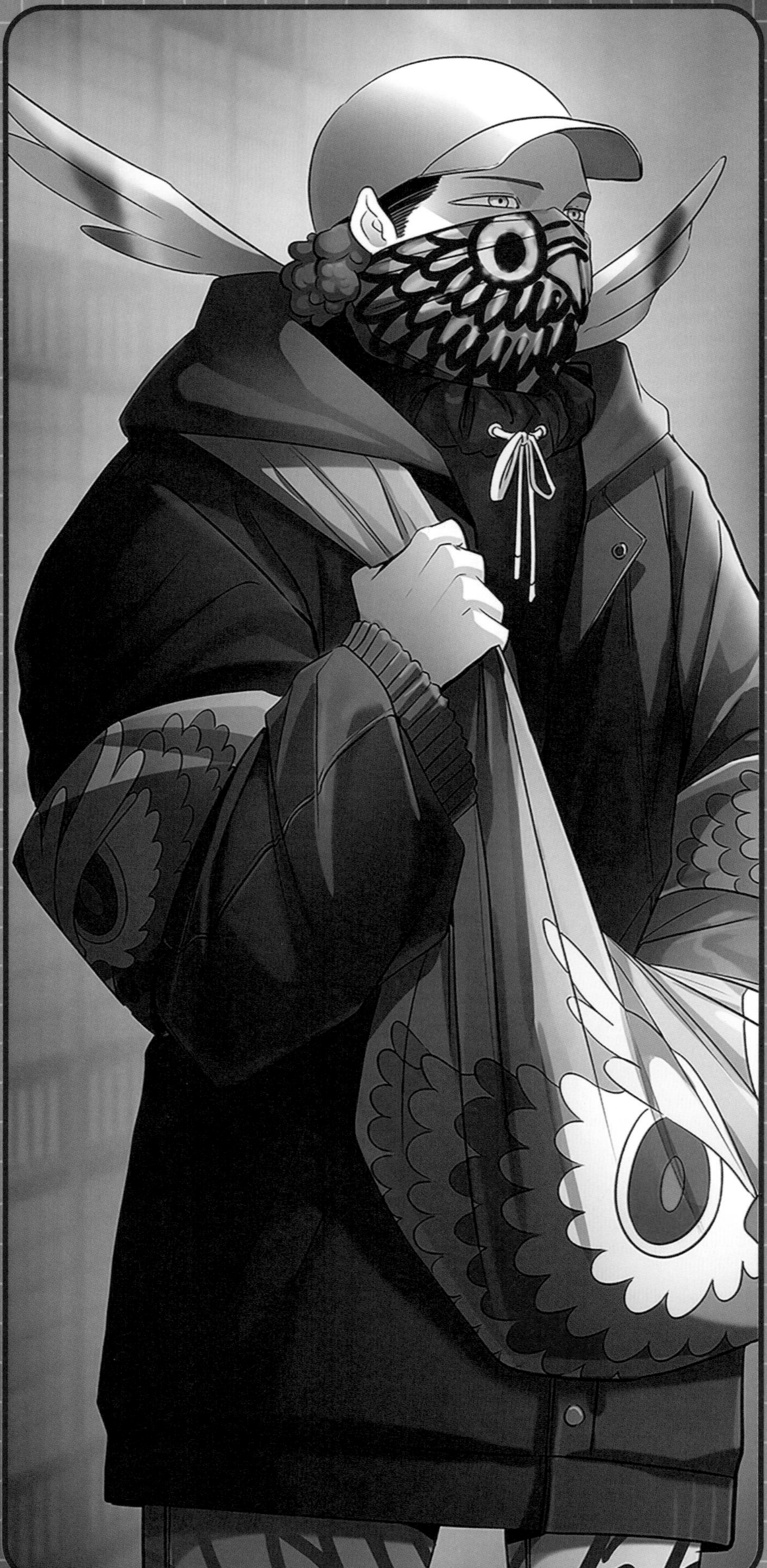

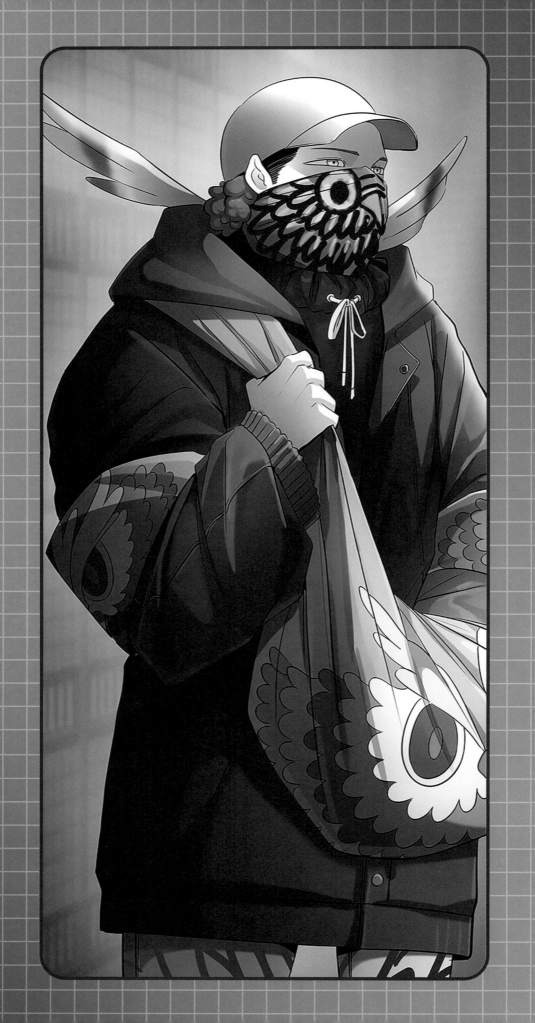

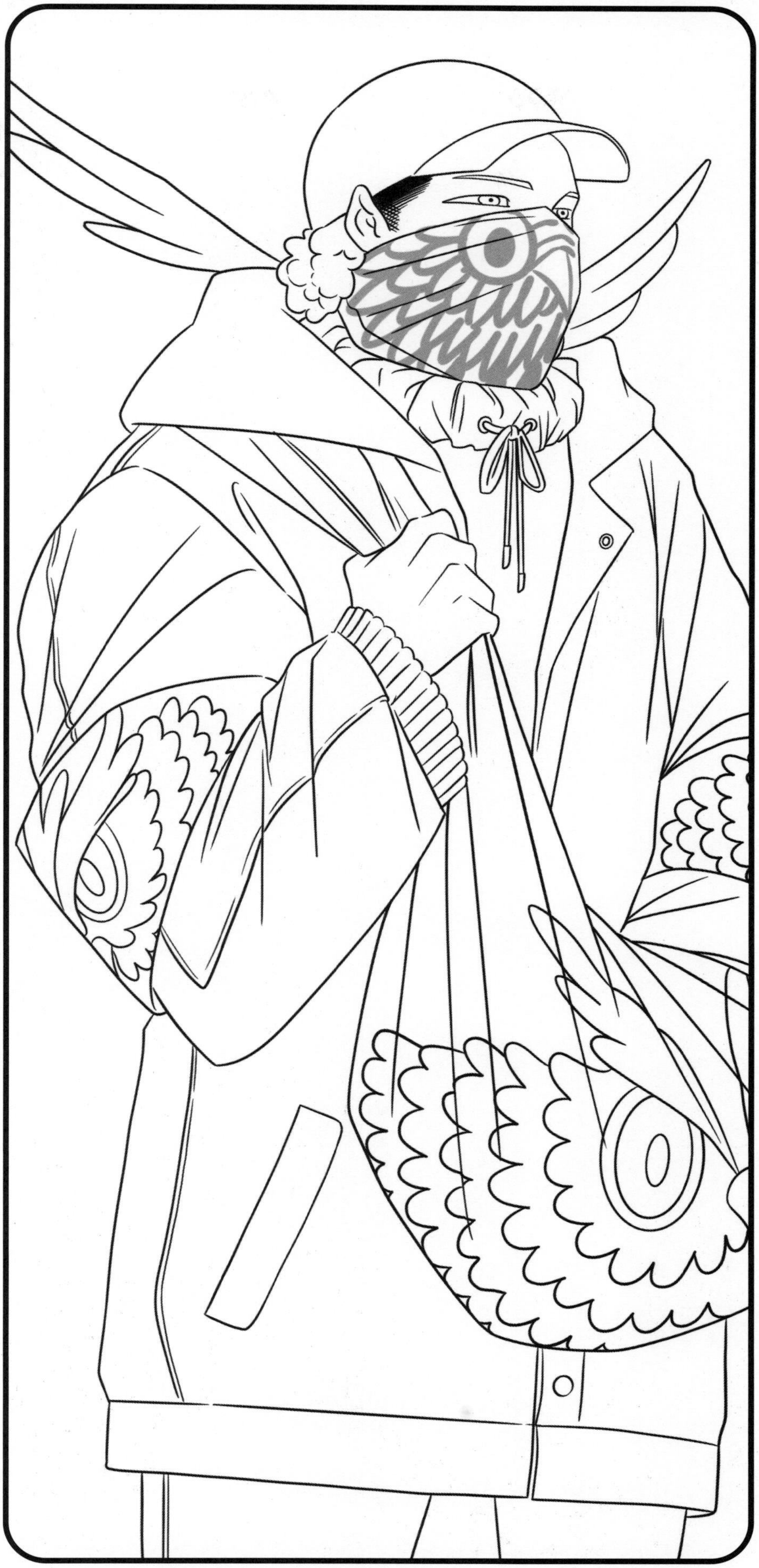

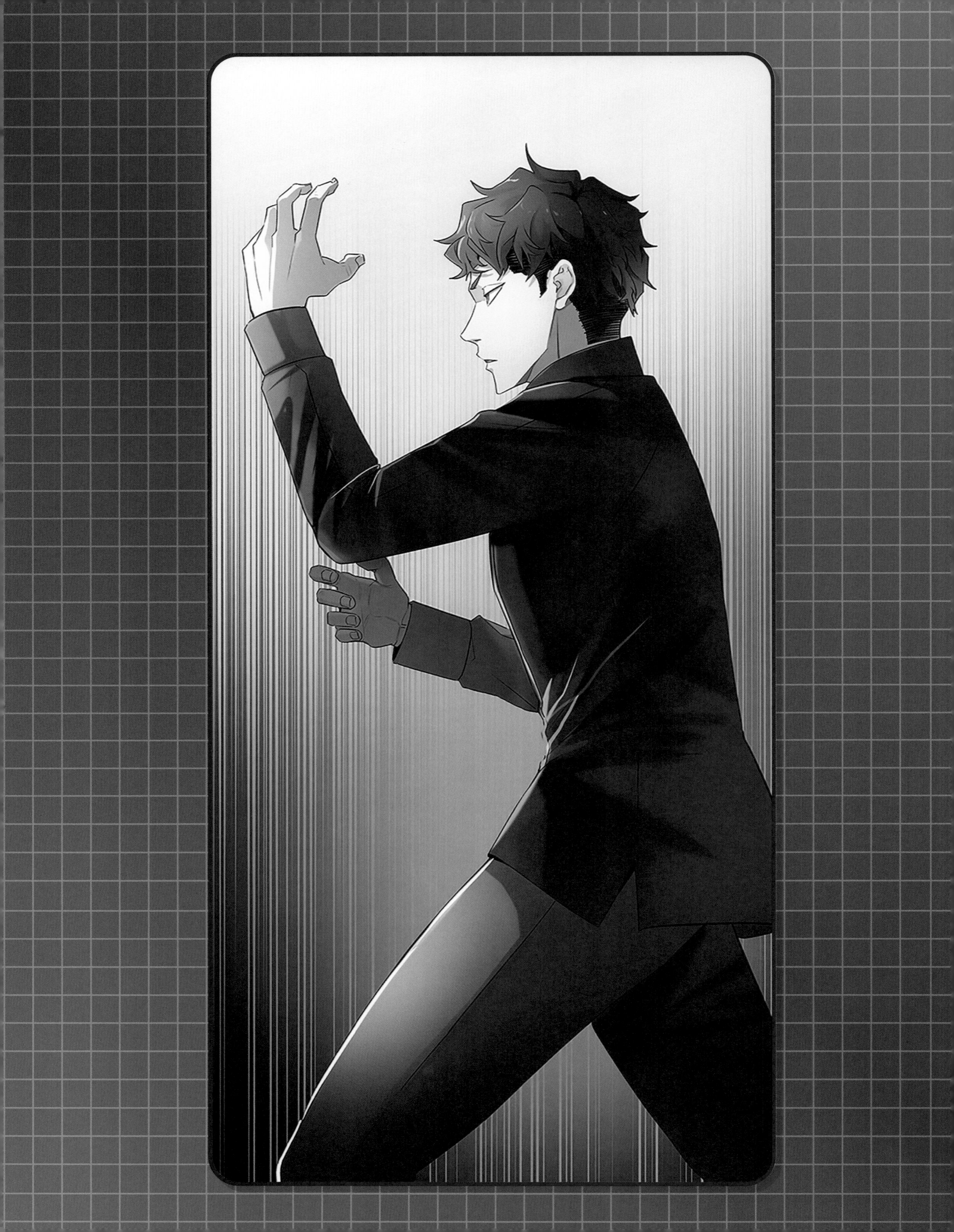

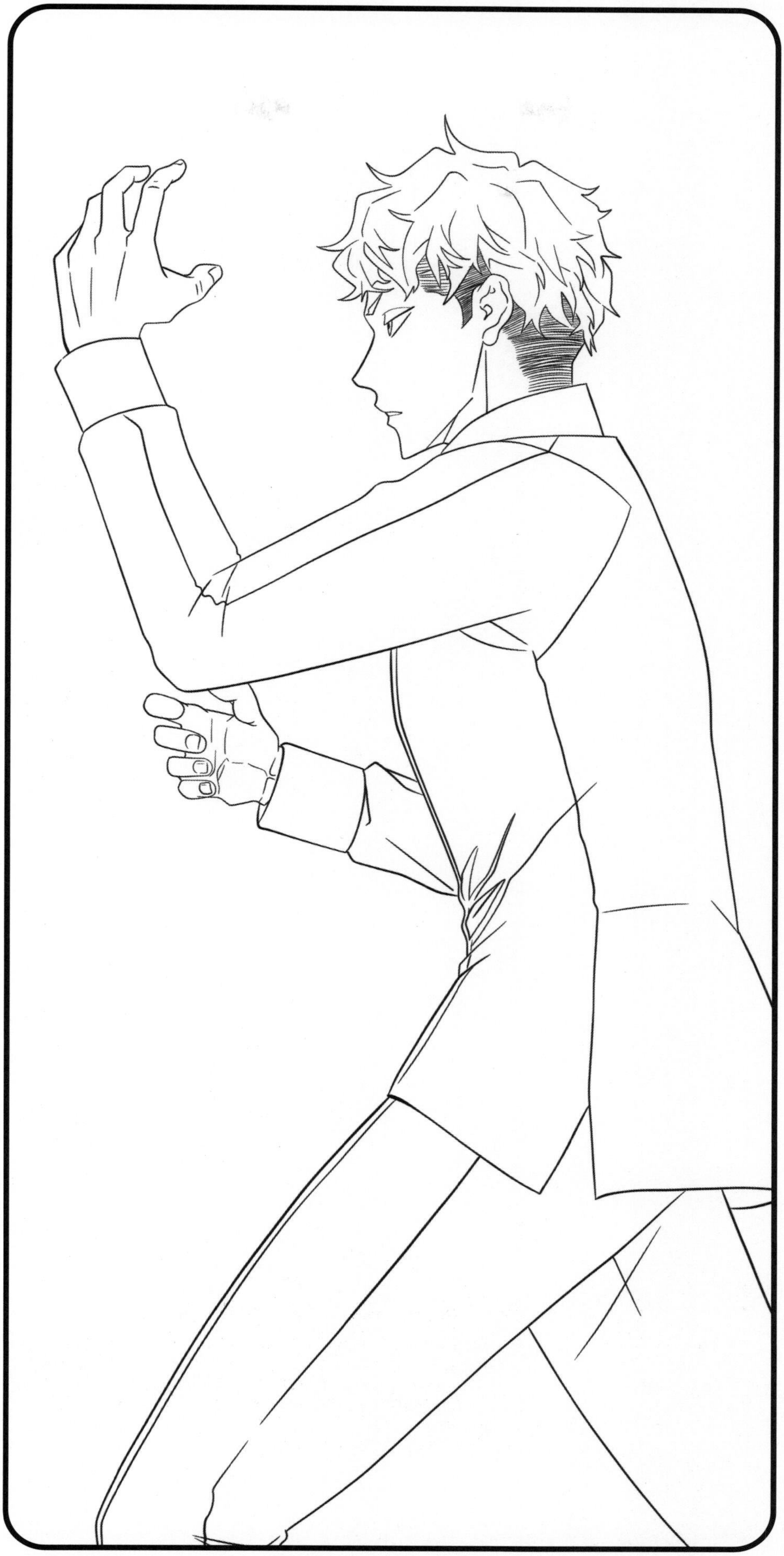

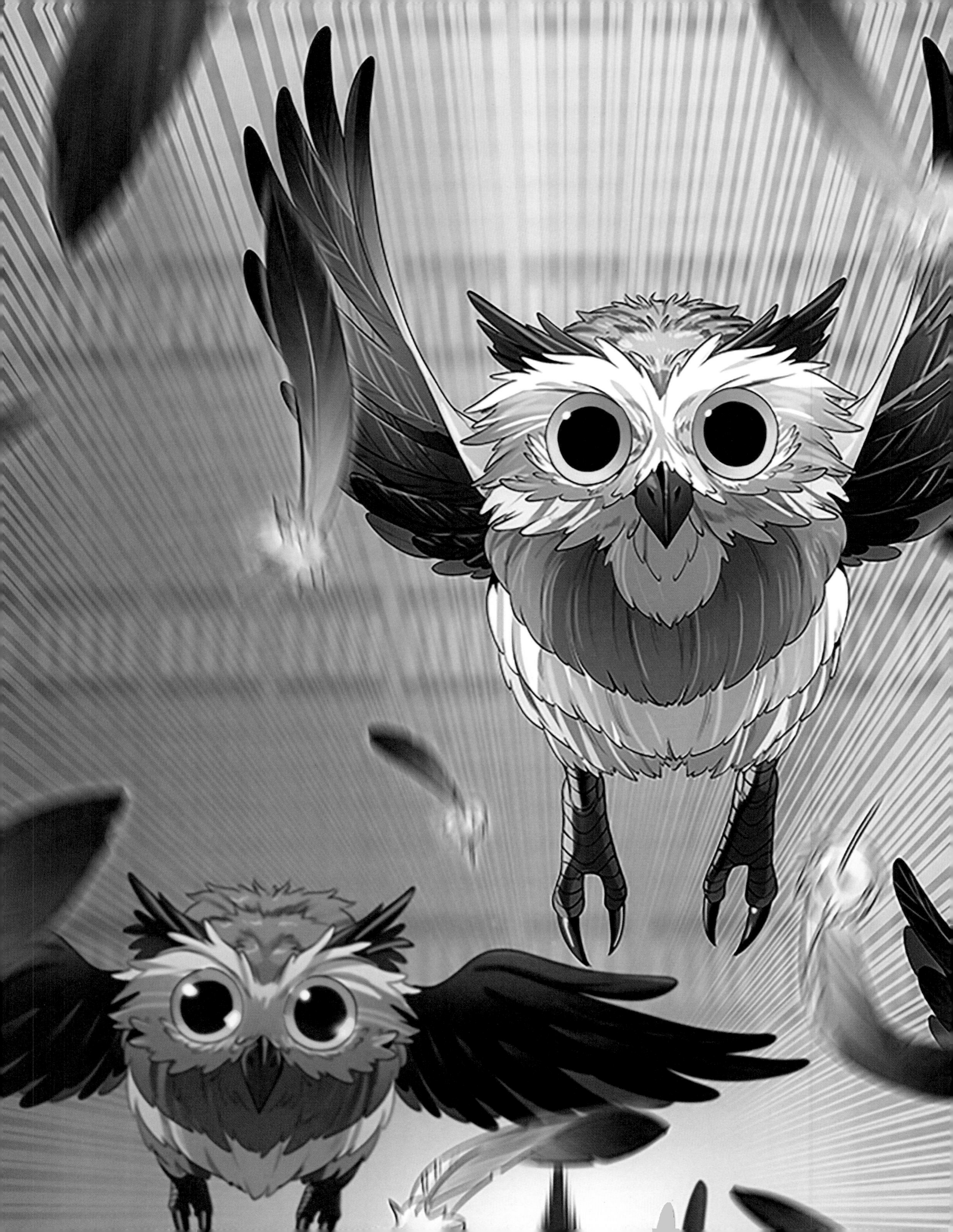

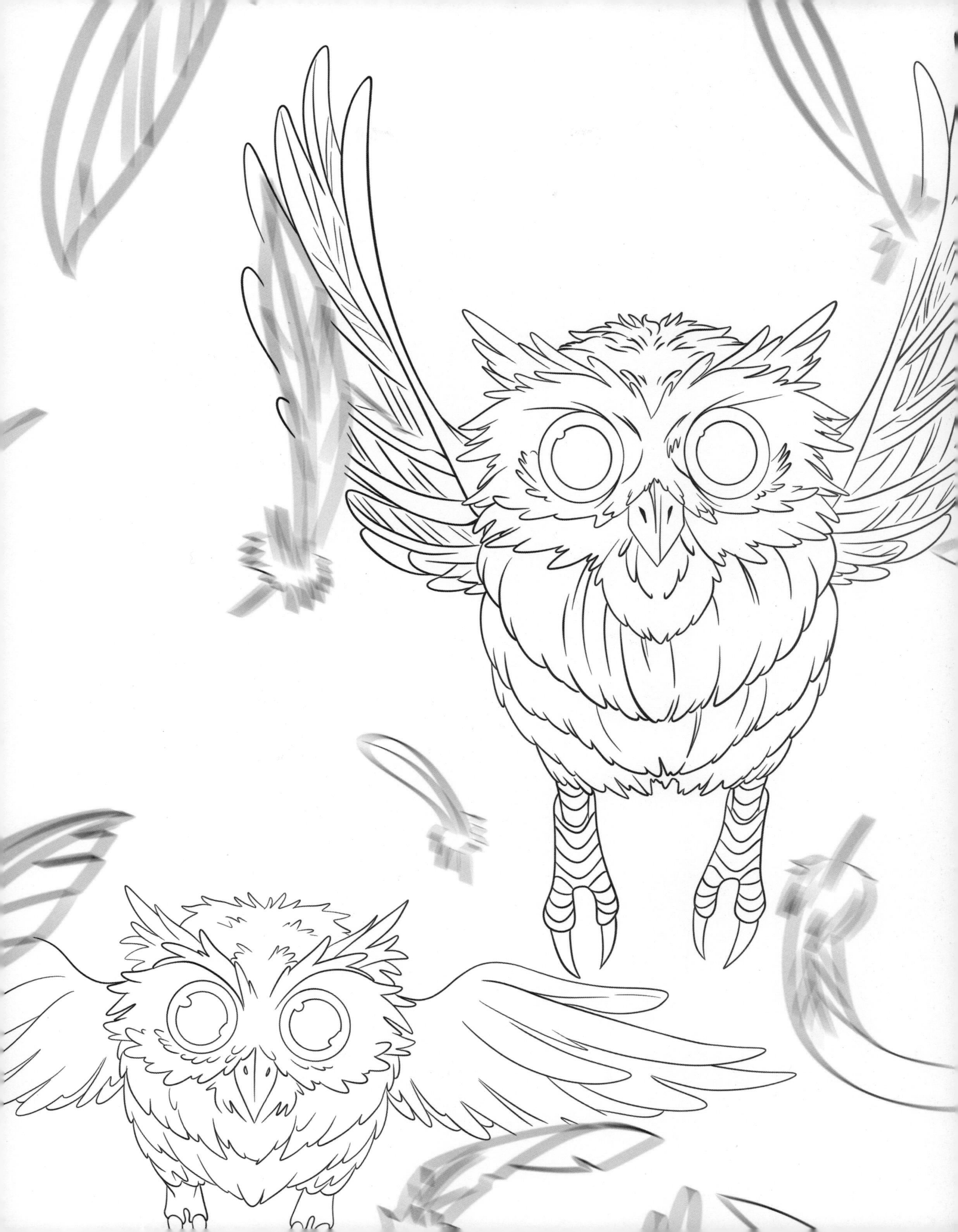

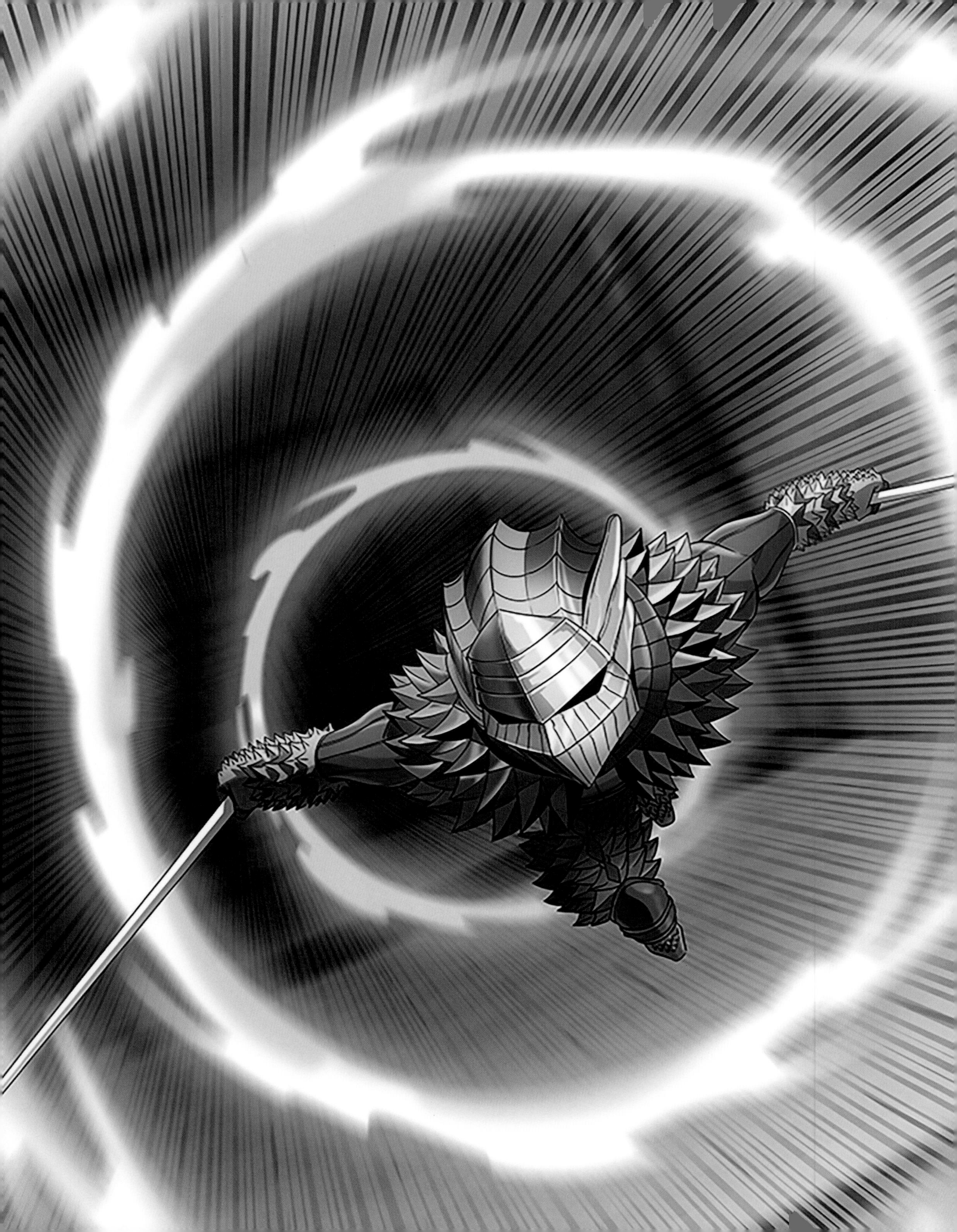

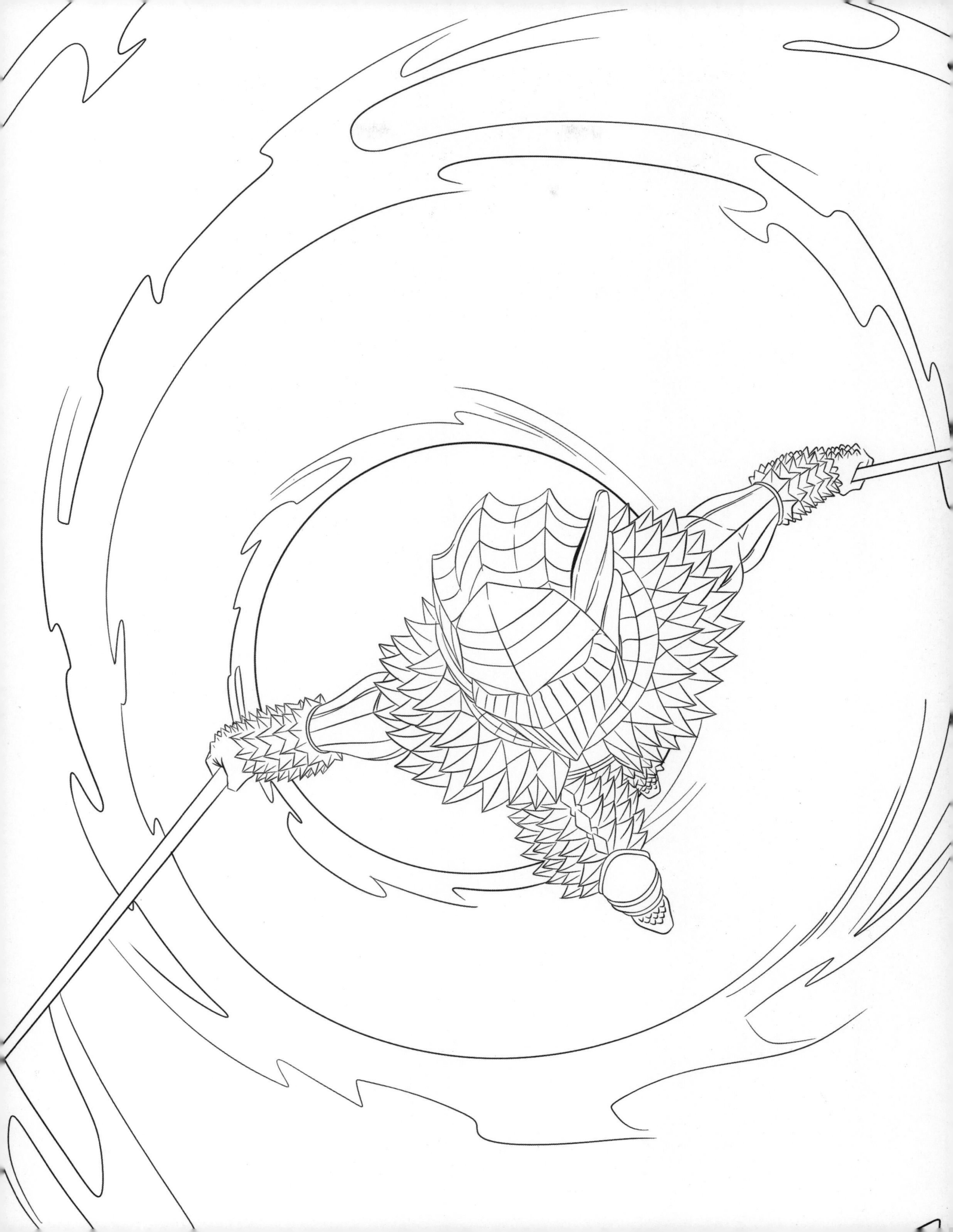

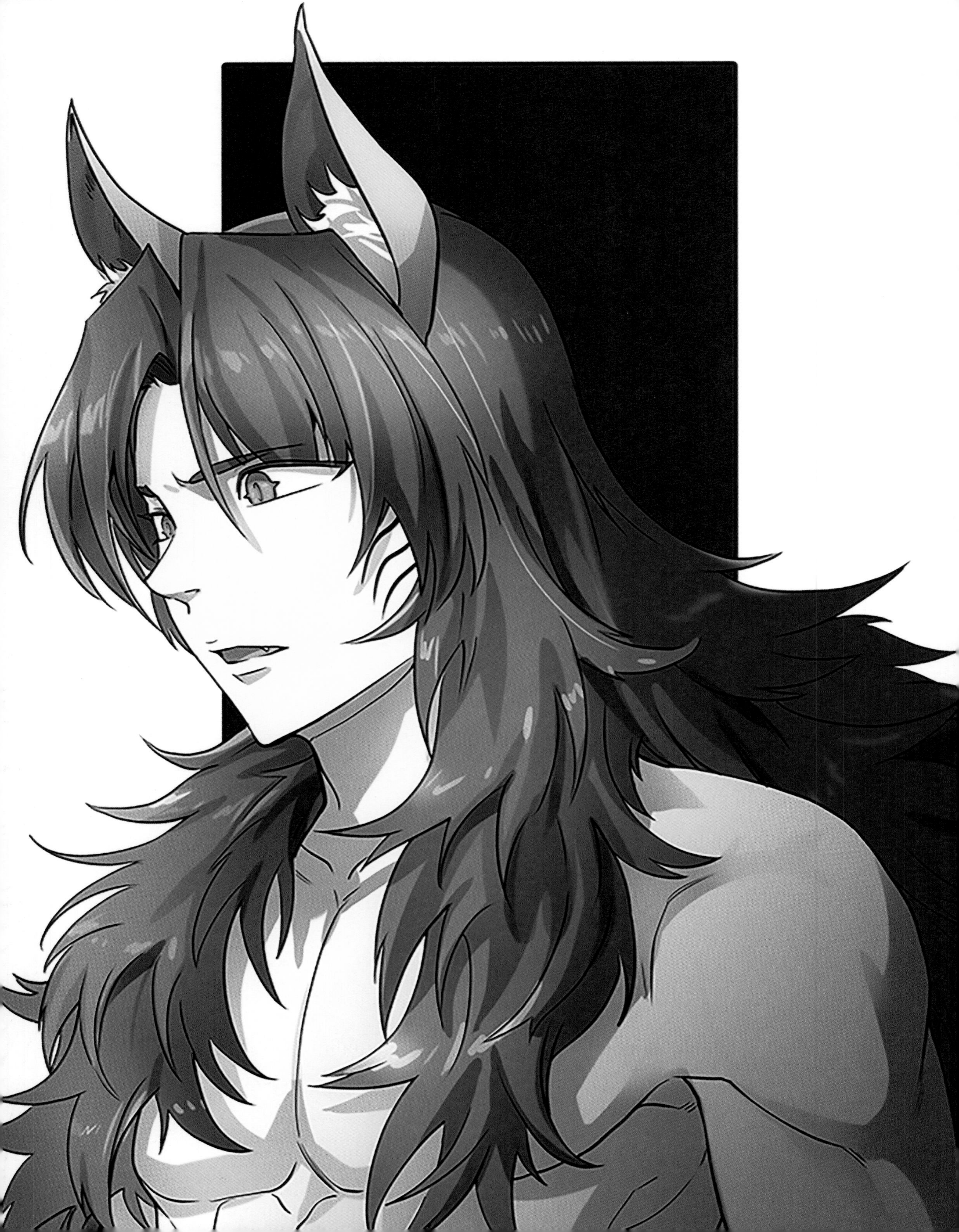

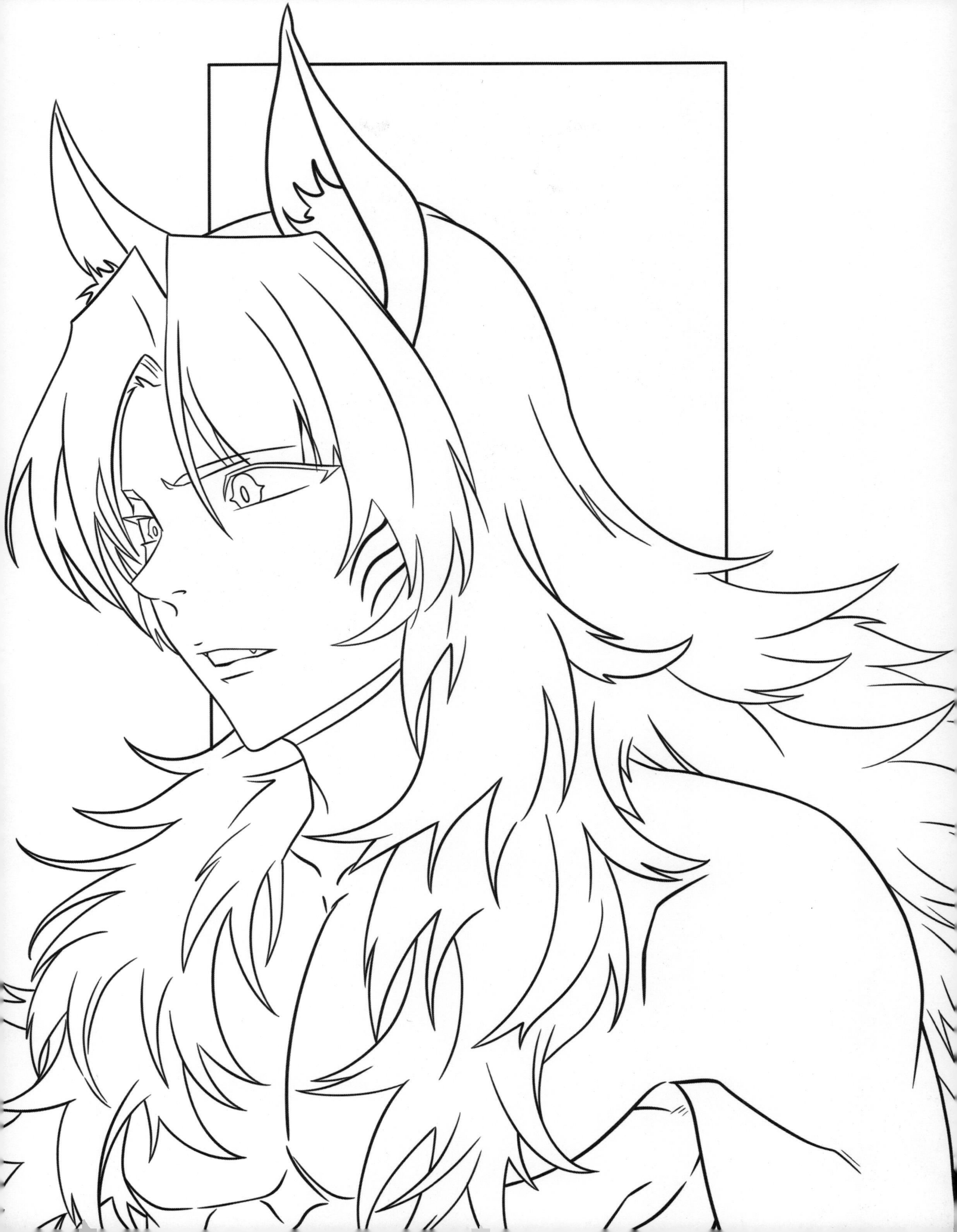

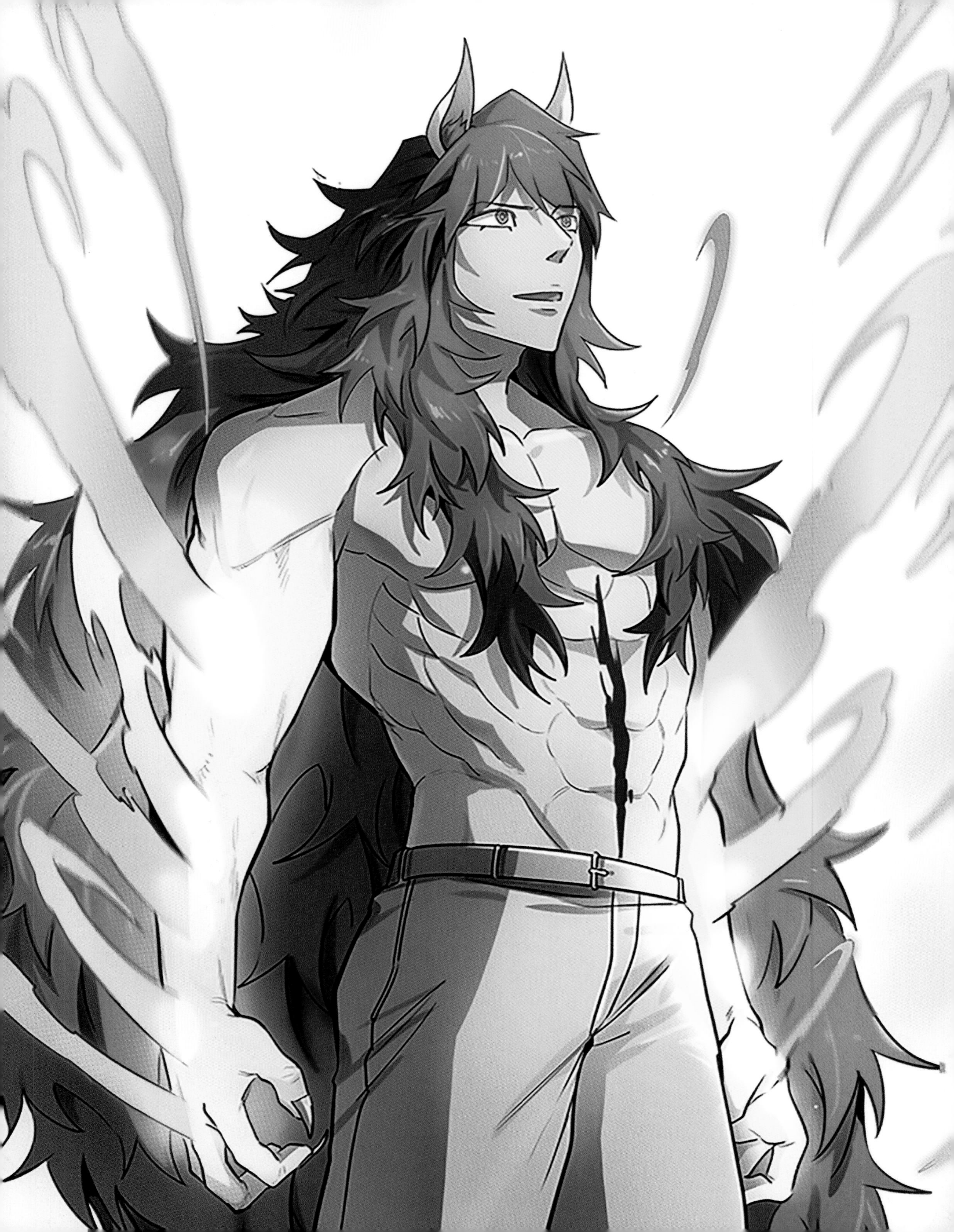

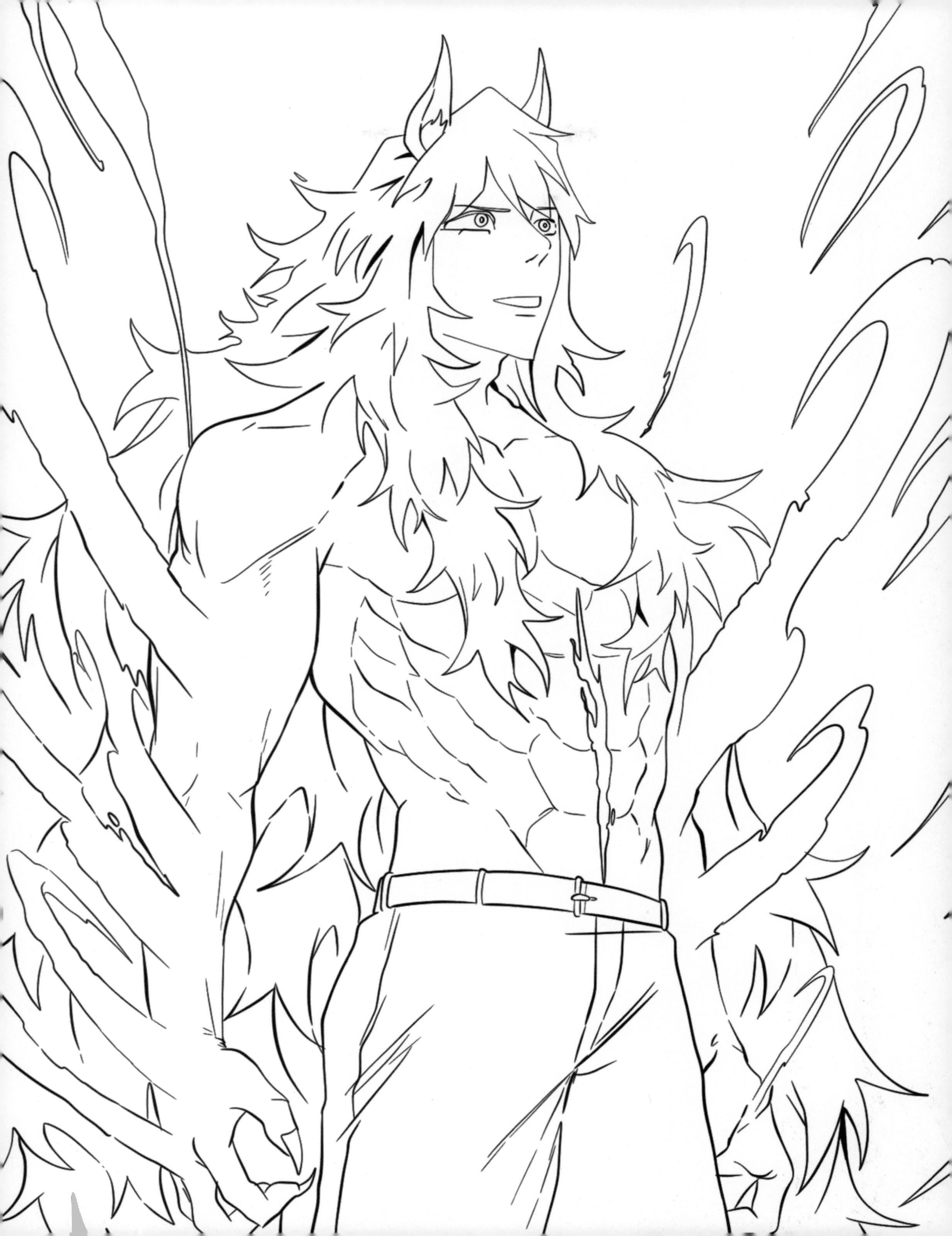

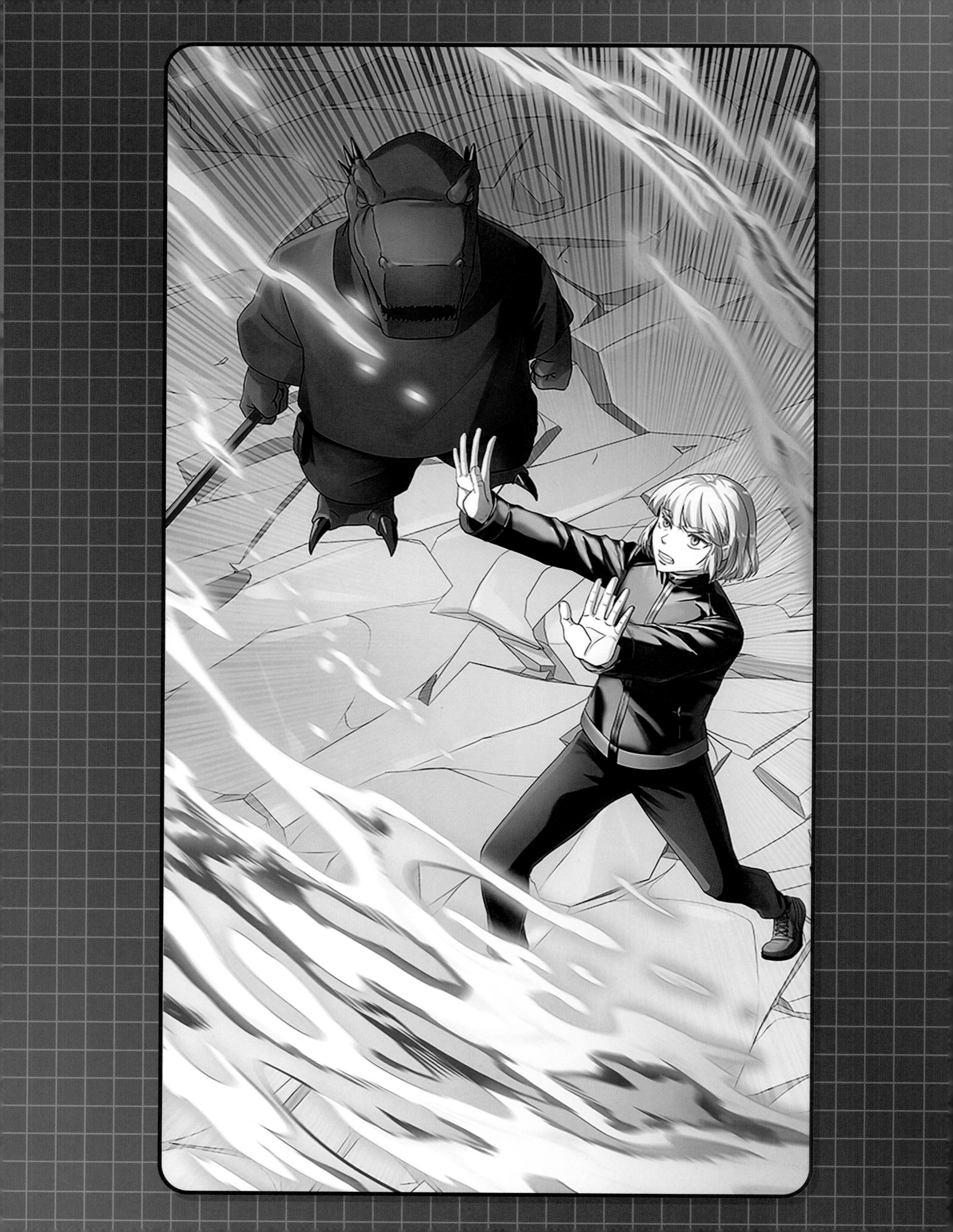

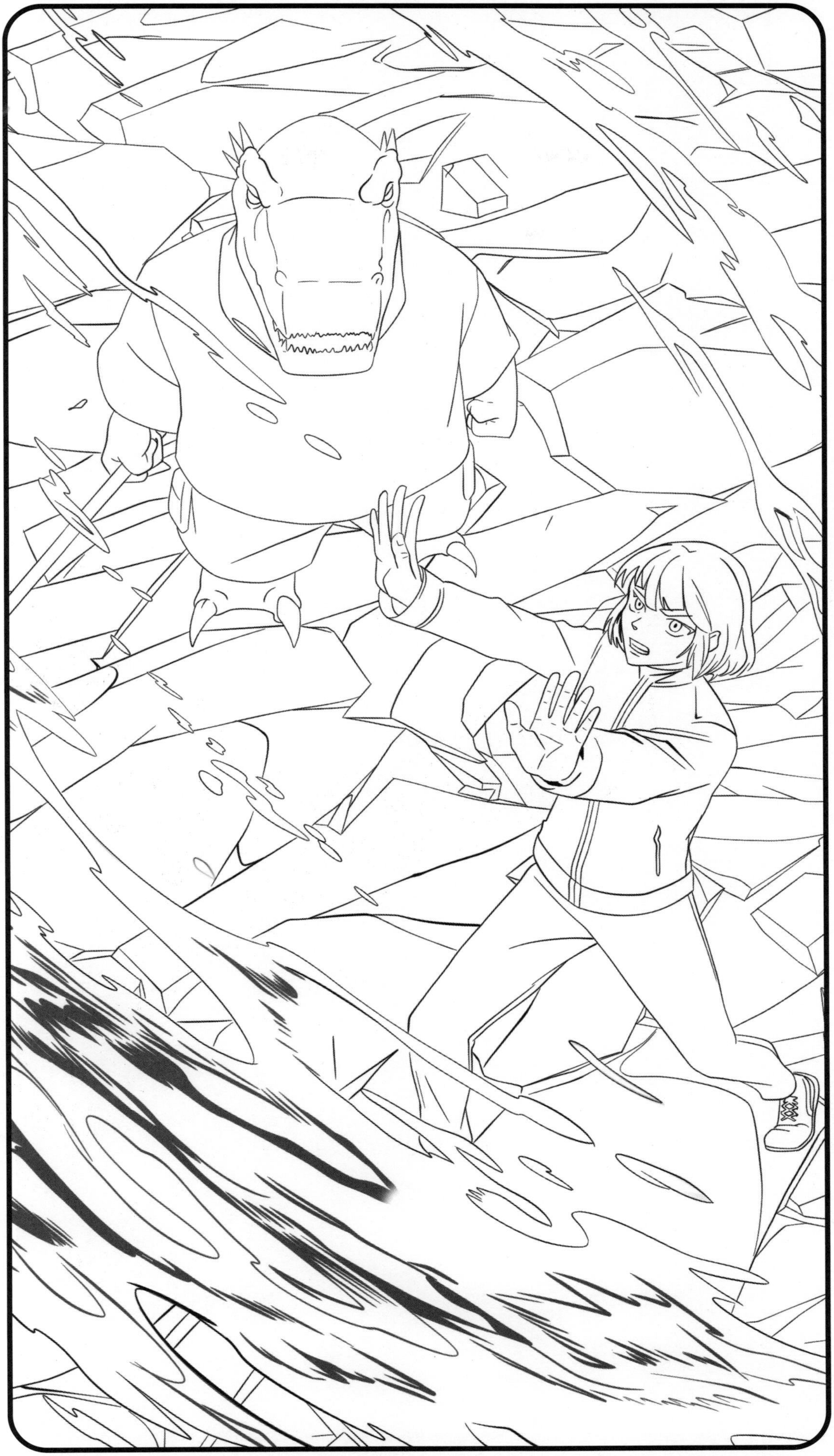

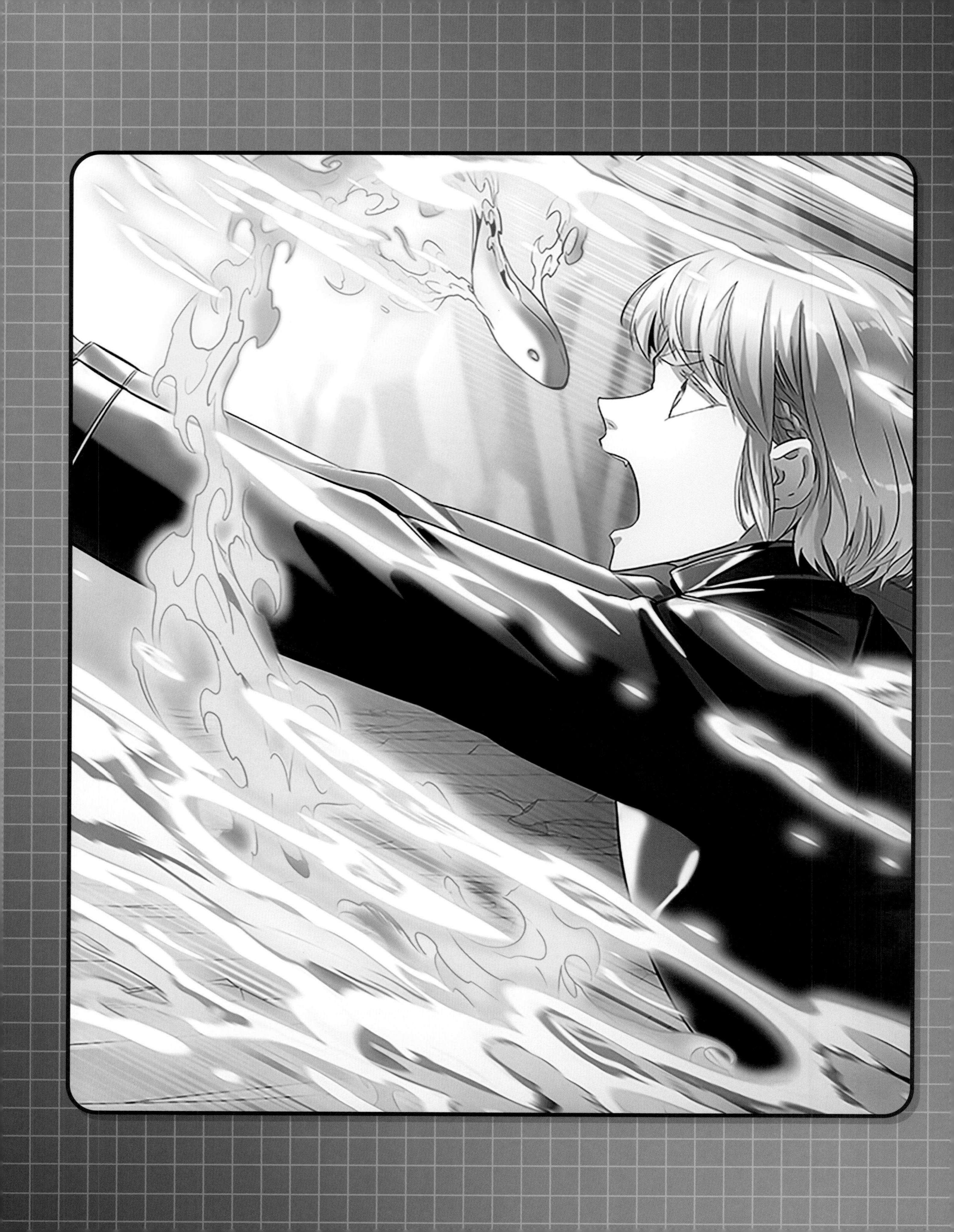

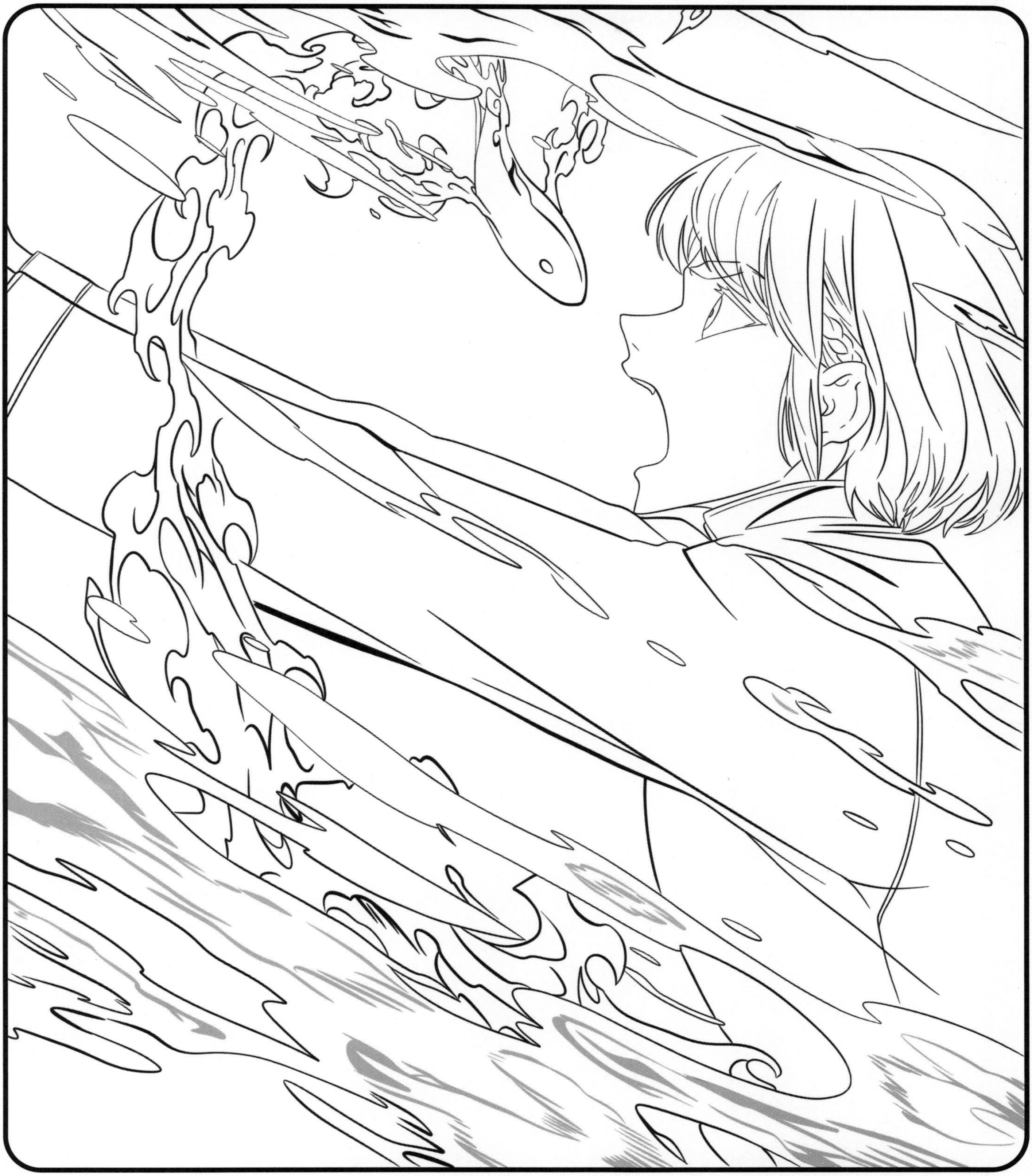

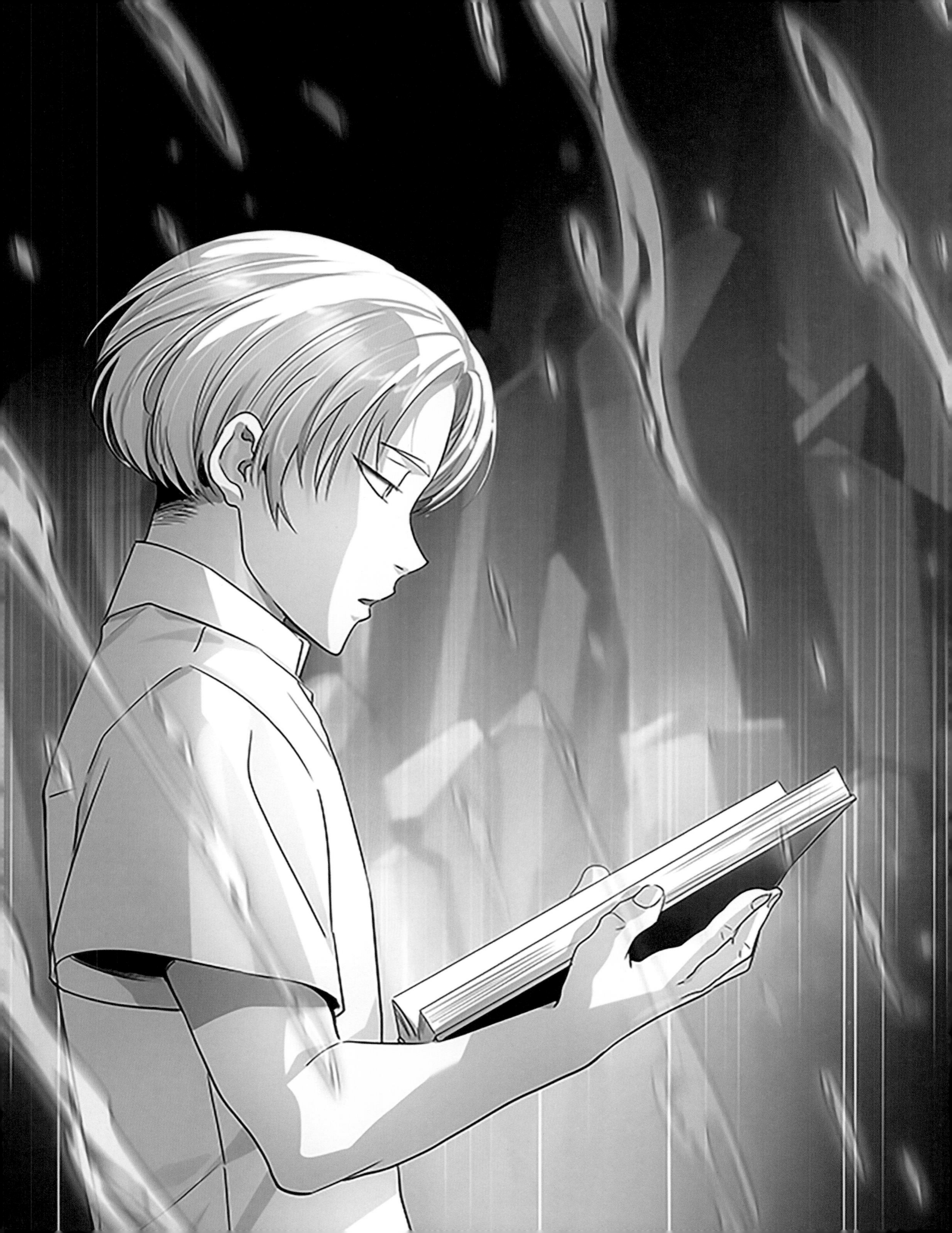

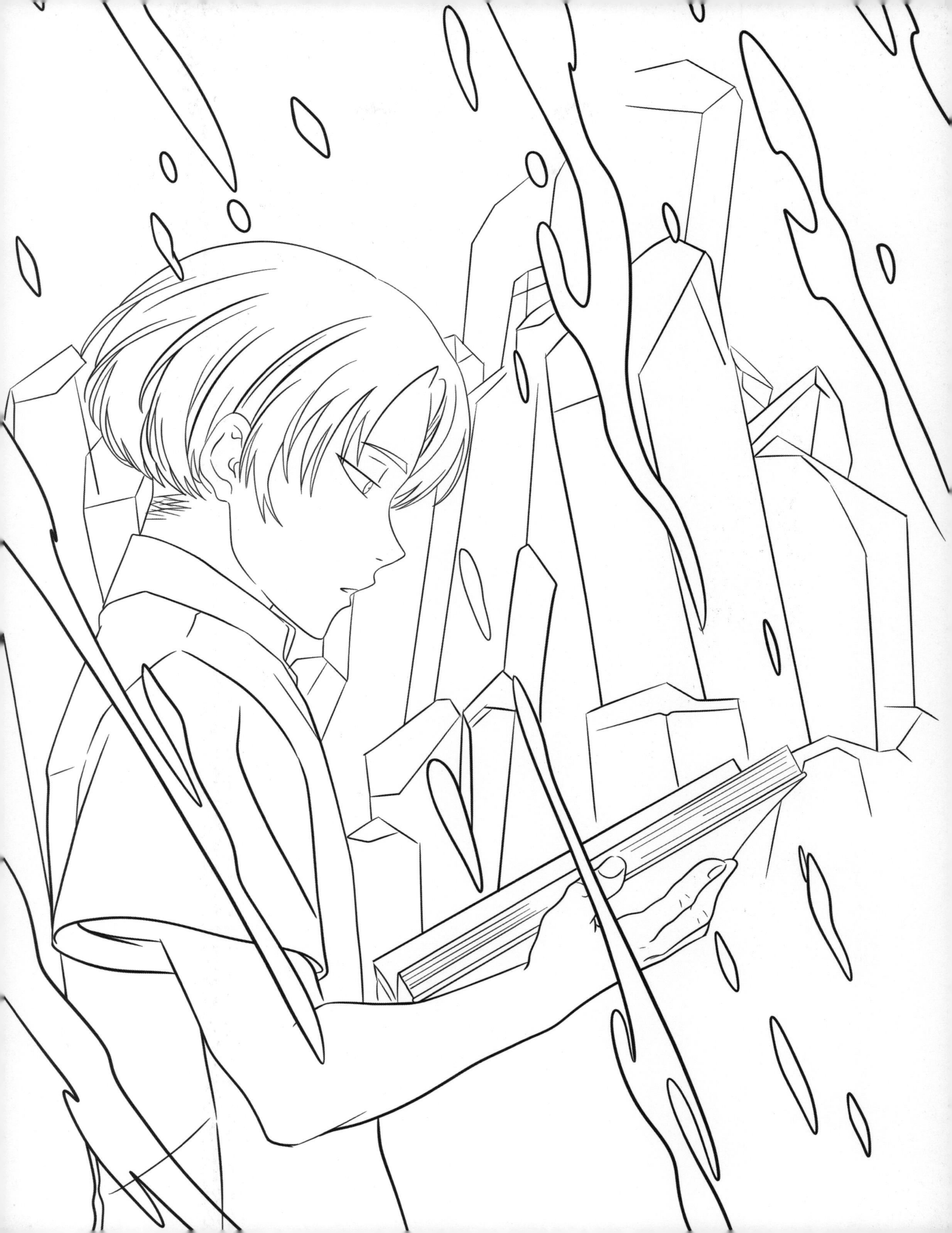

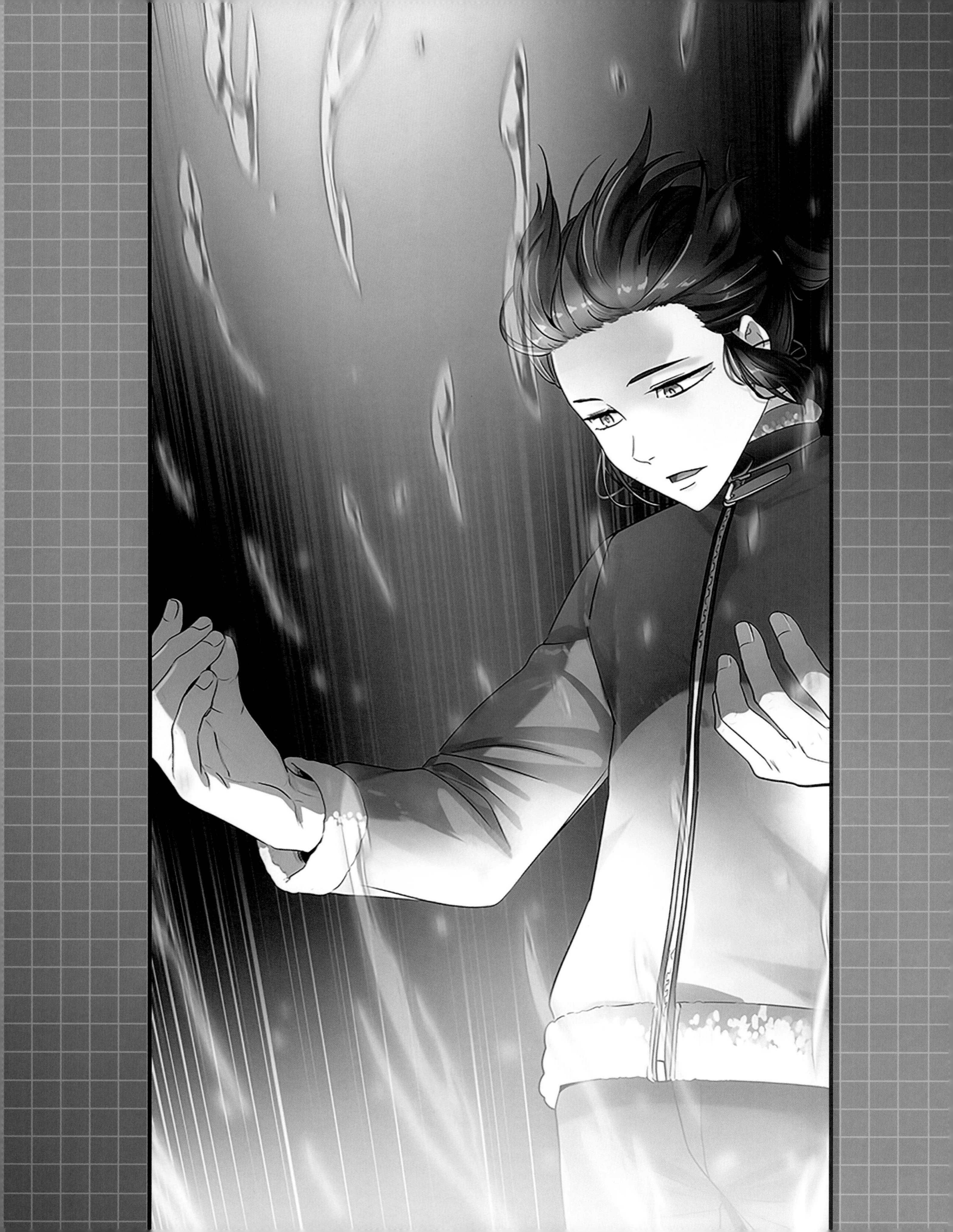

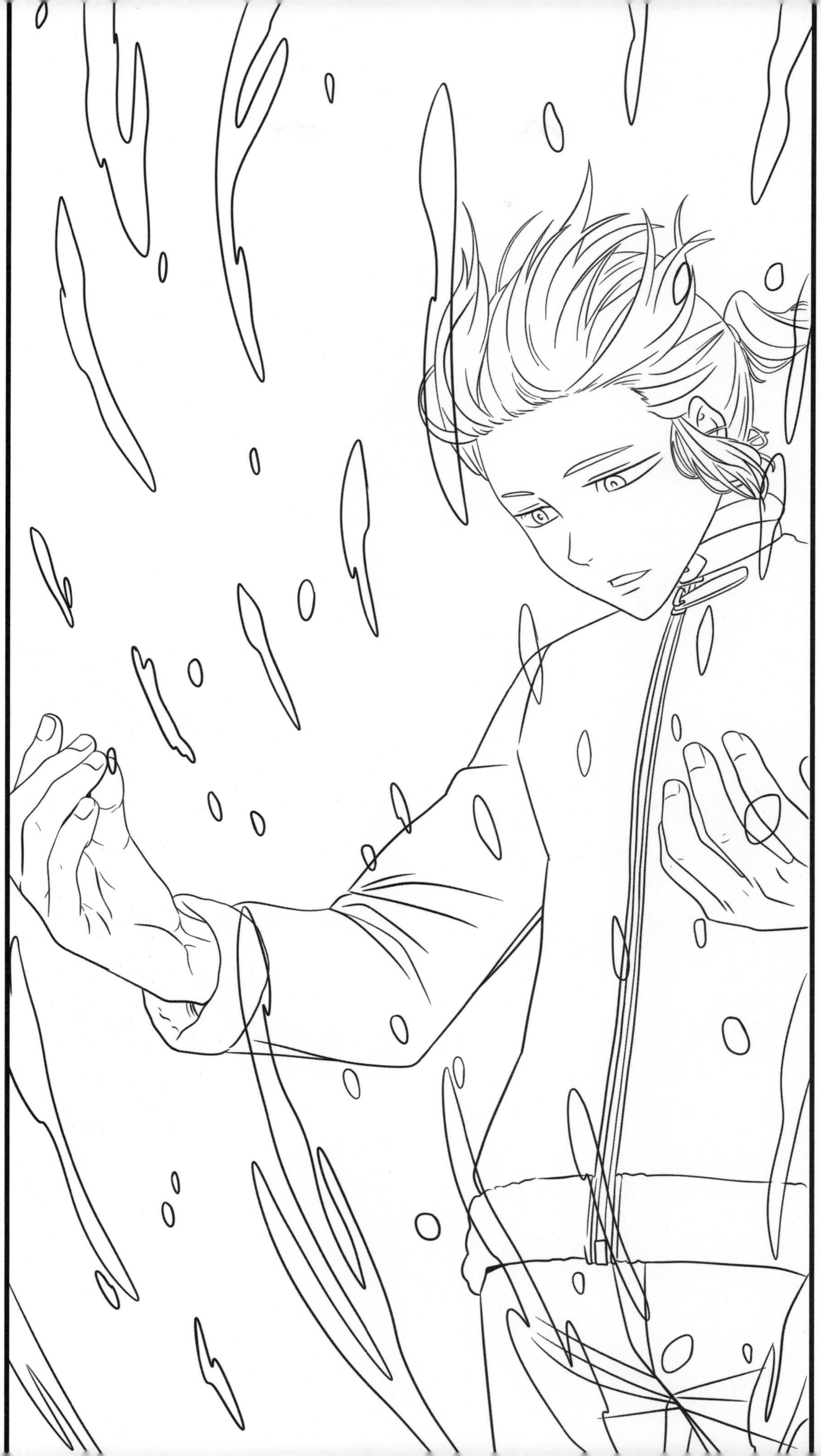

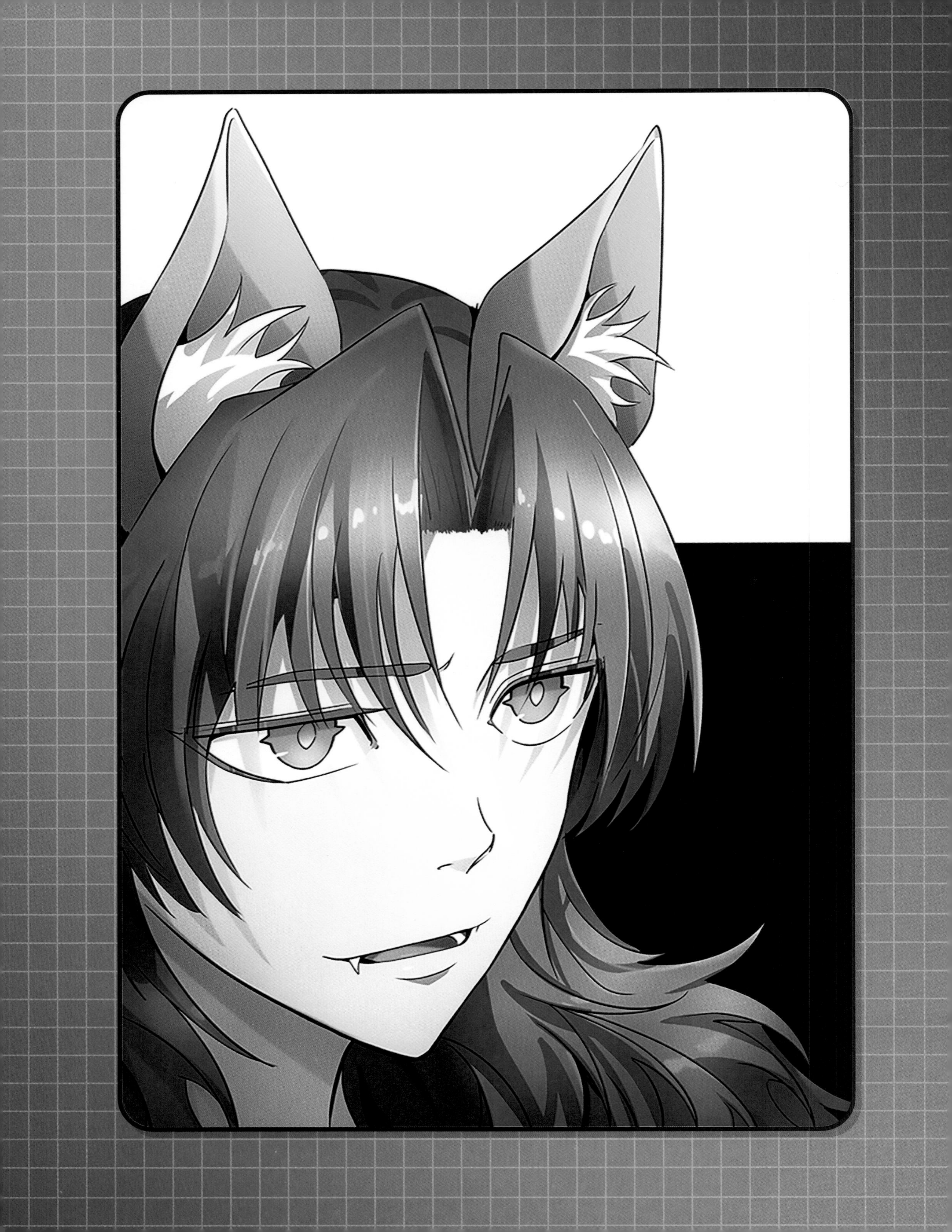

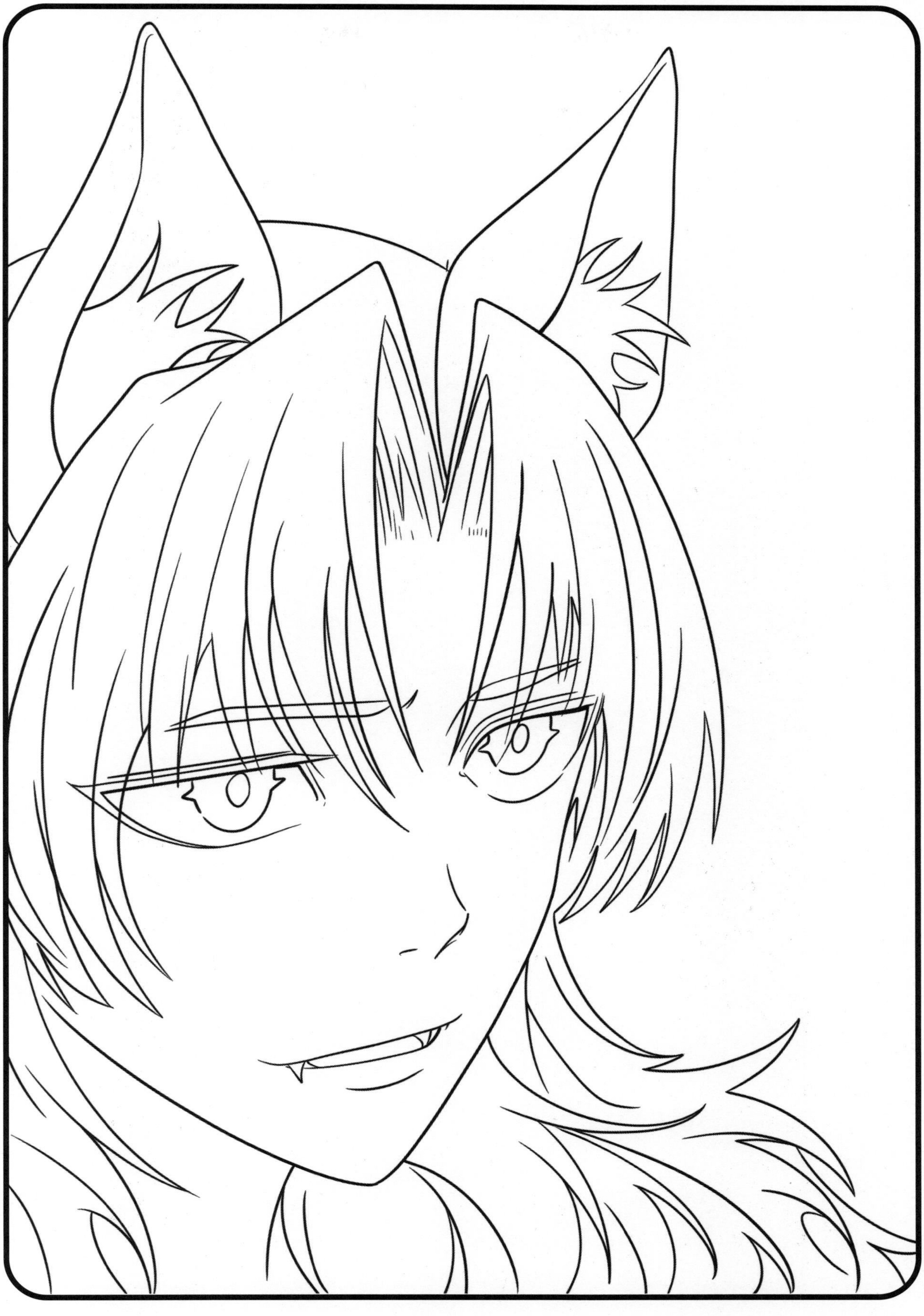

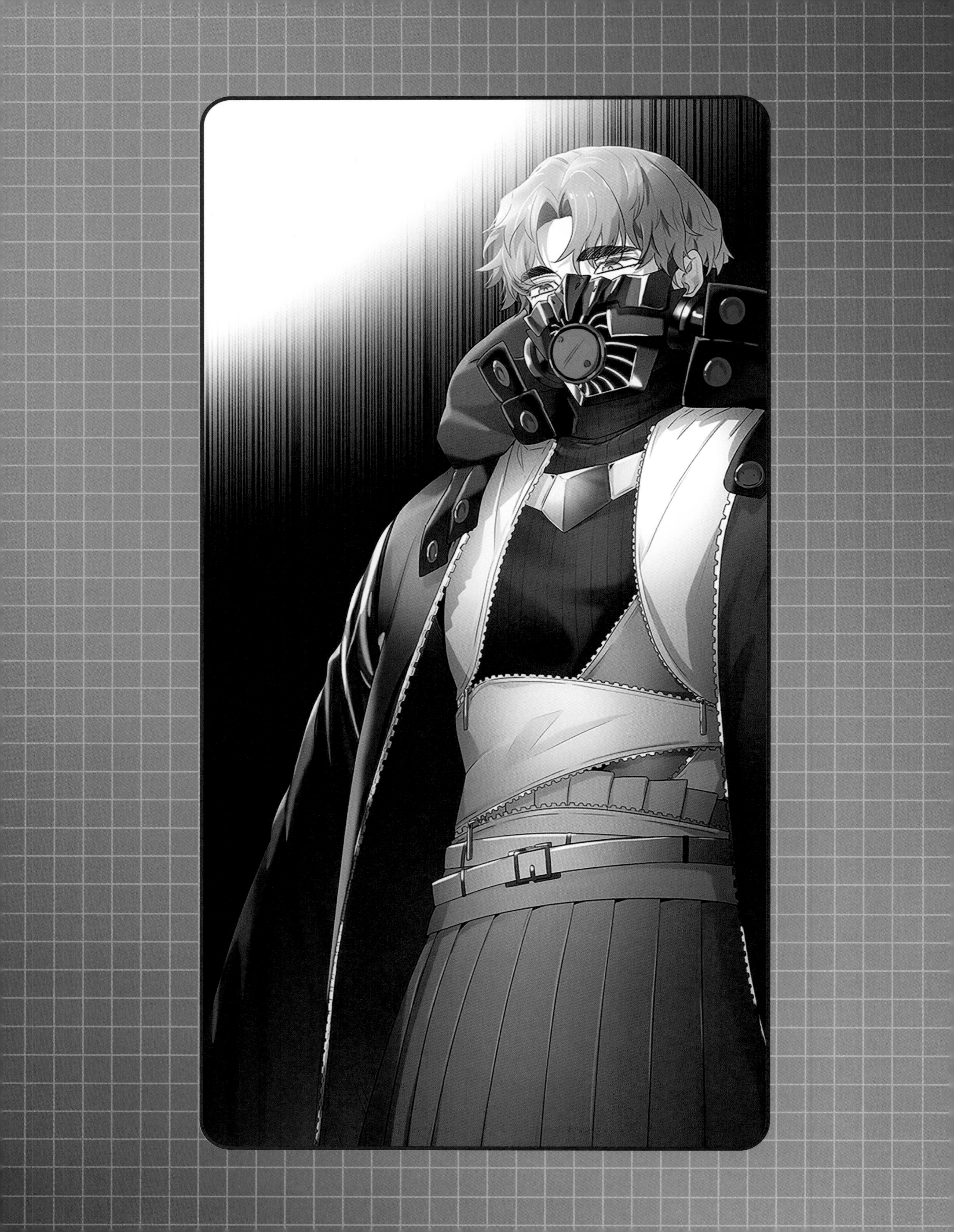

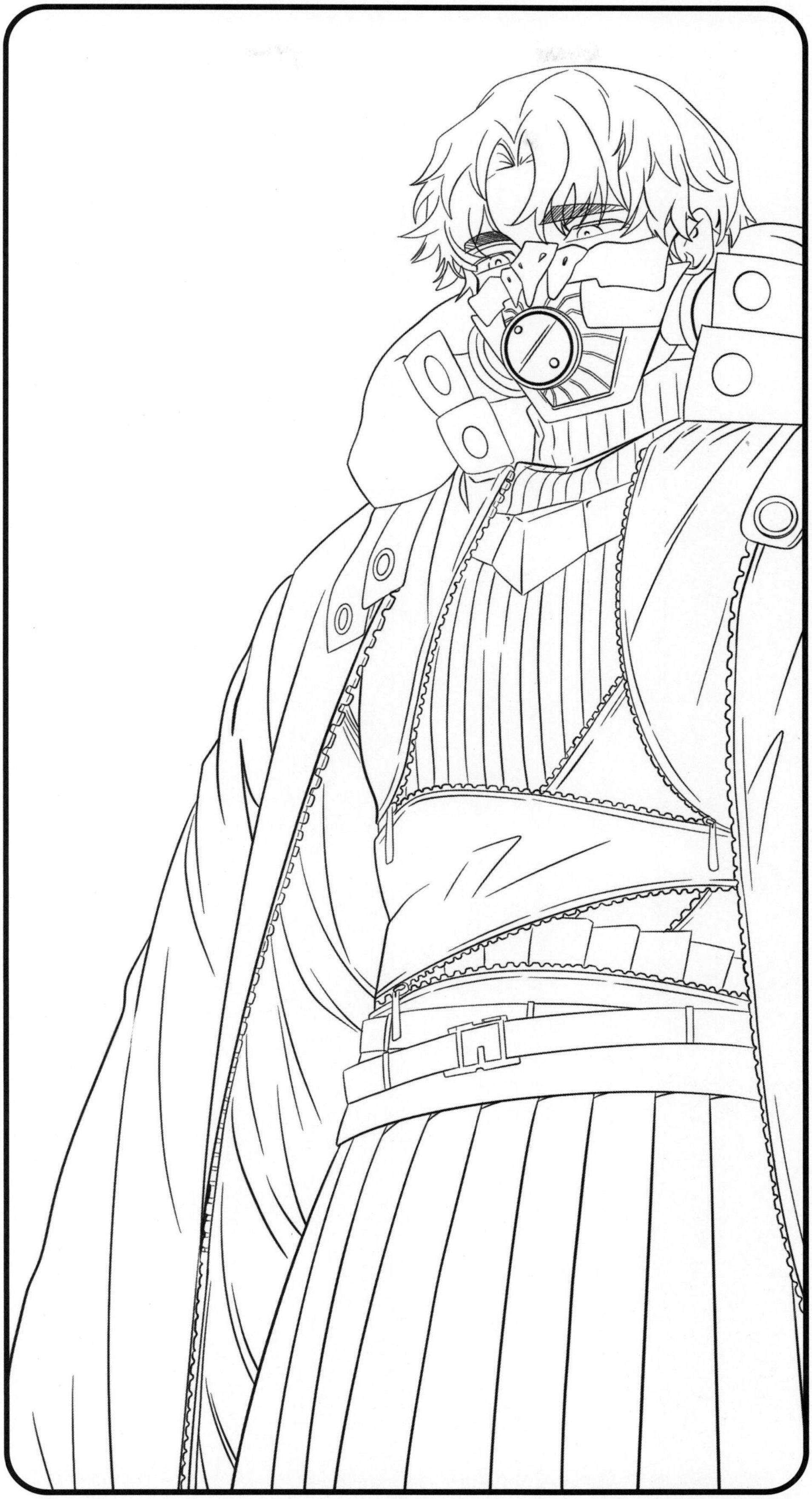

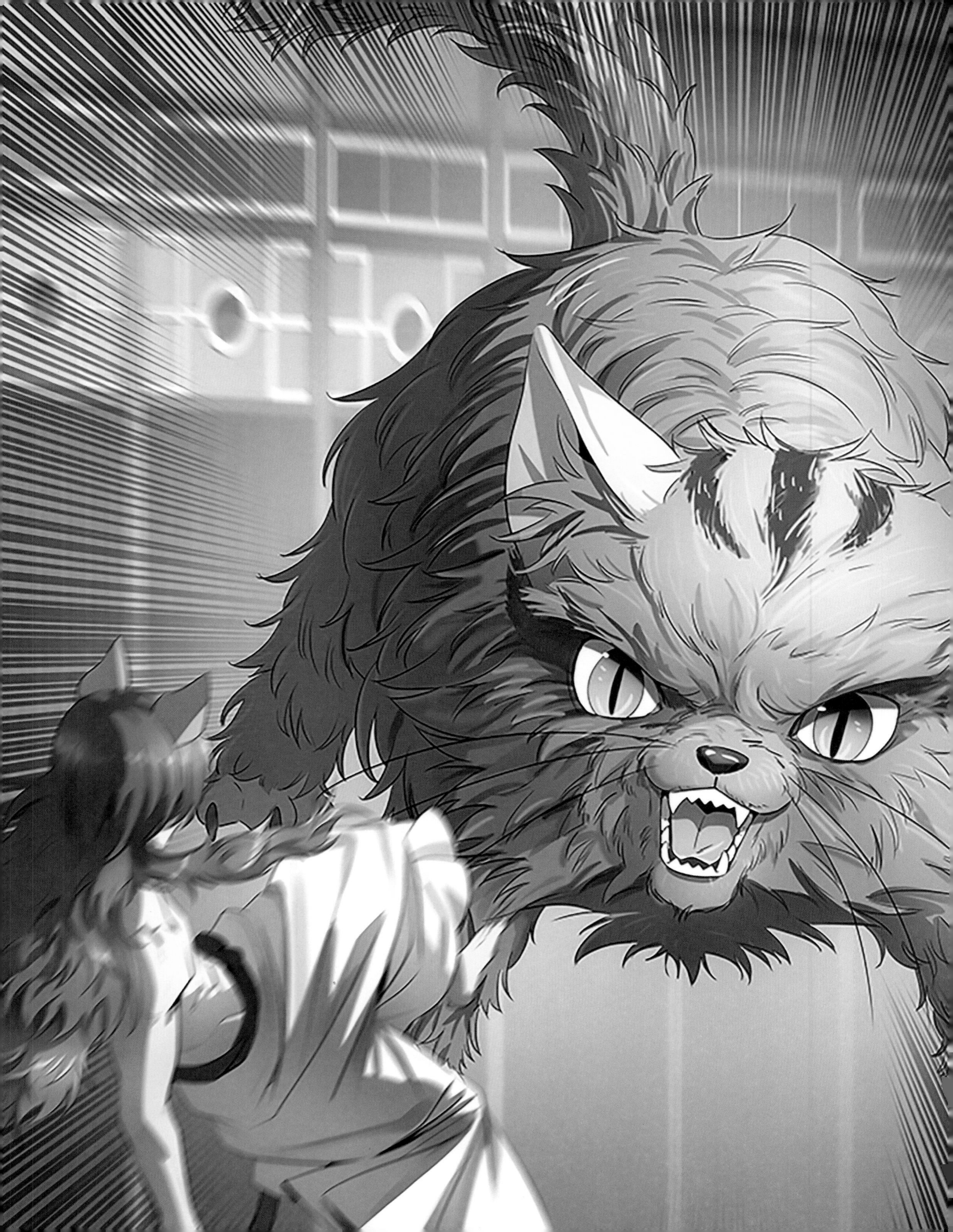

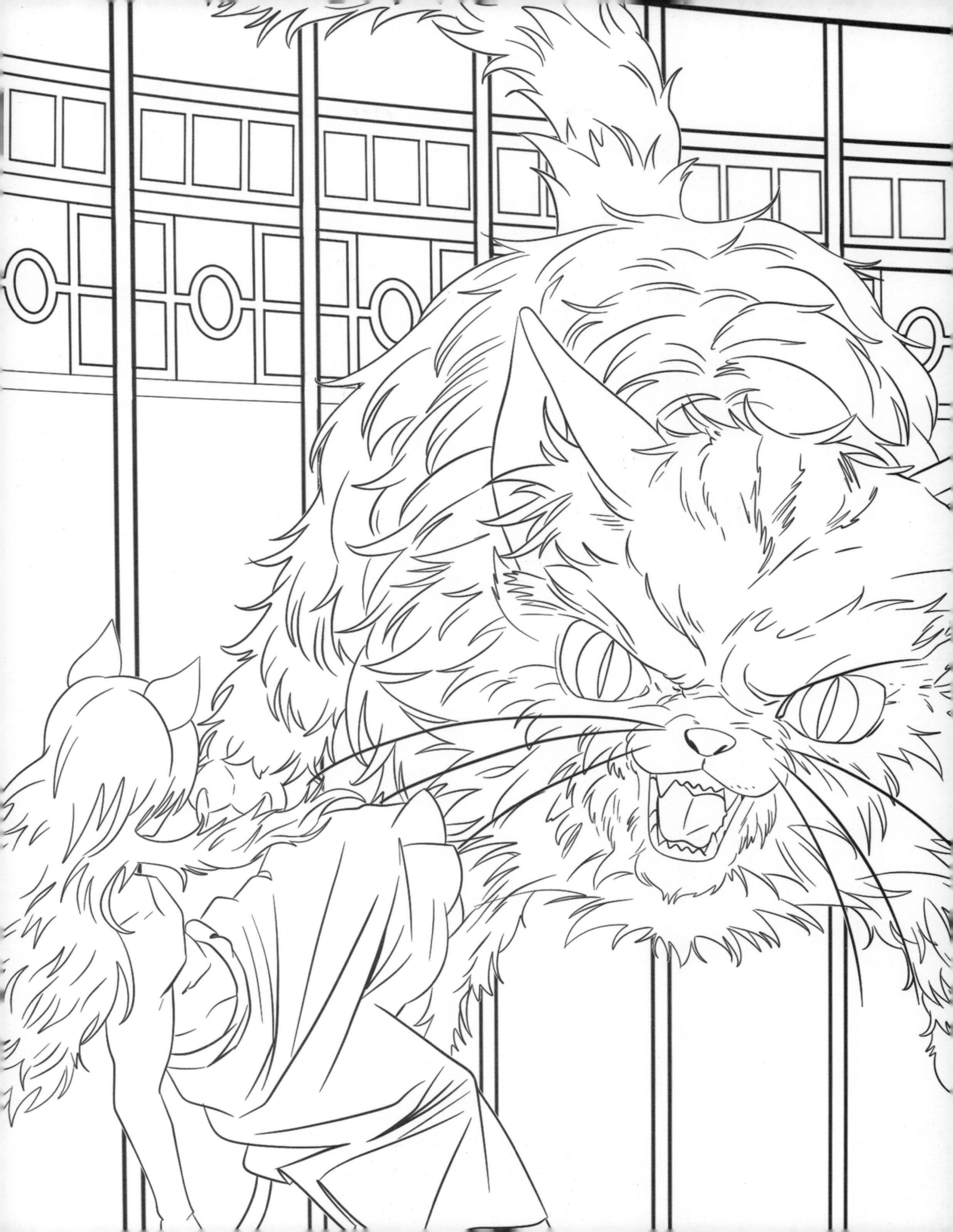

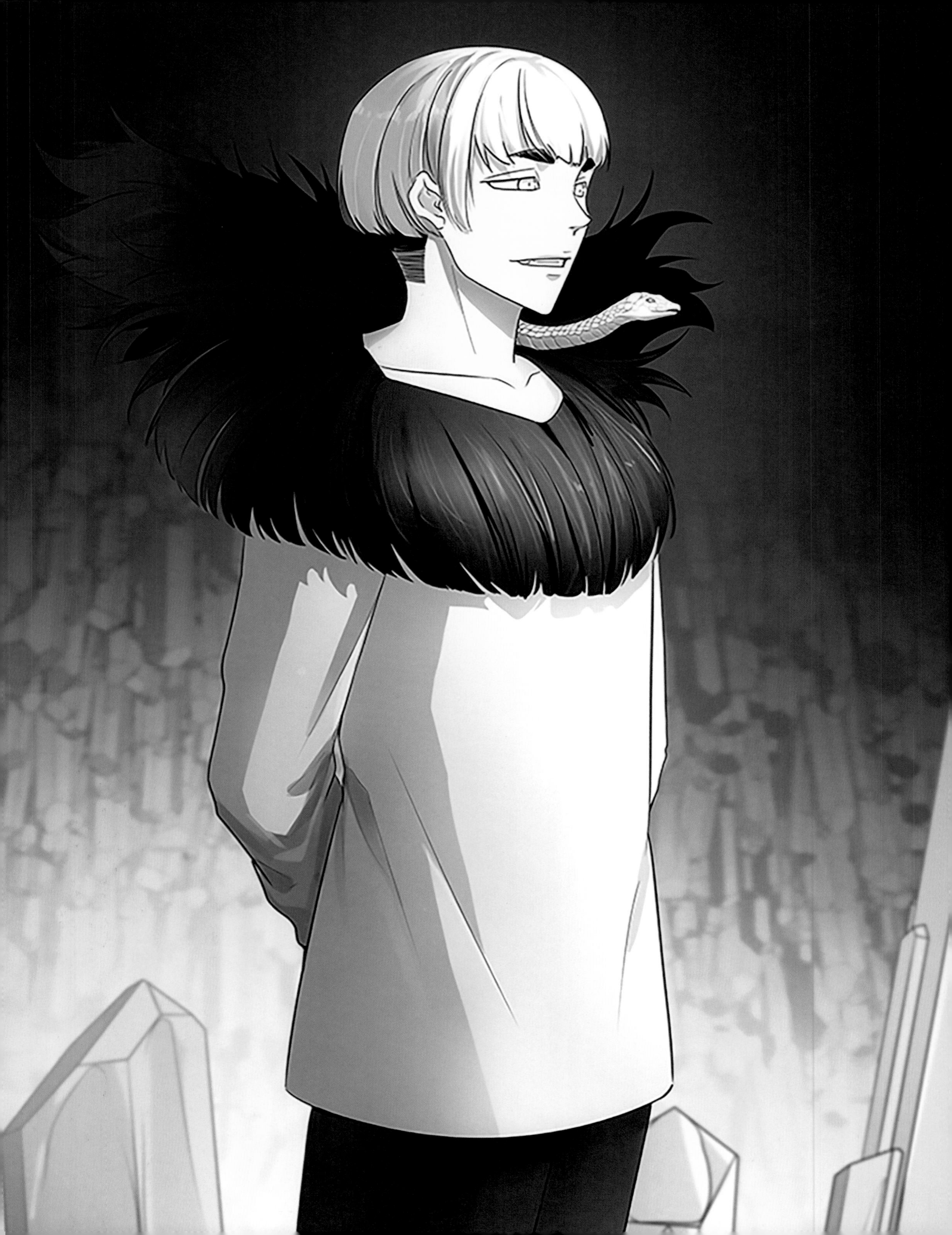

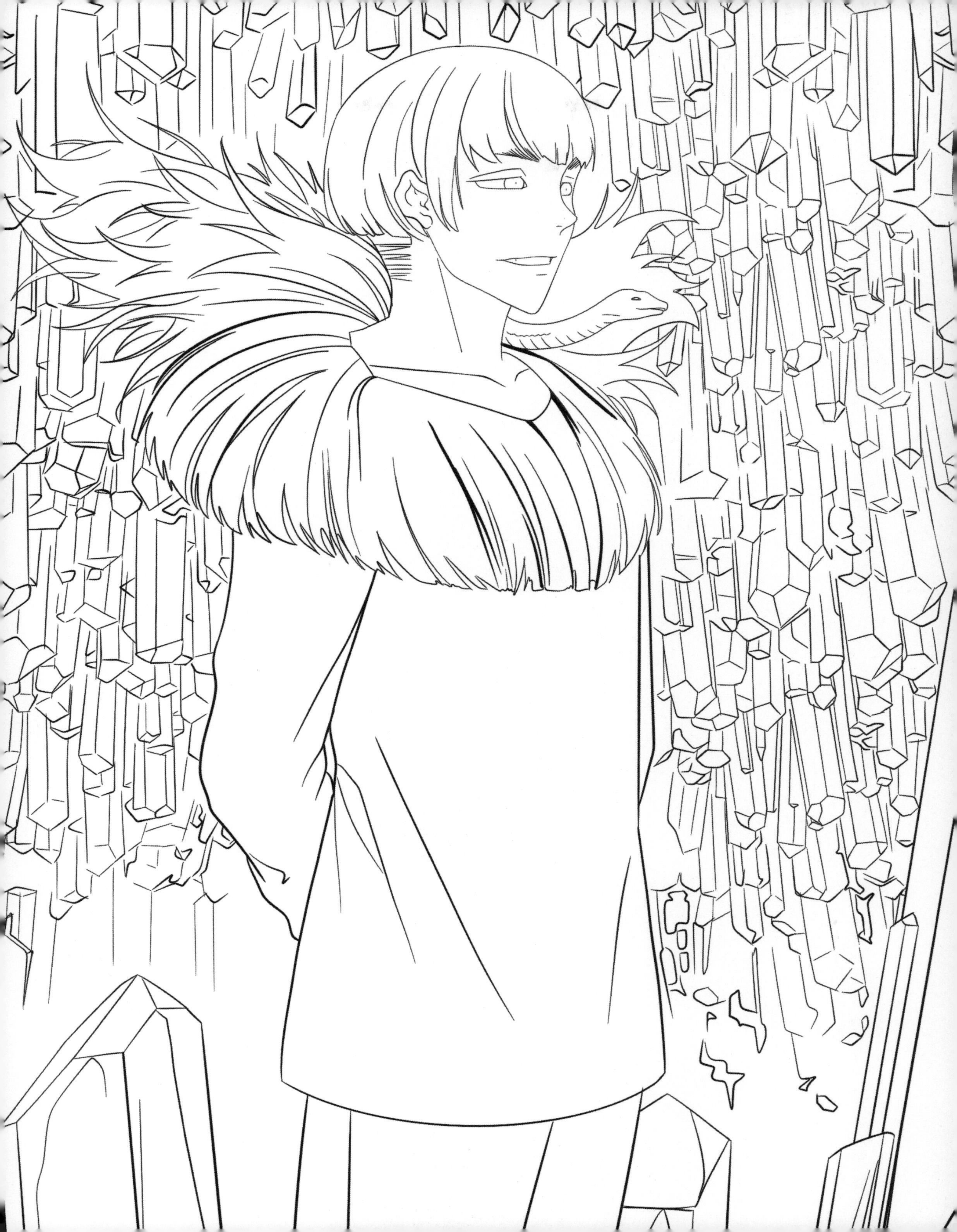

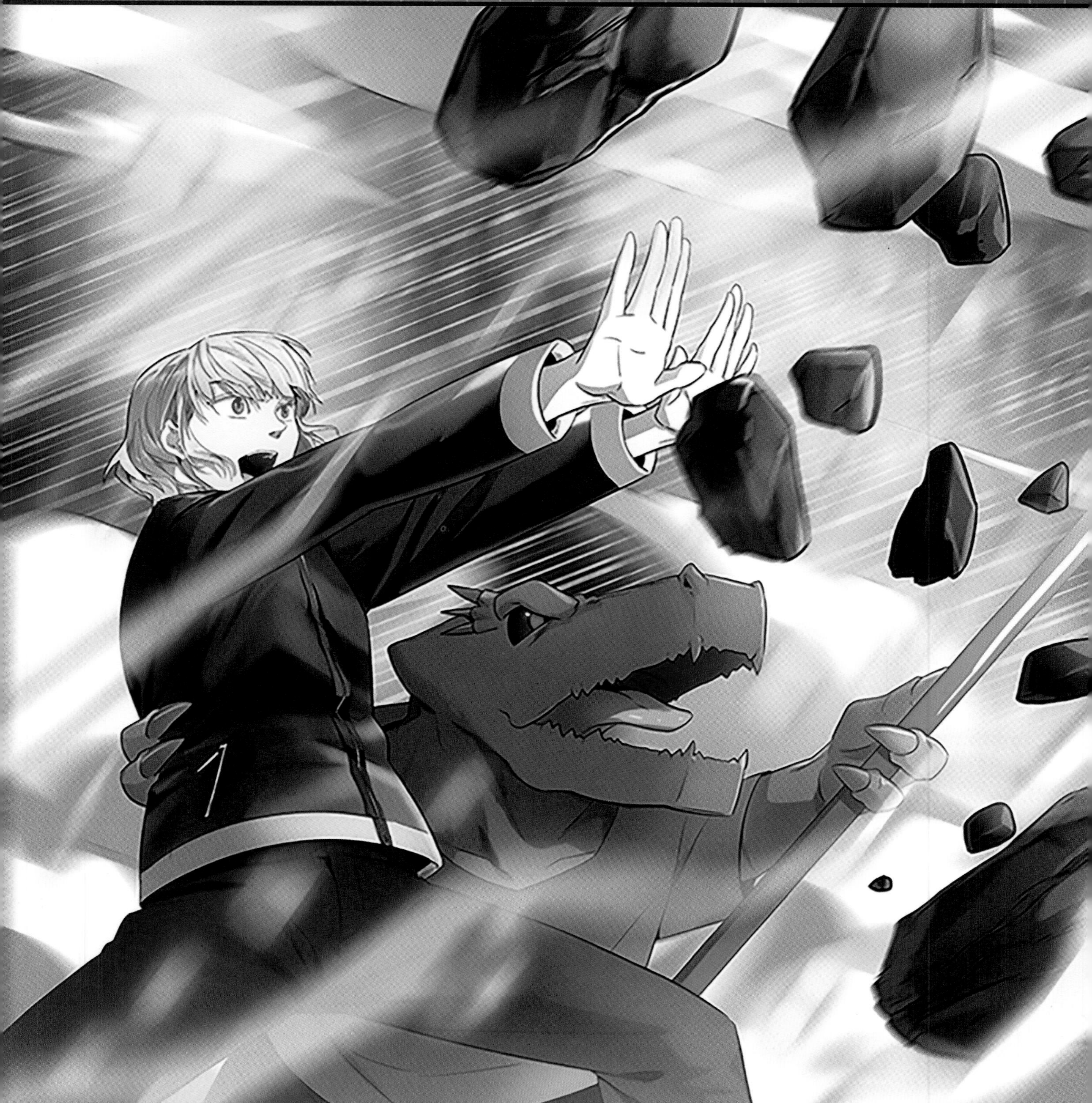

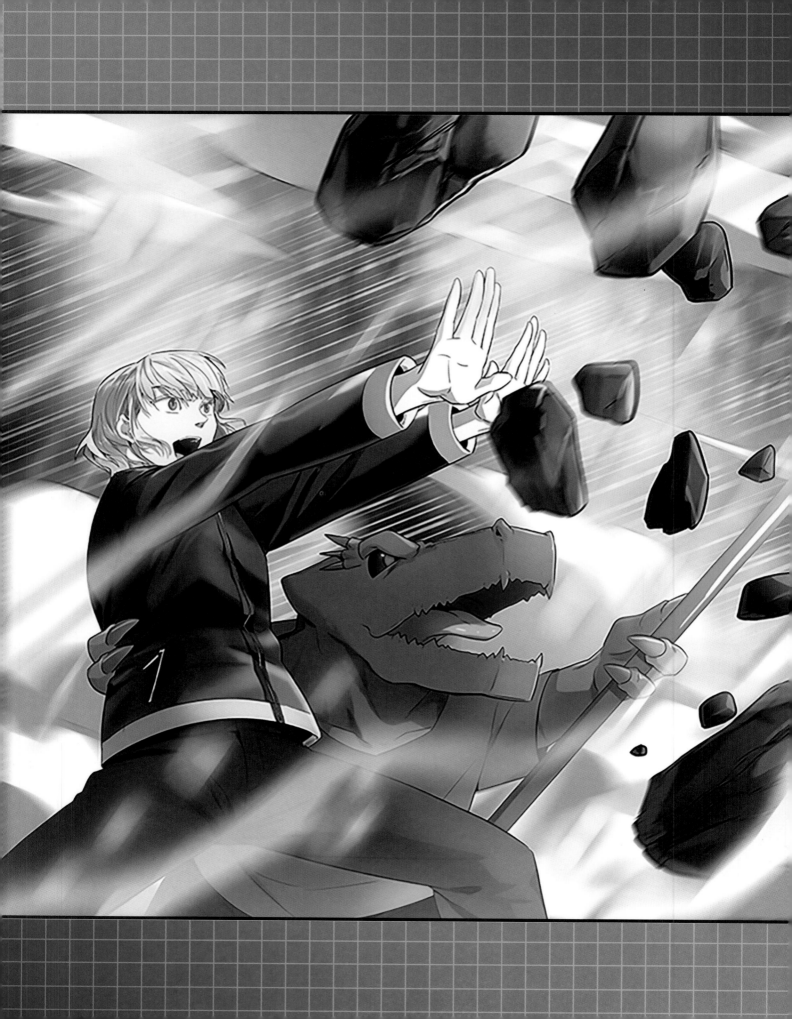

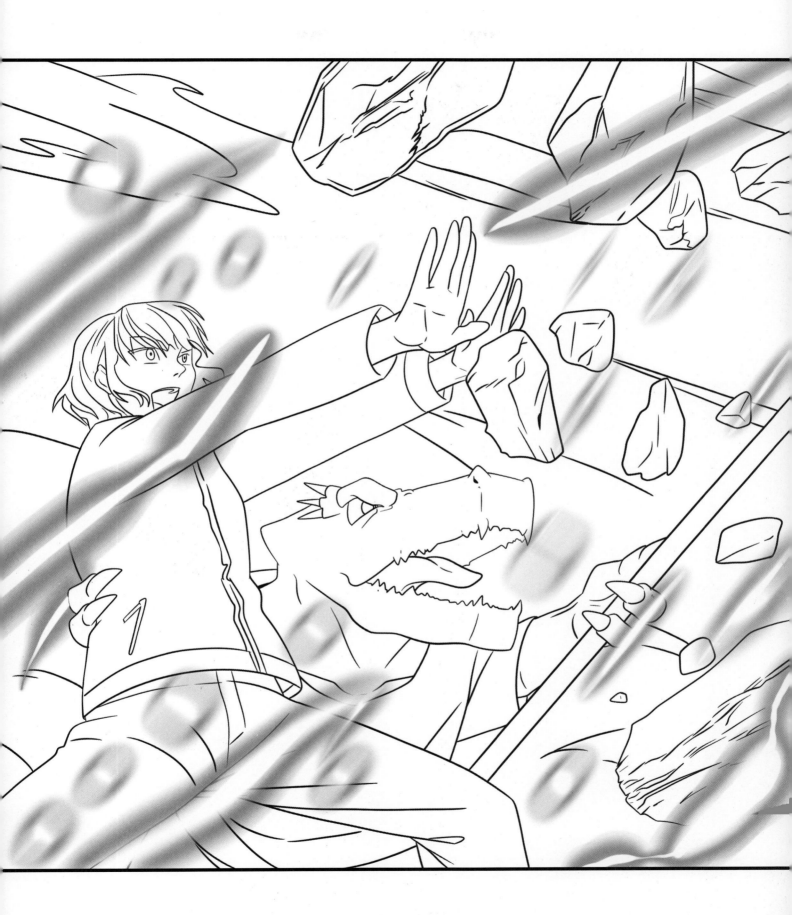

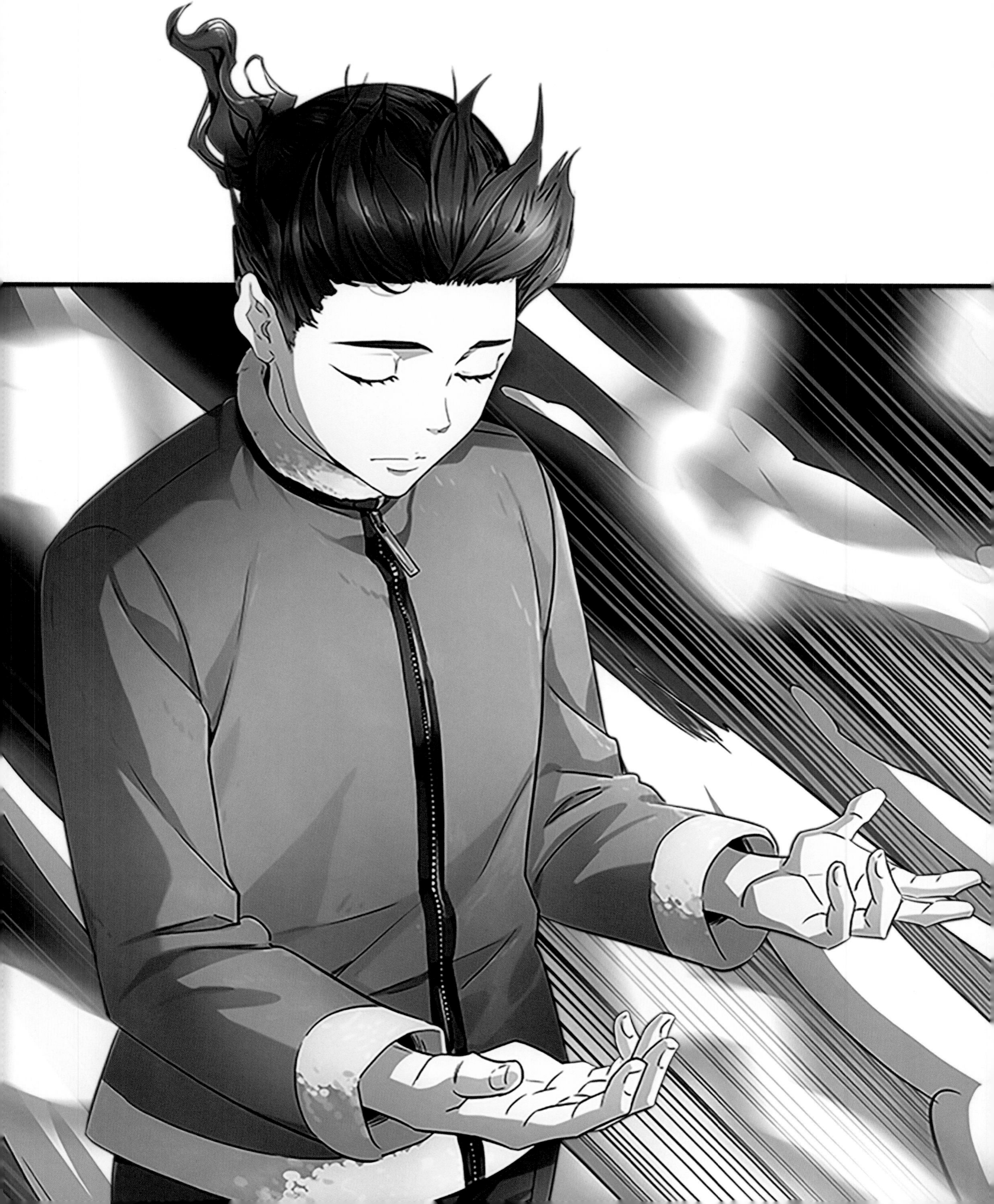

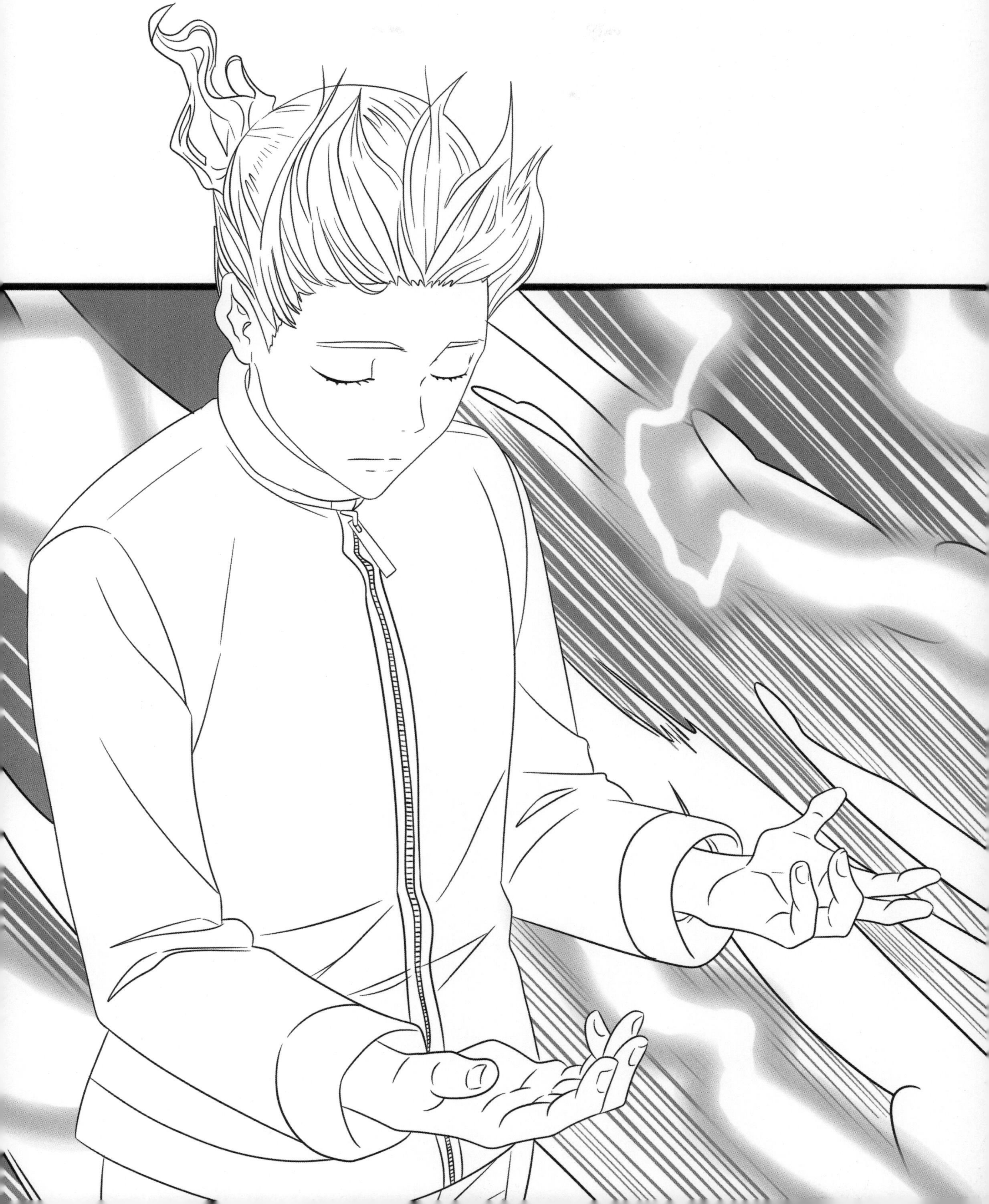

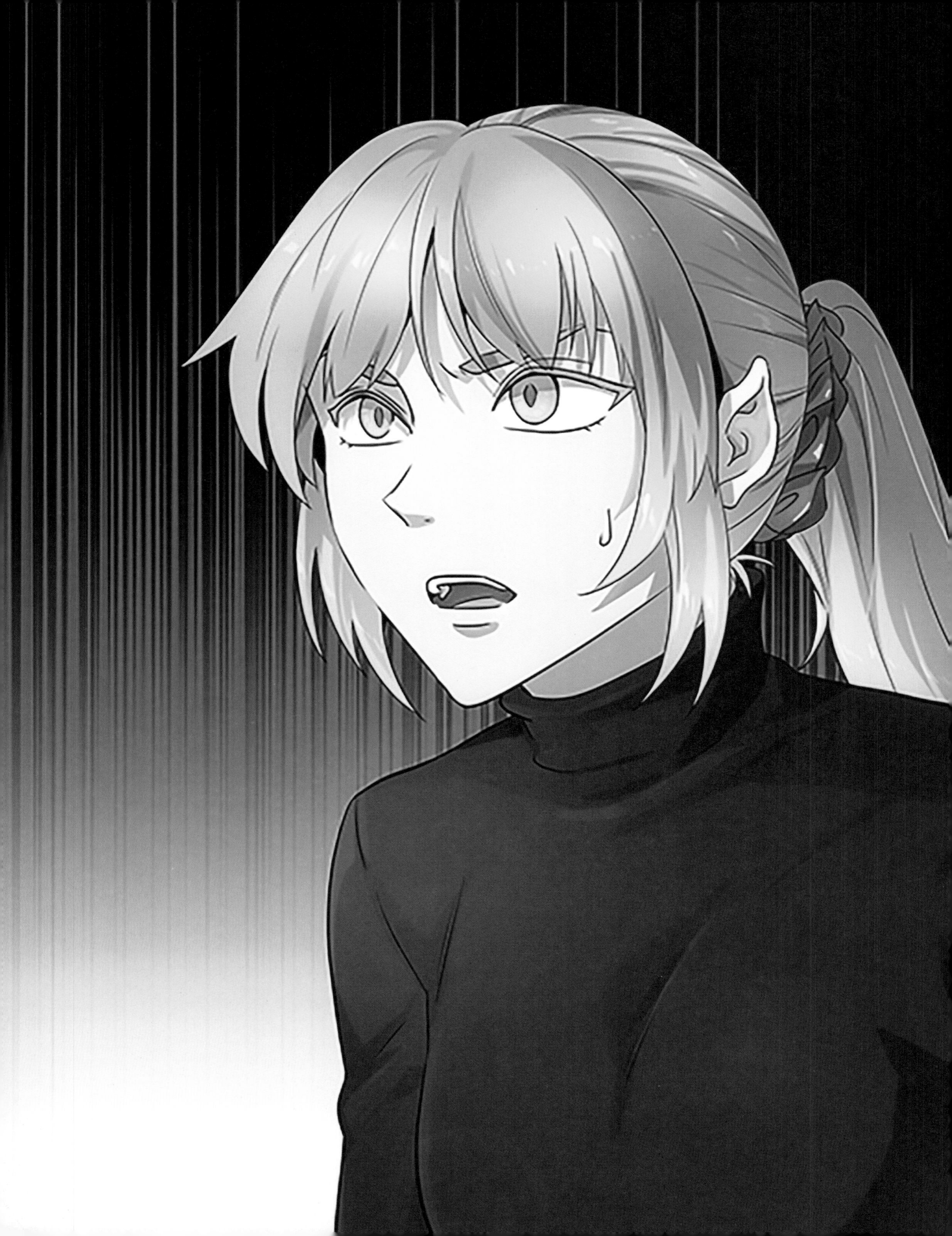

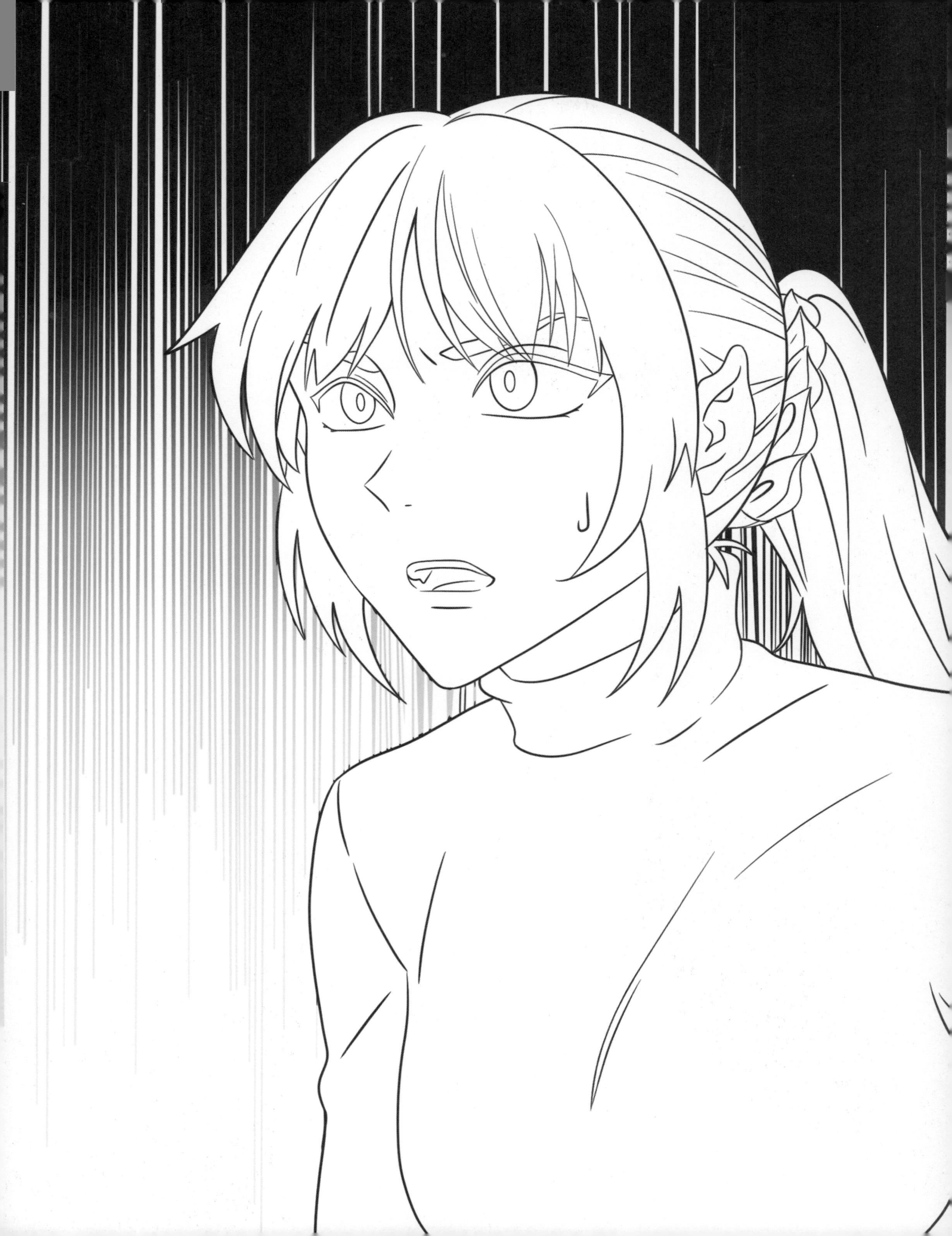

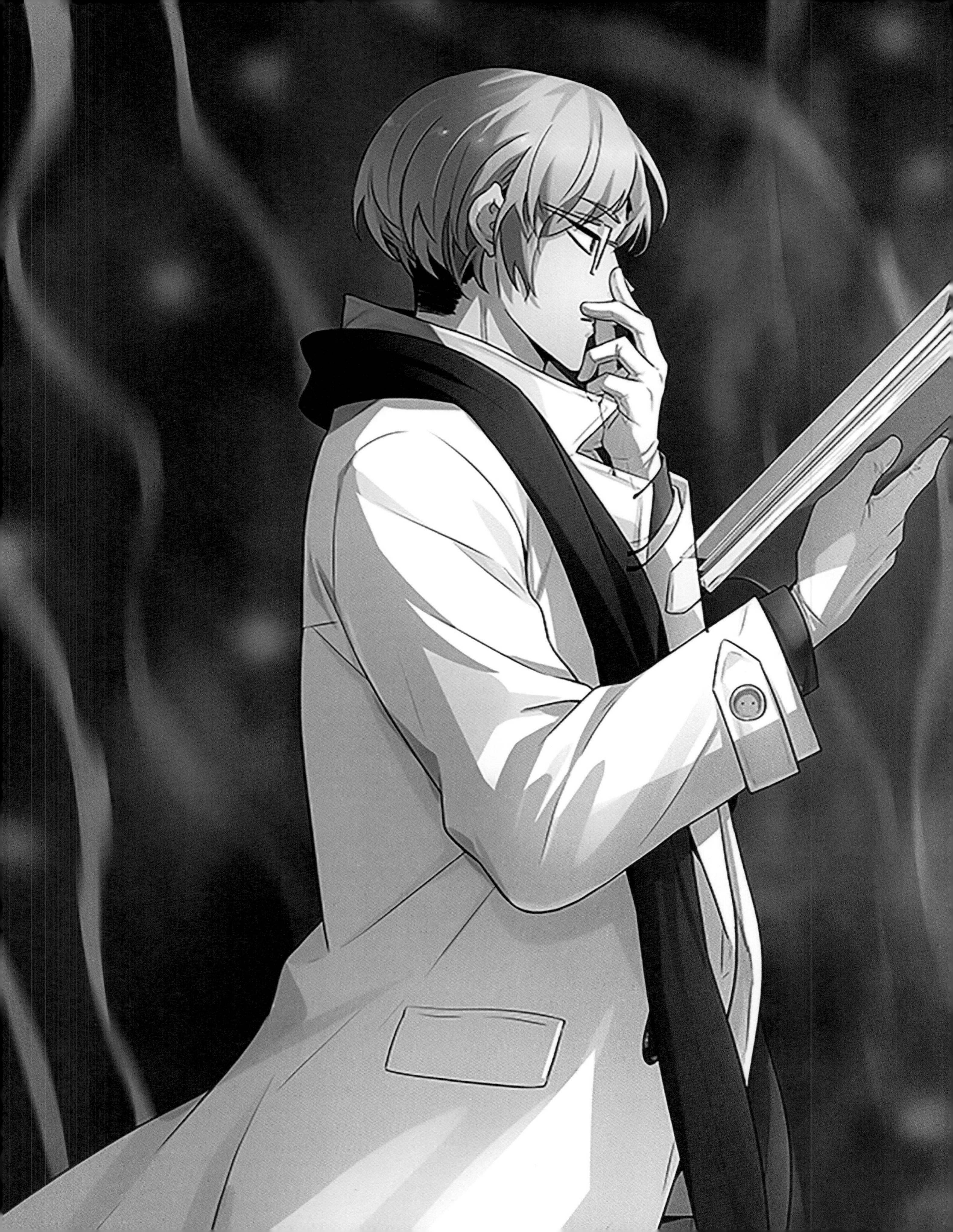

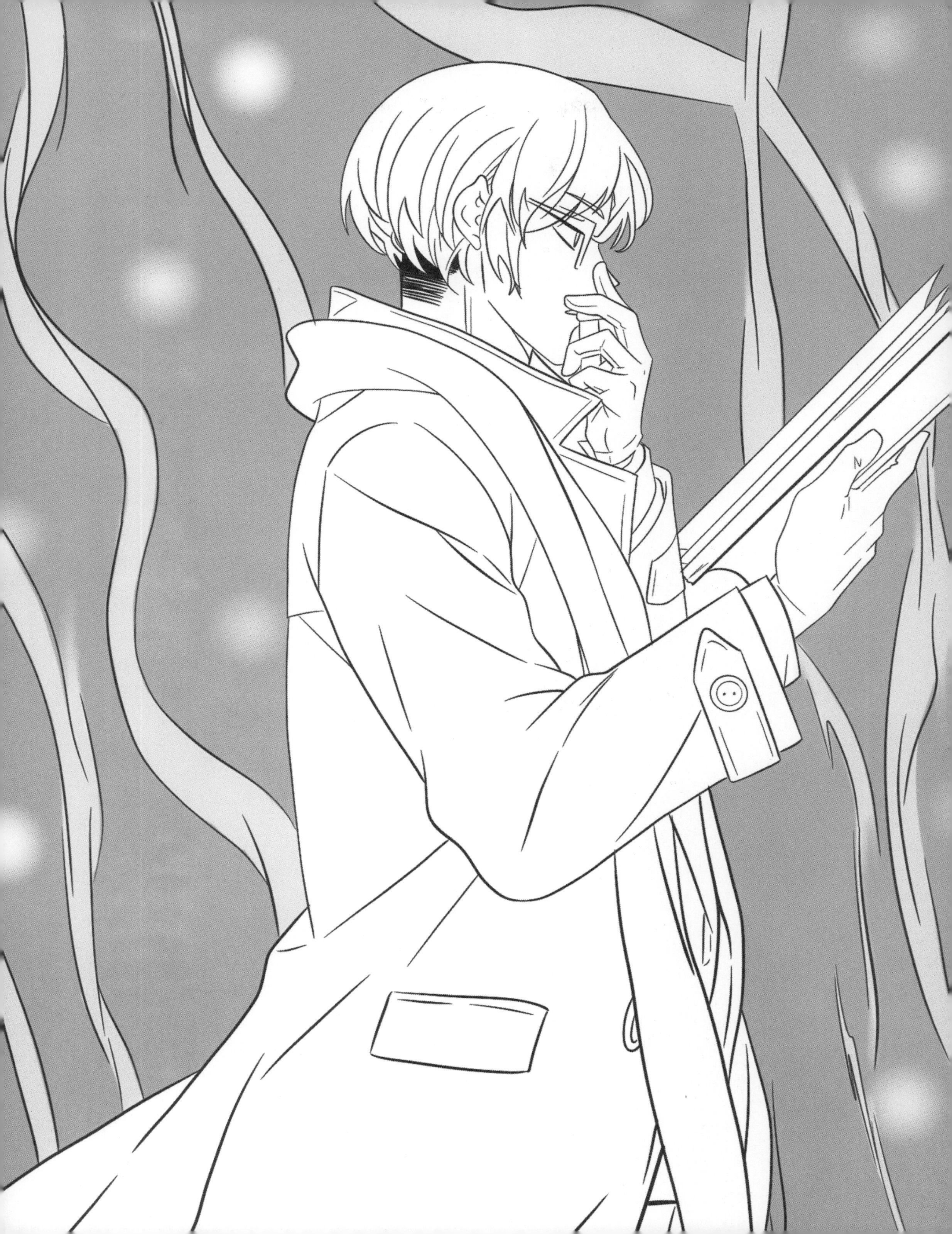

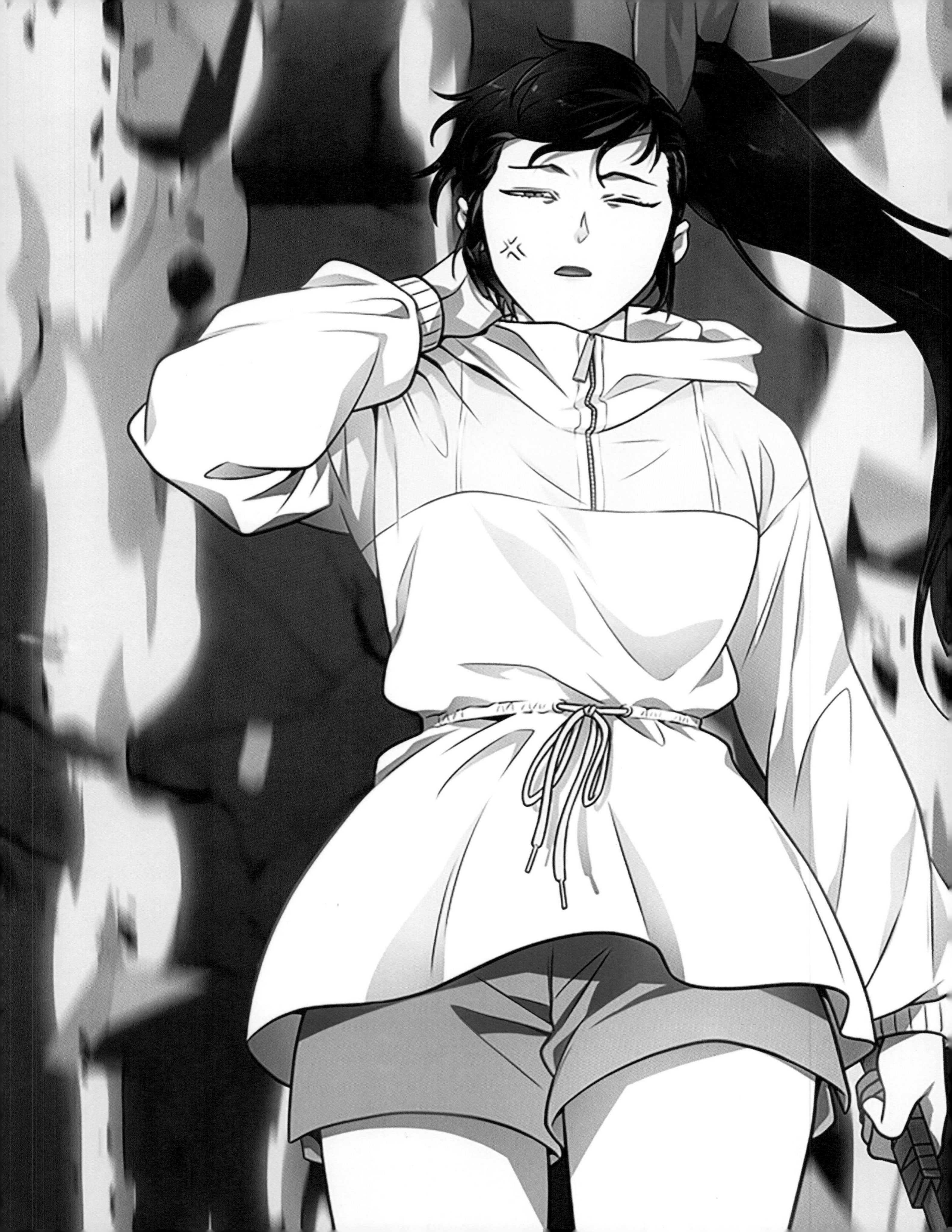

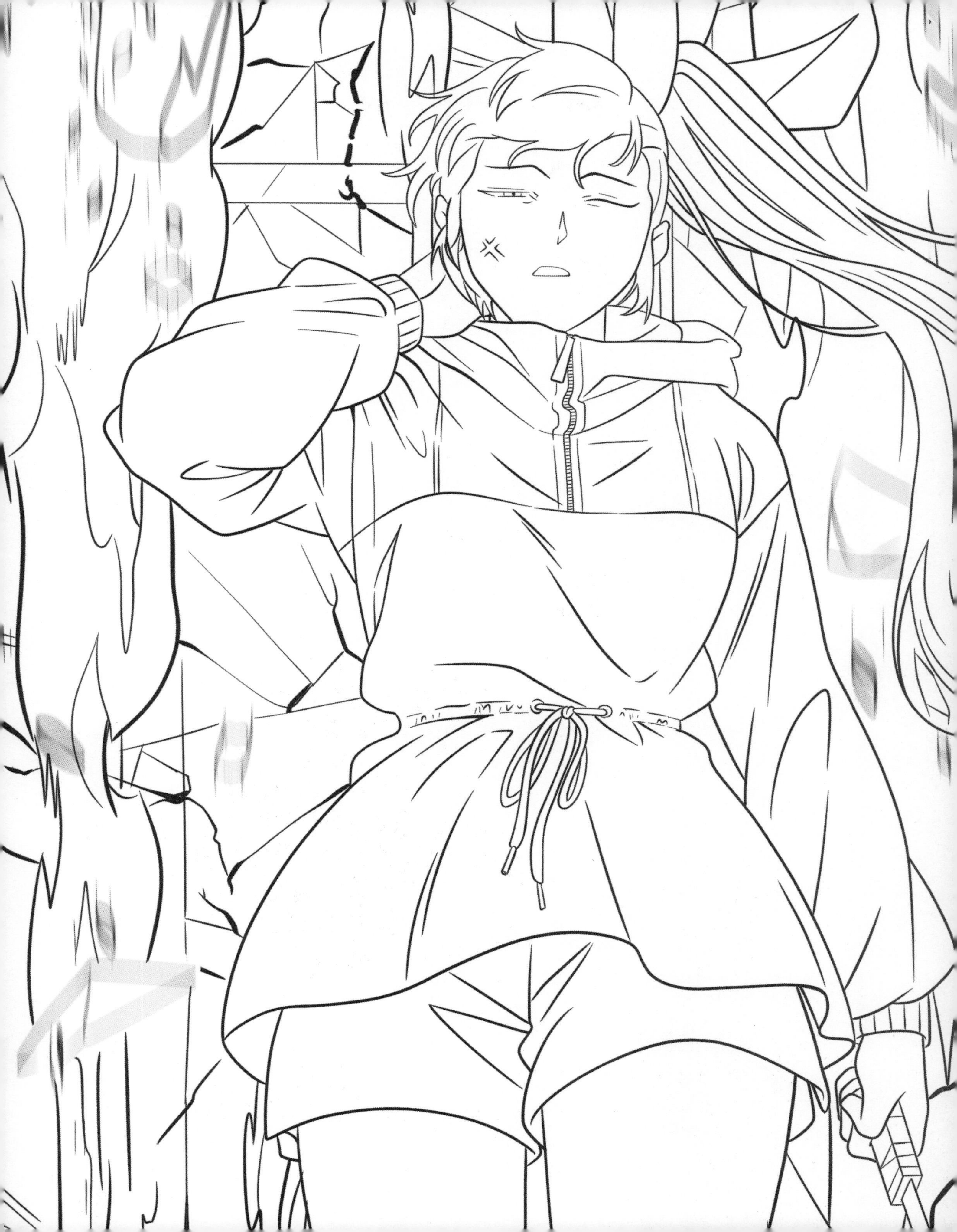

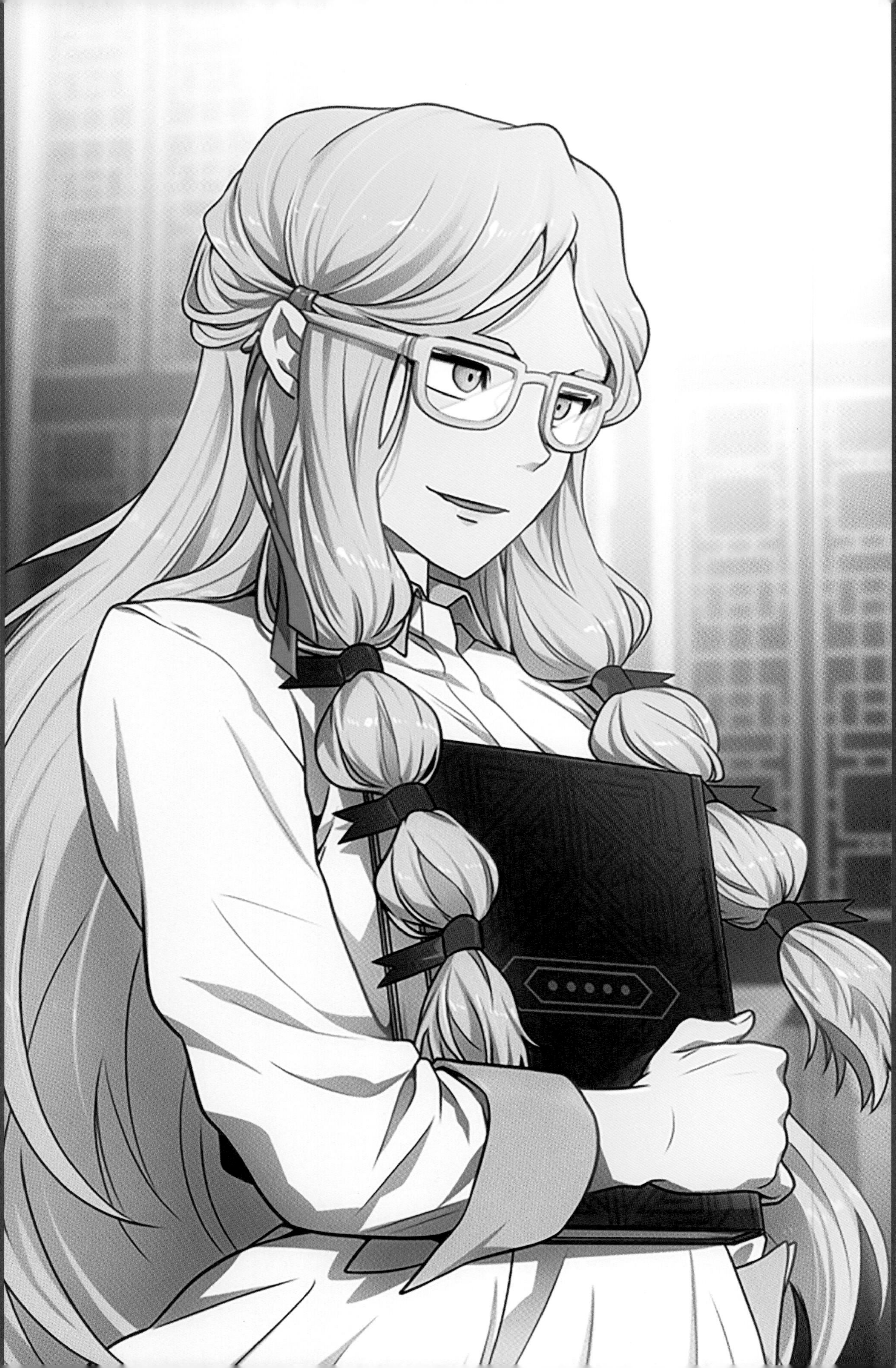

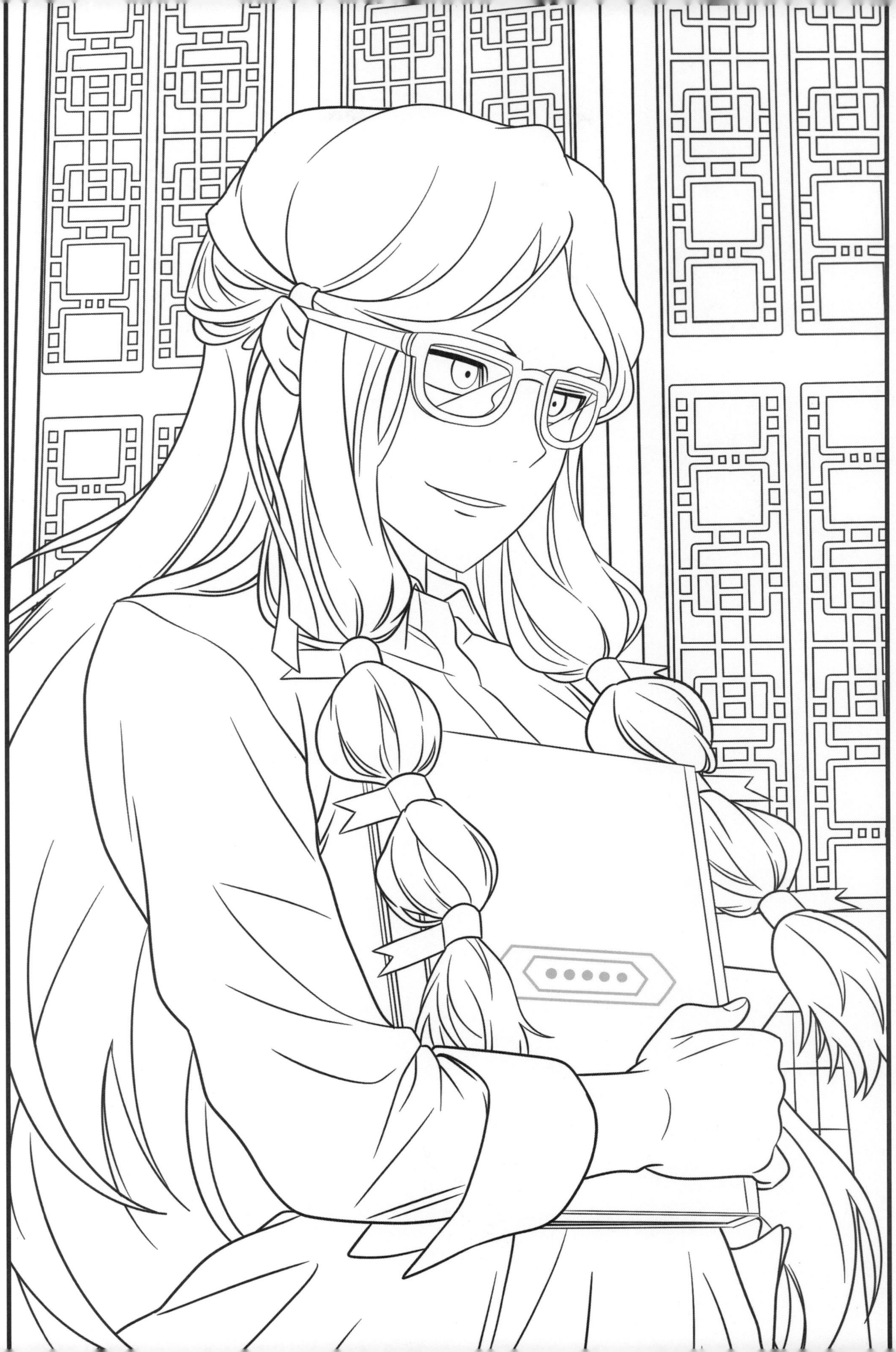

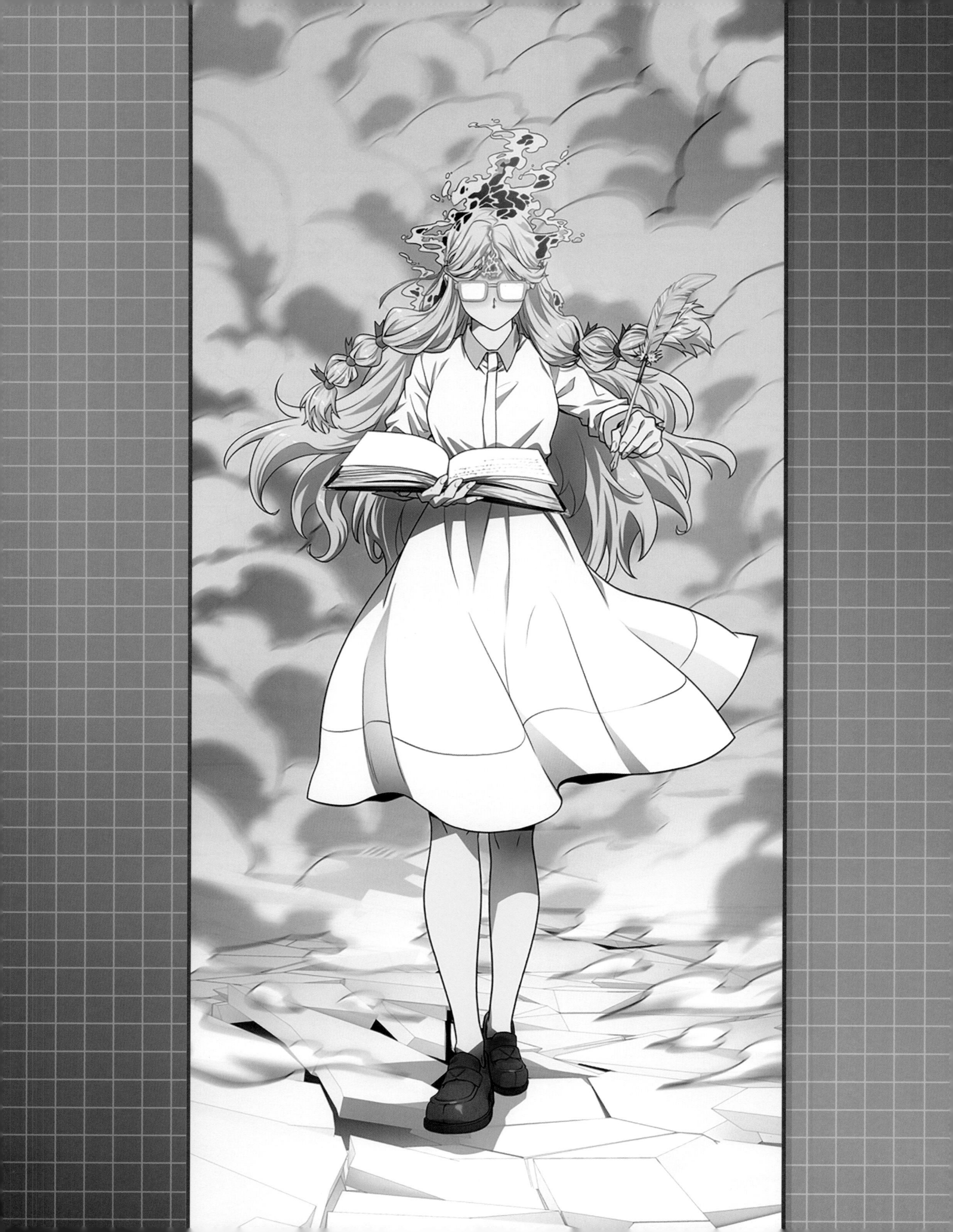

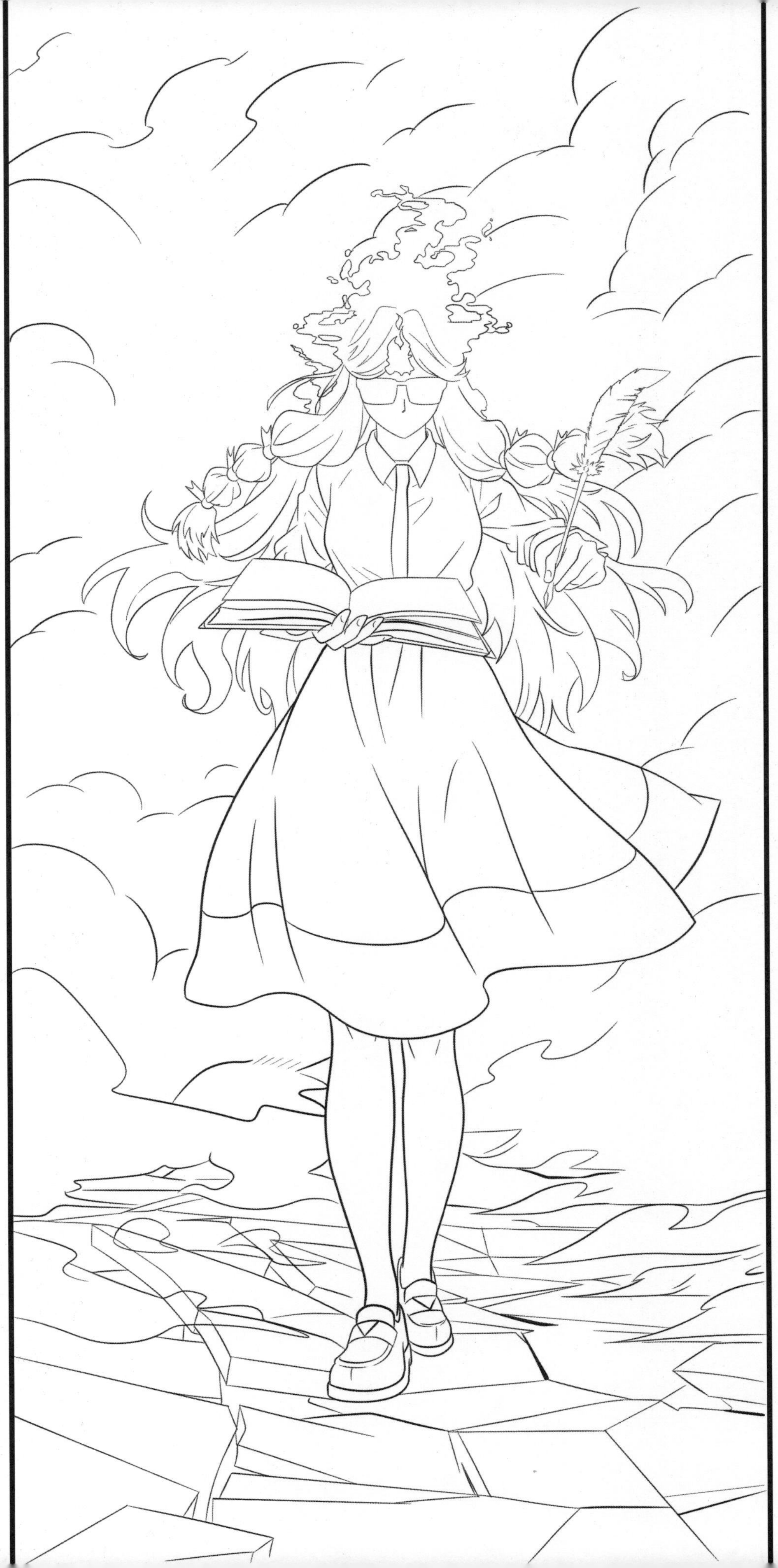

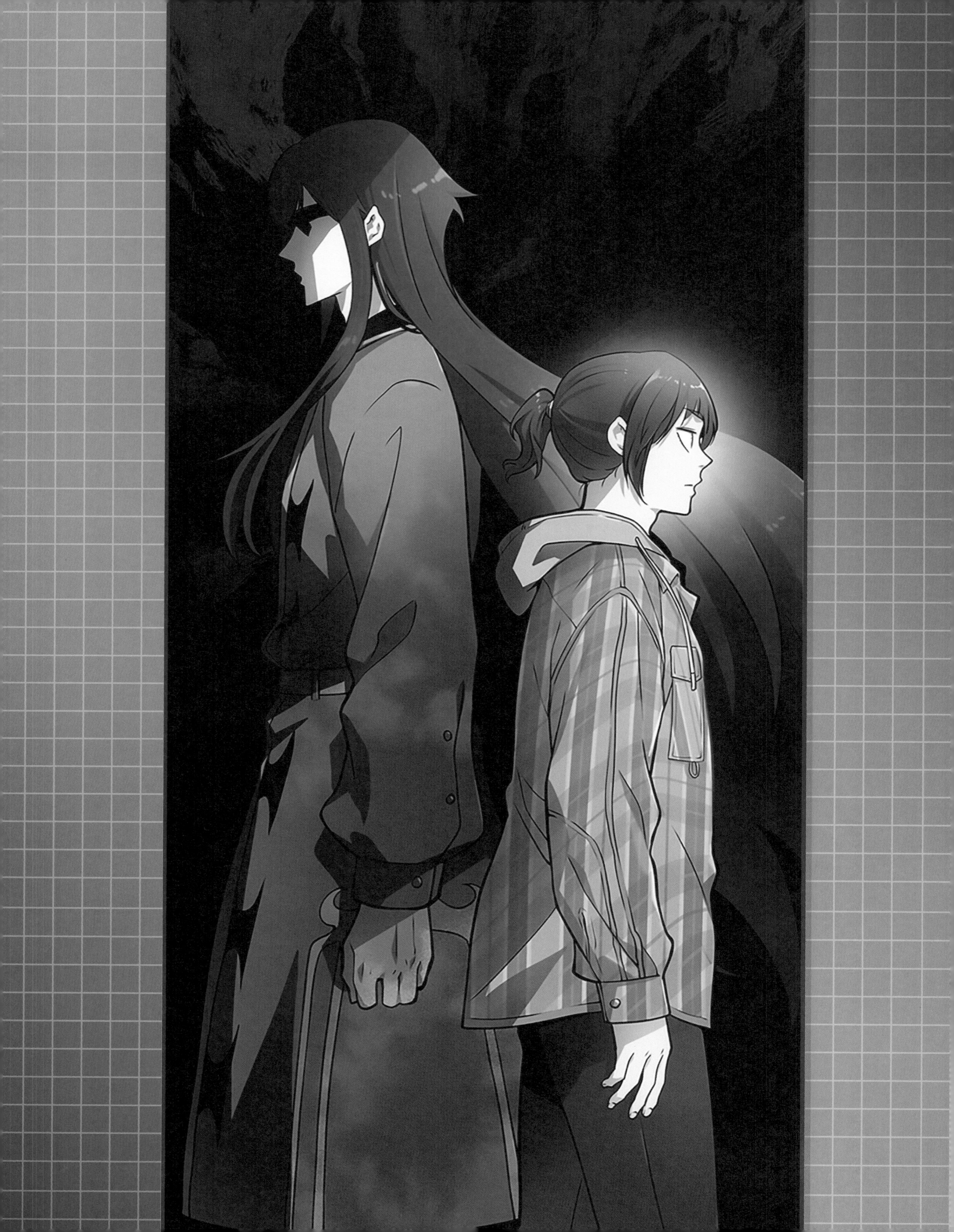

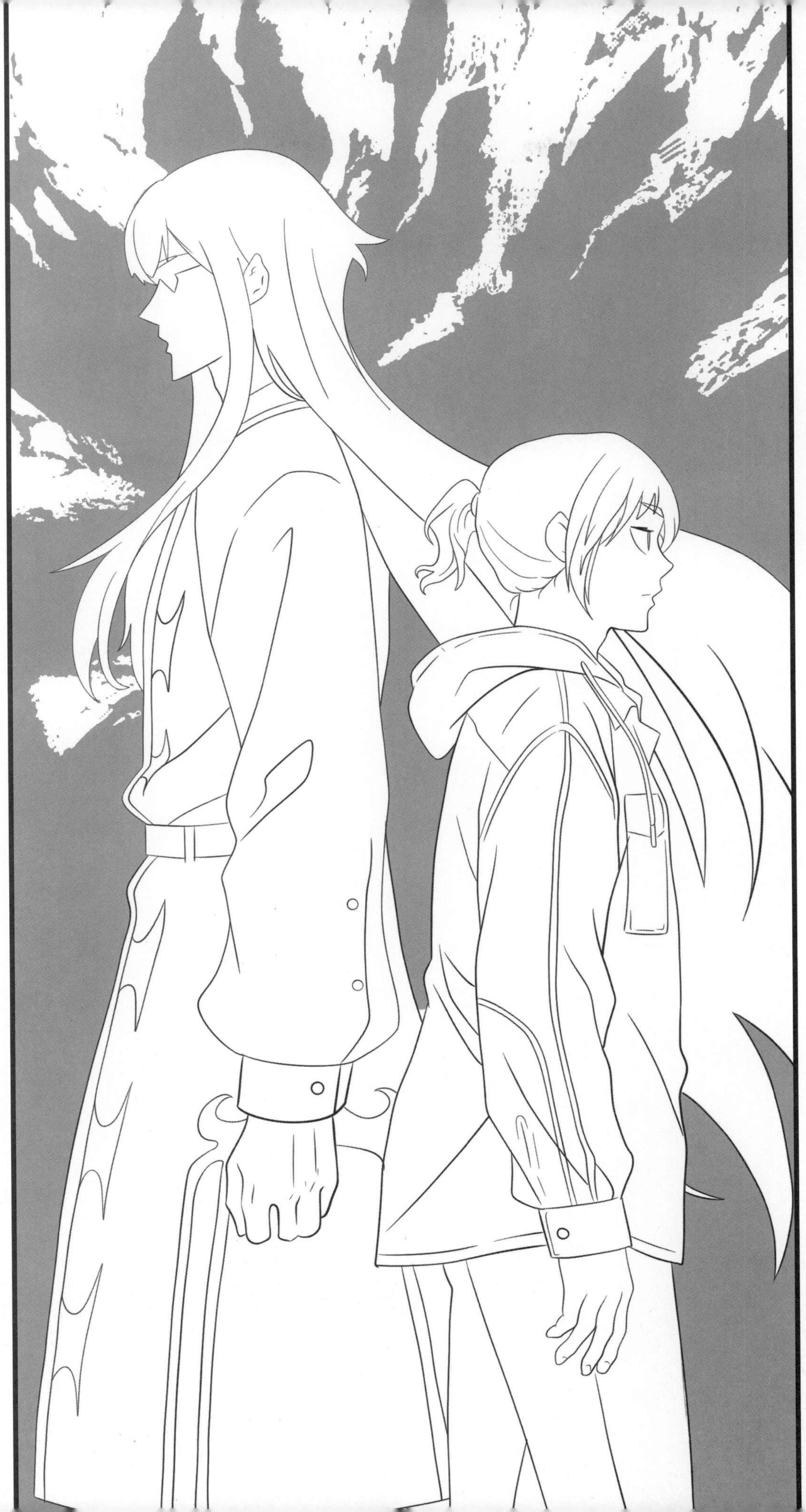

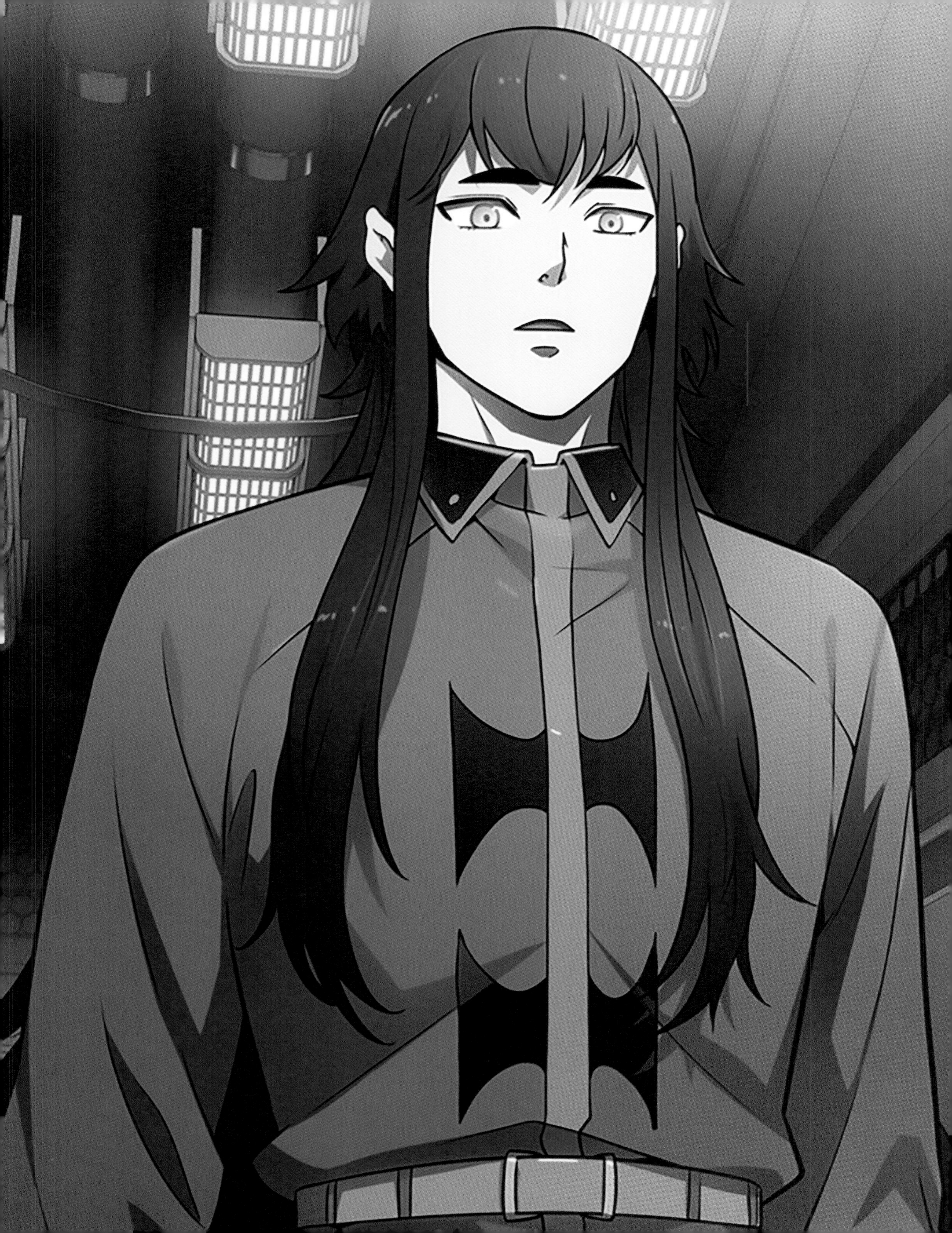

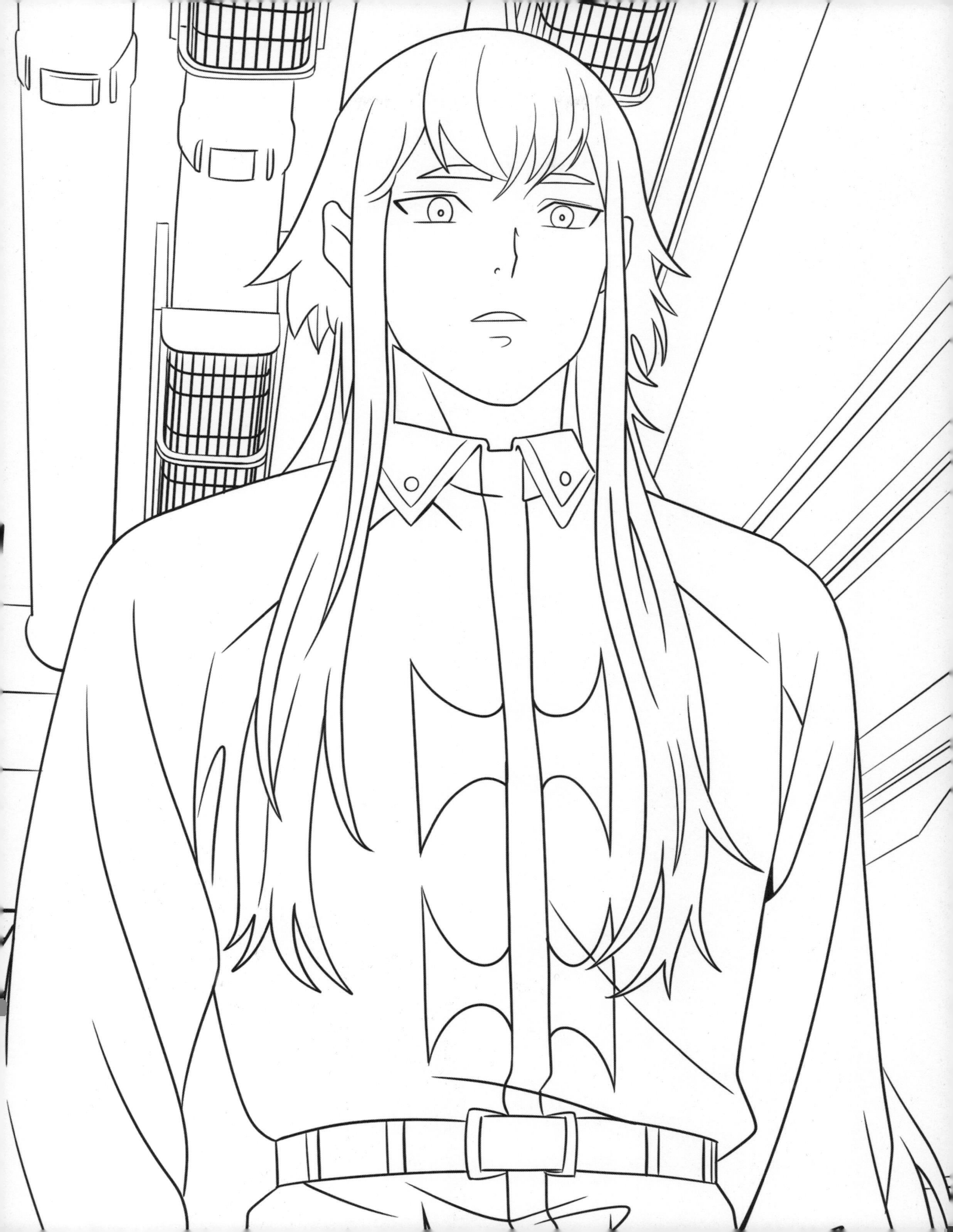

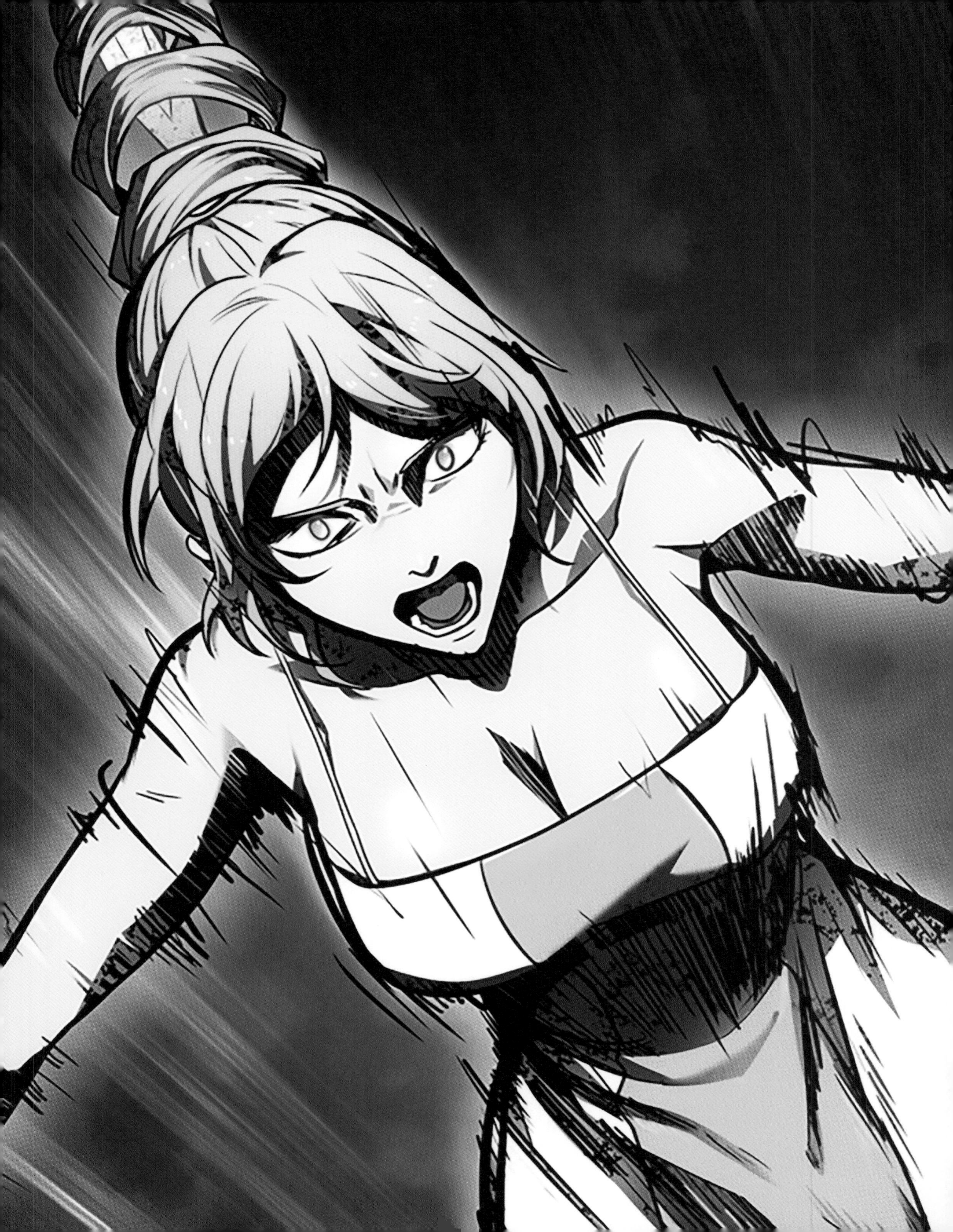

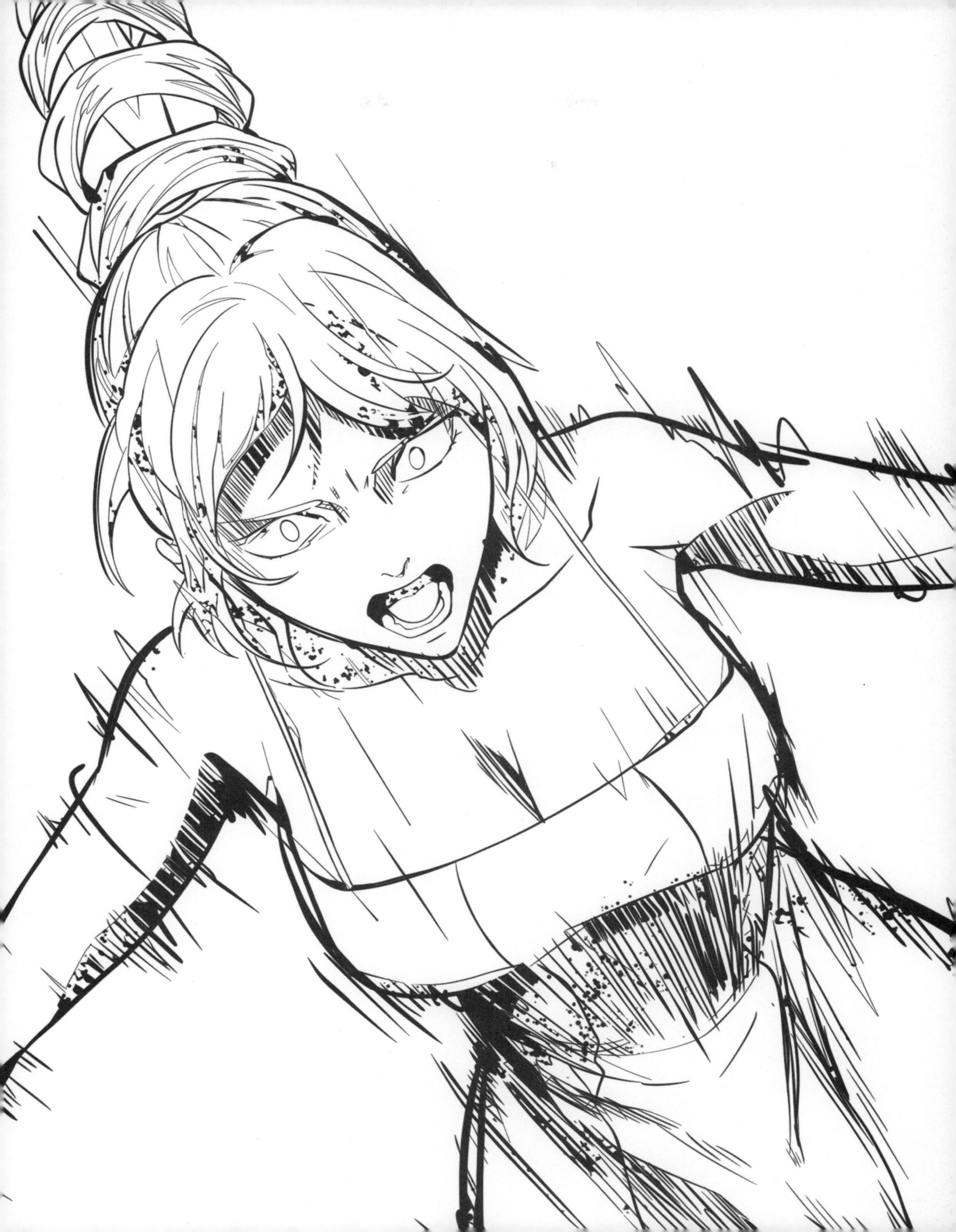

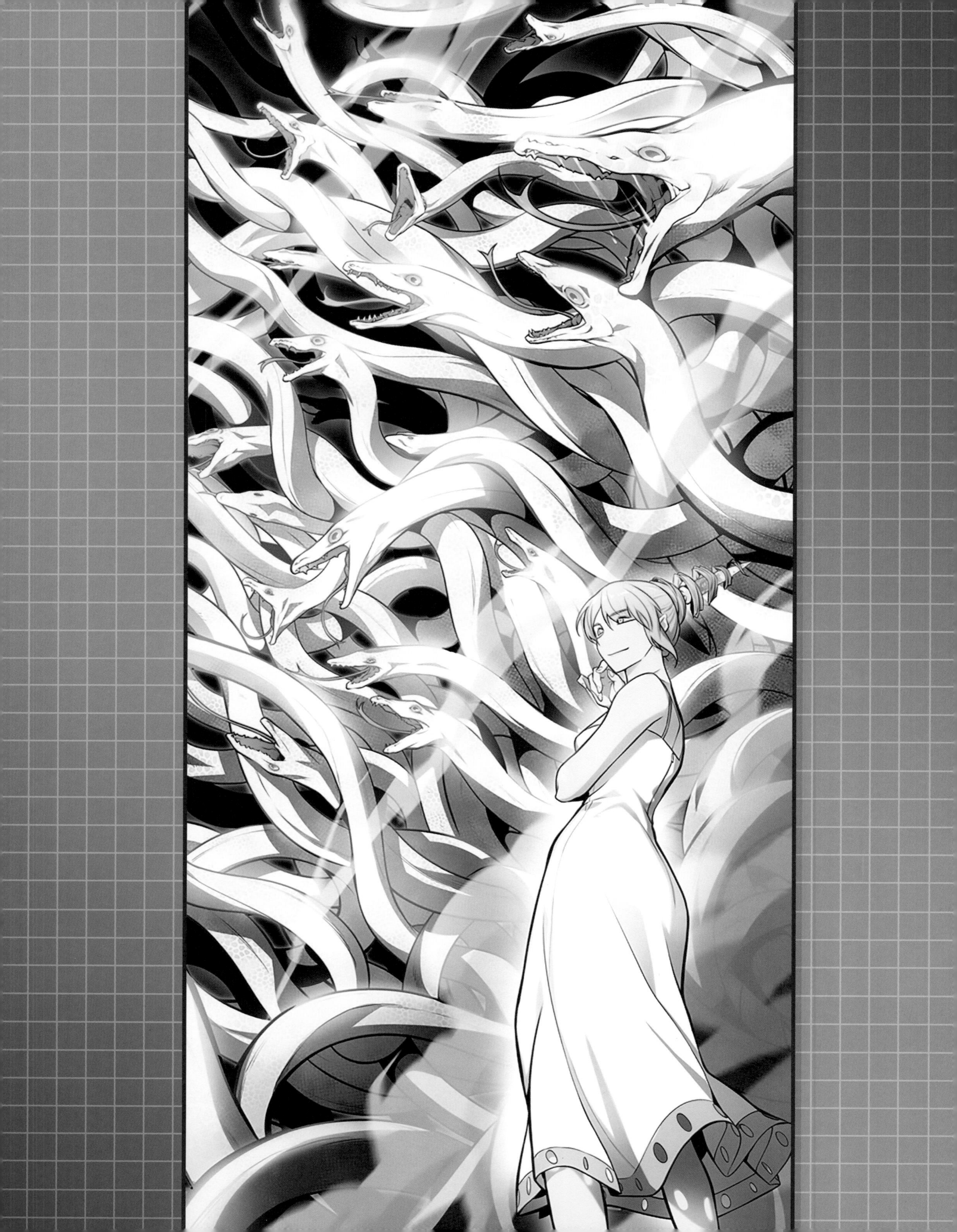

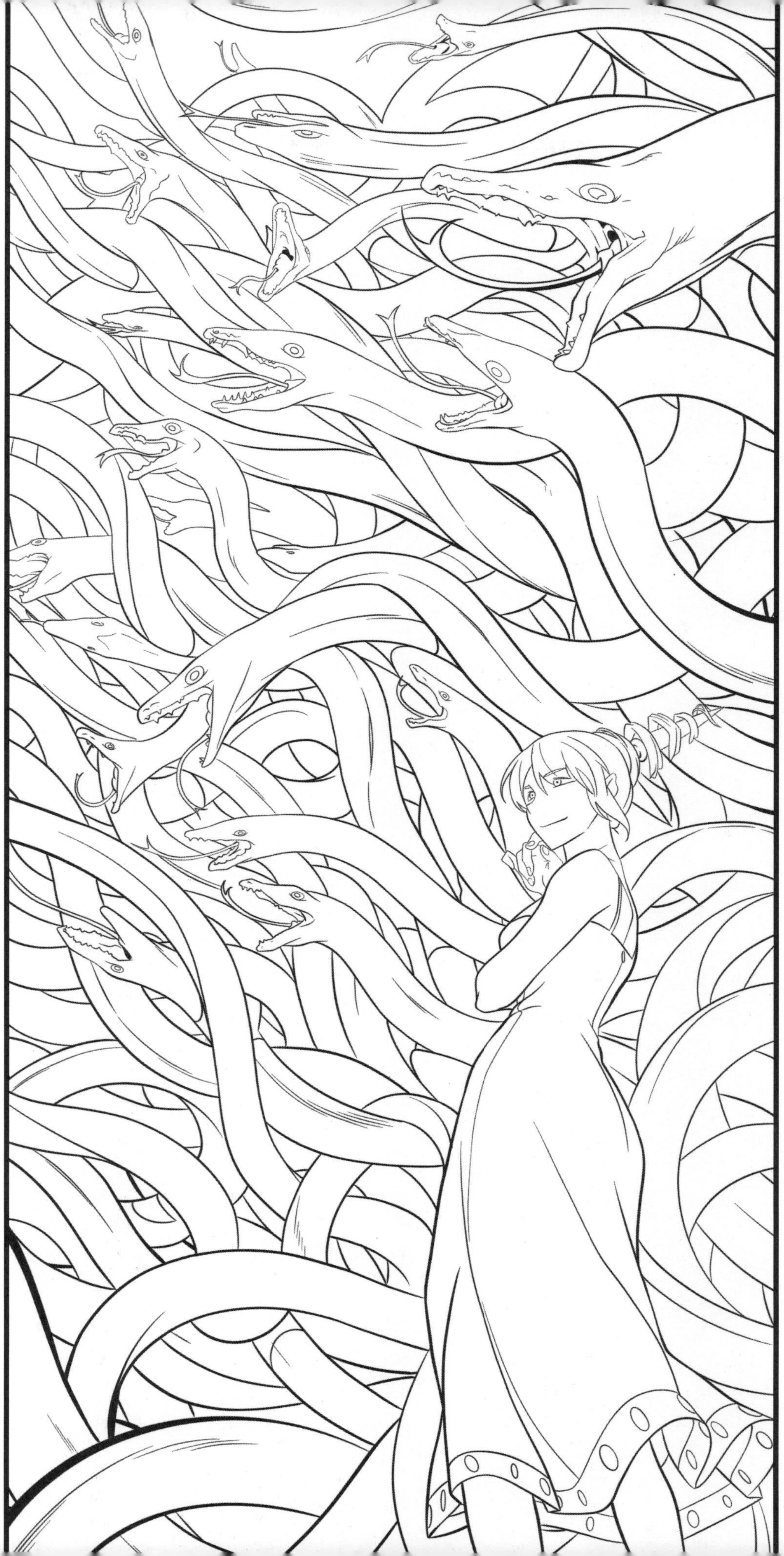

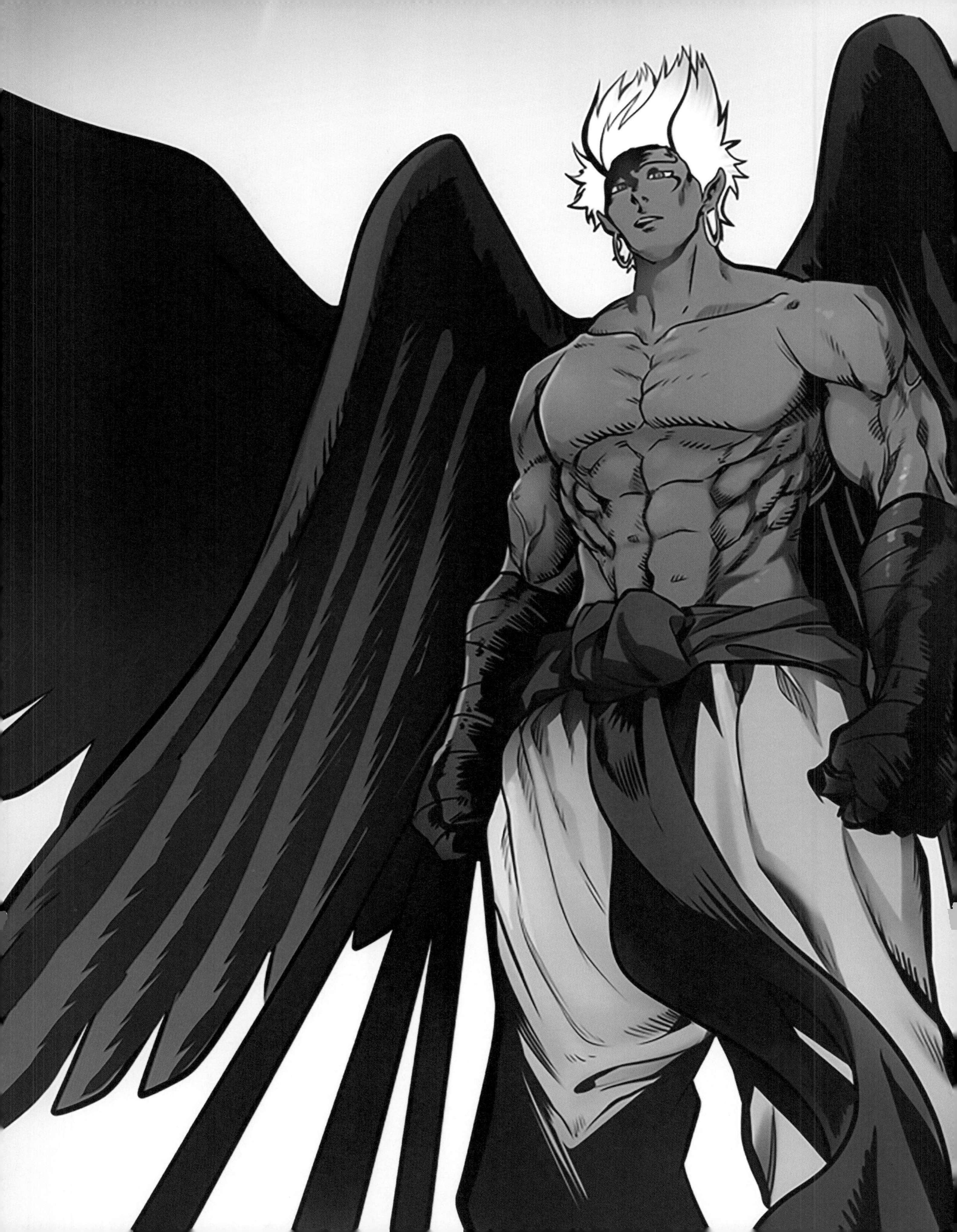

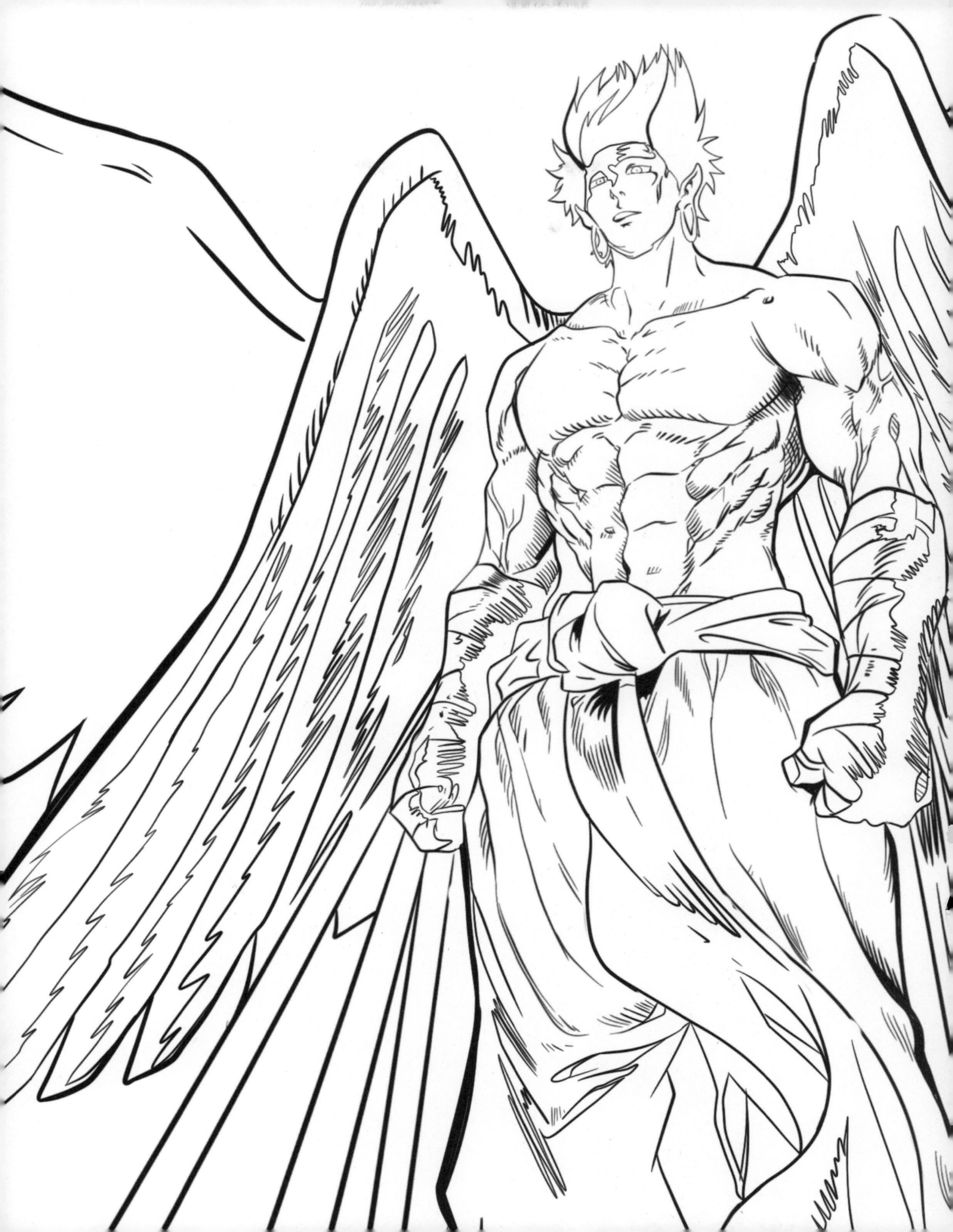

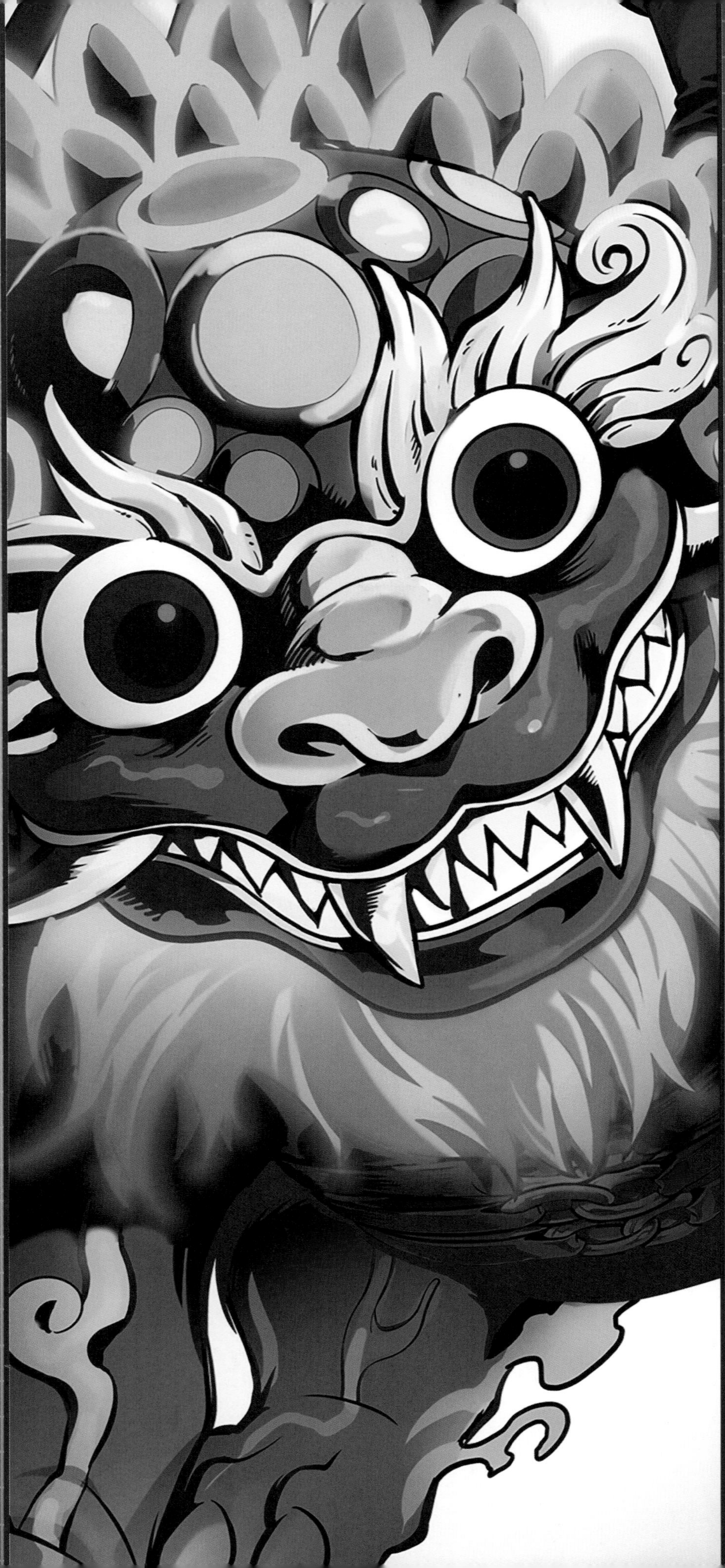

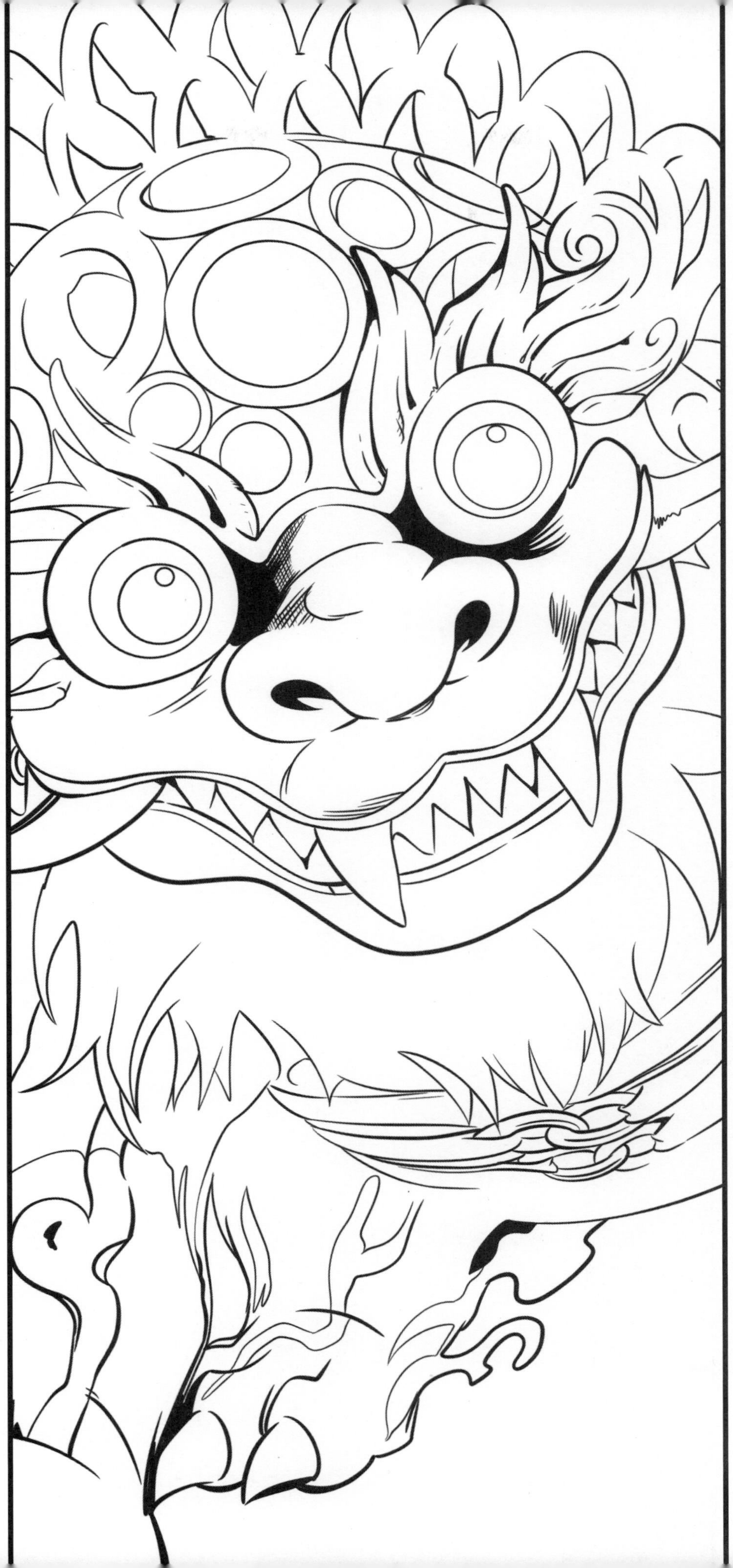

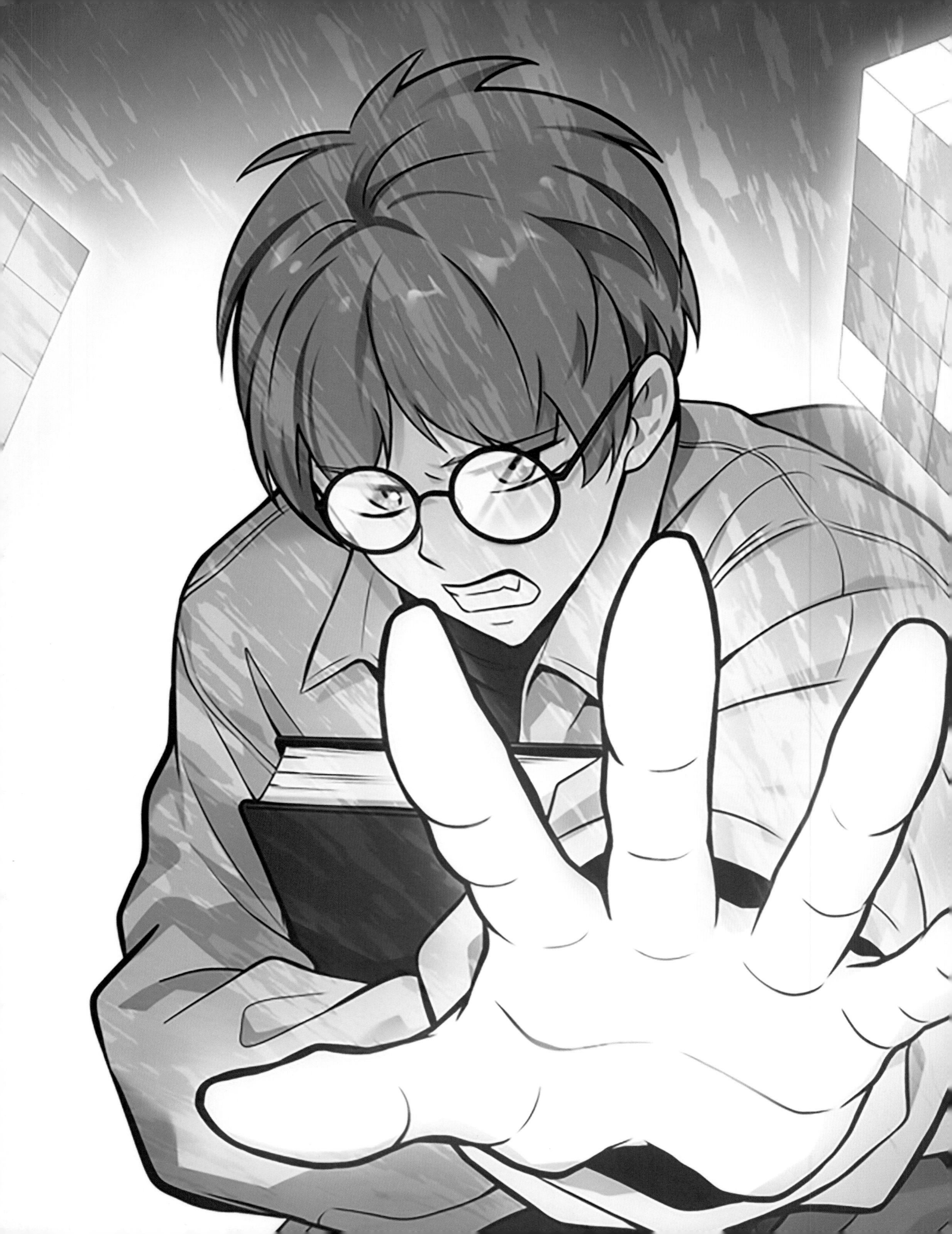

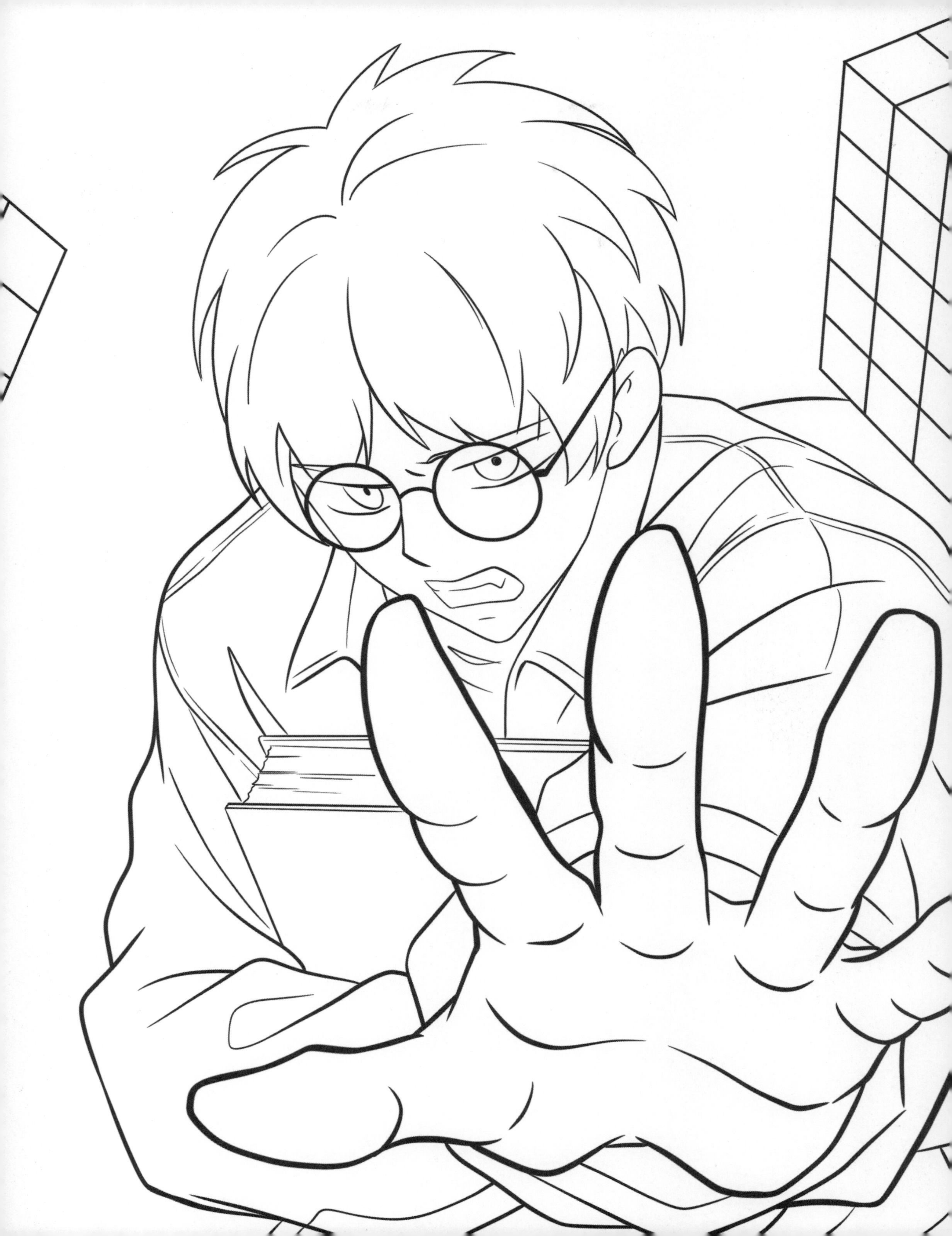

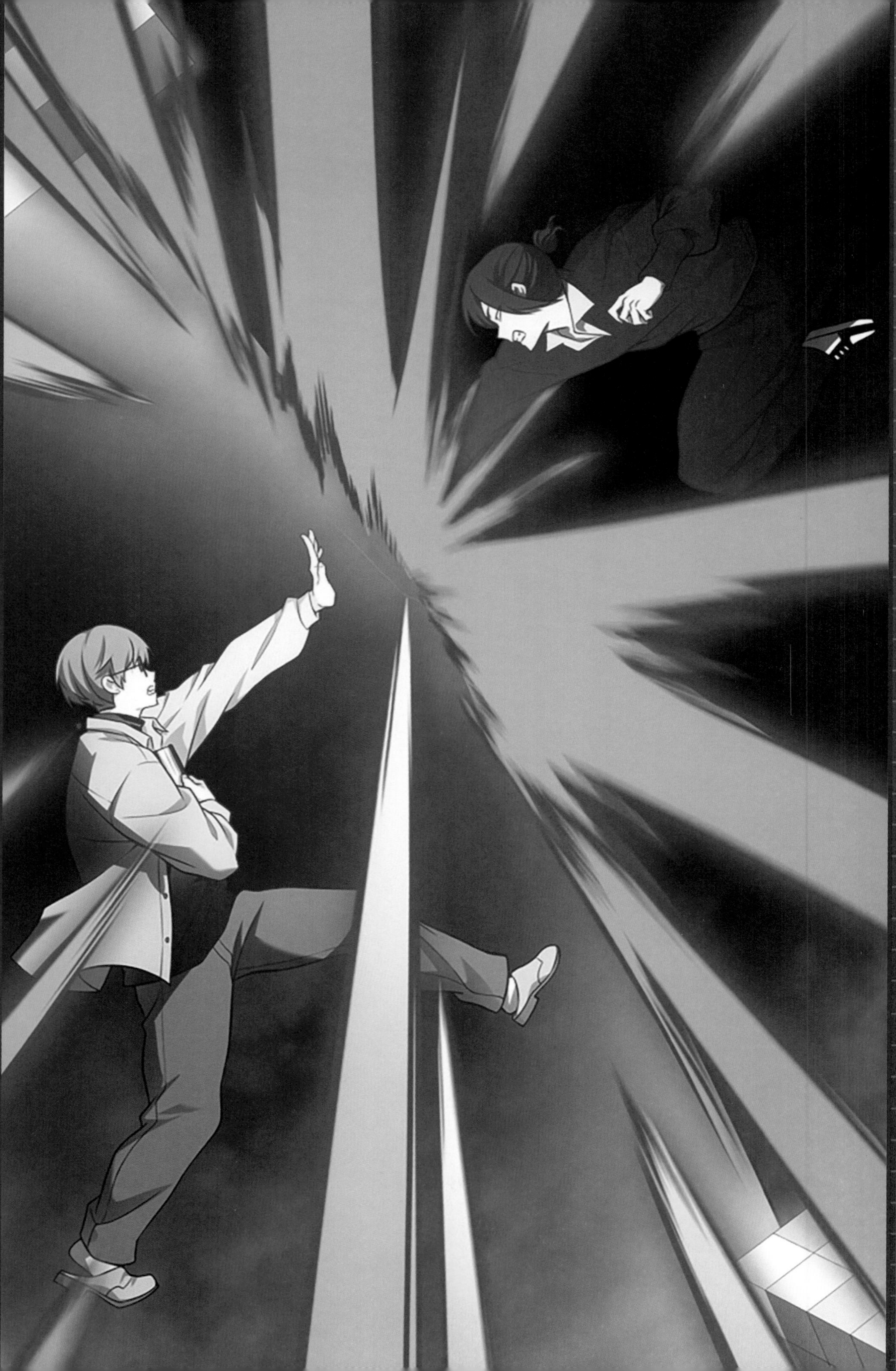

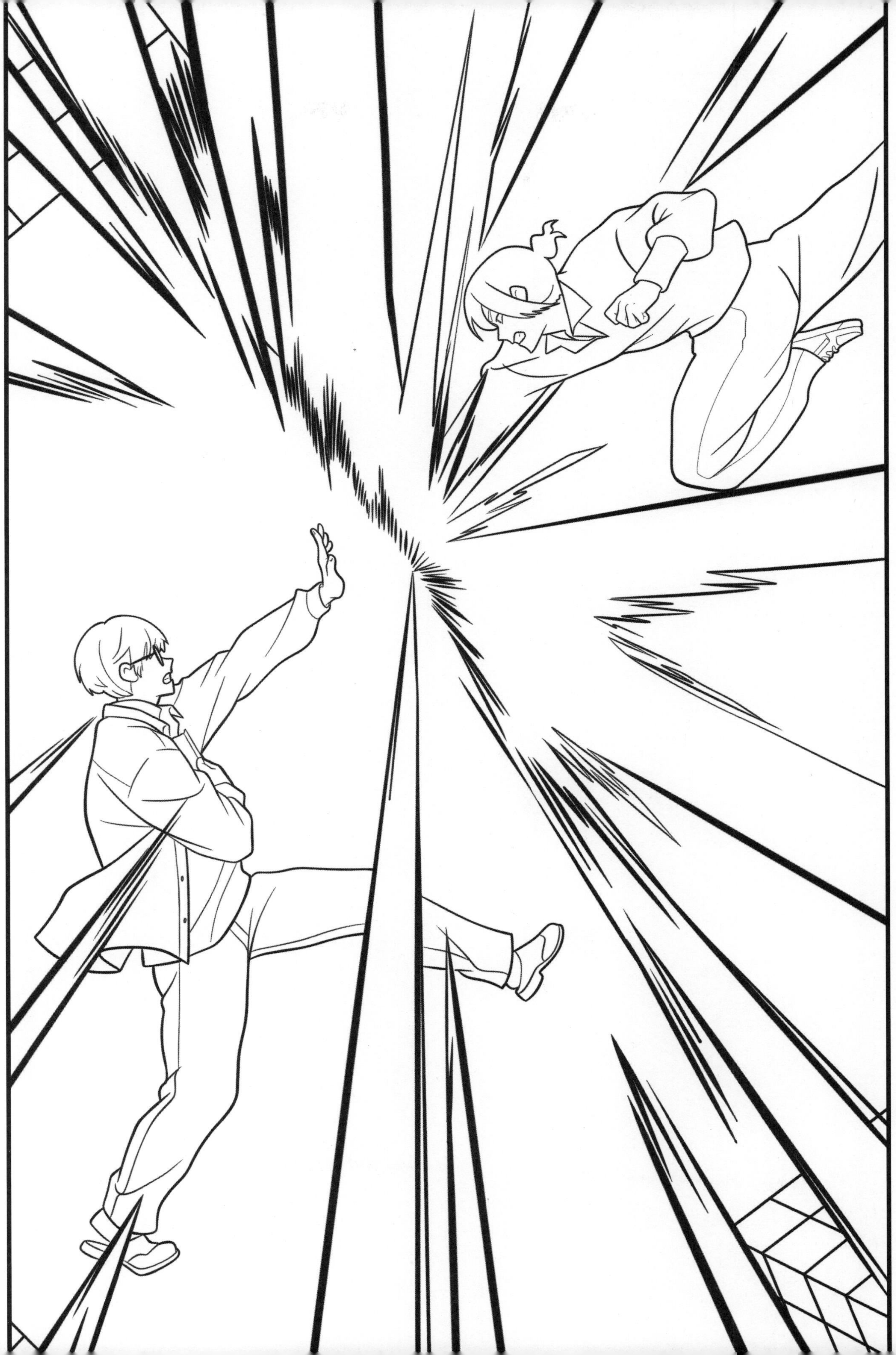

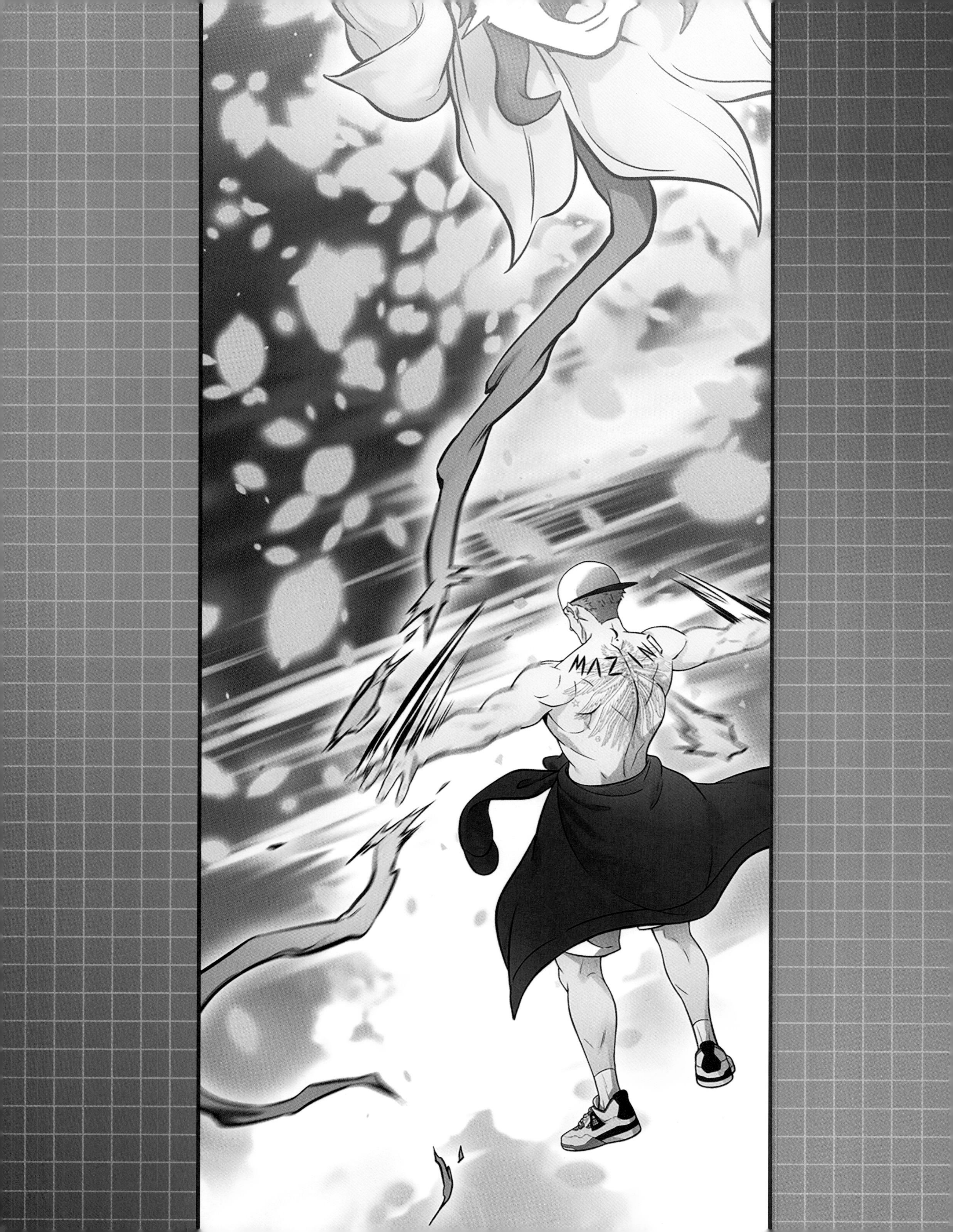

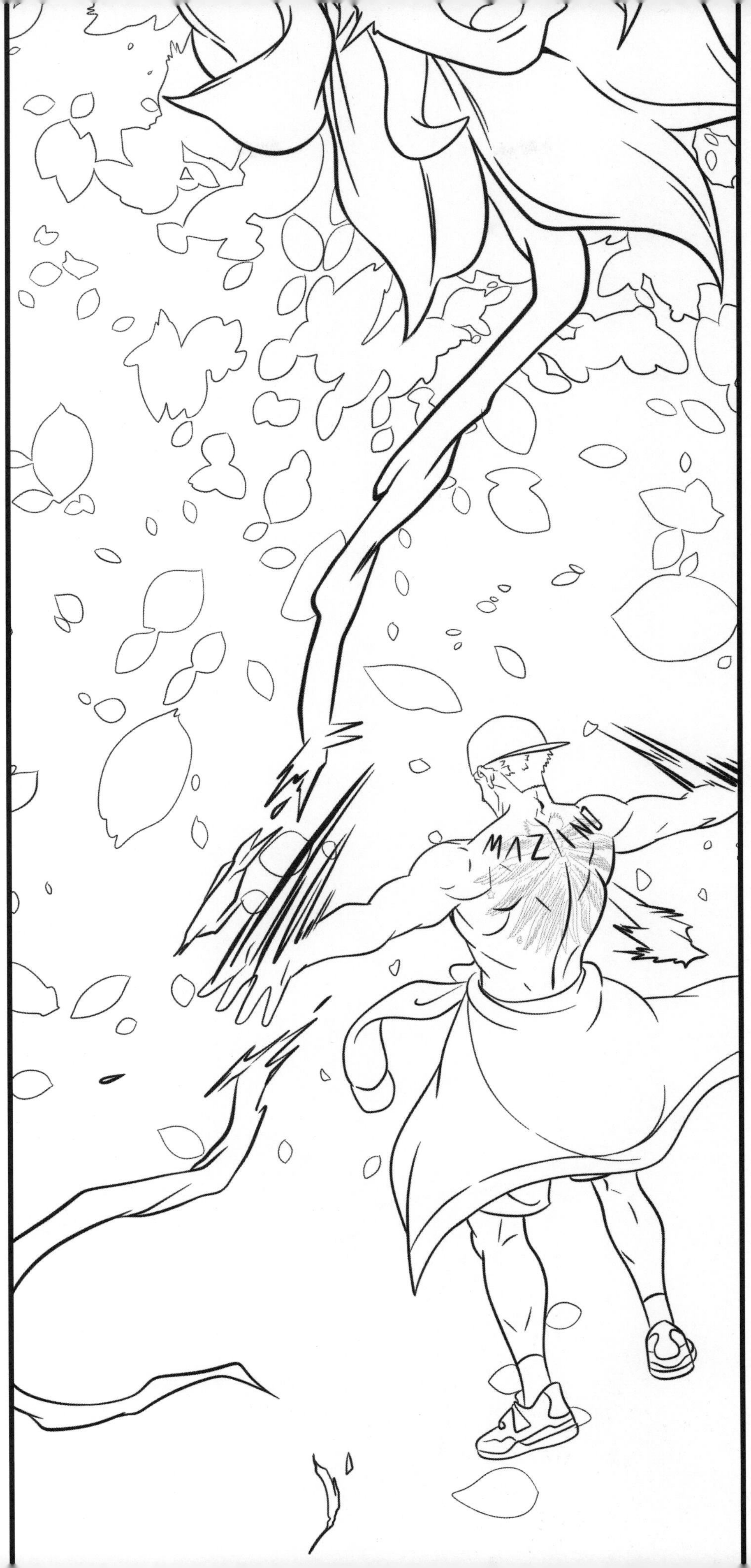
MAZINO

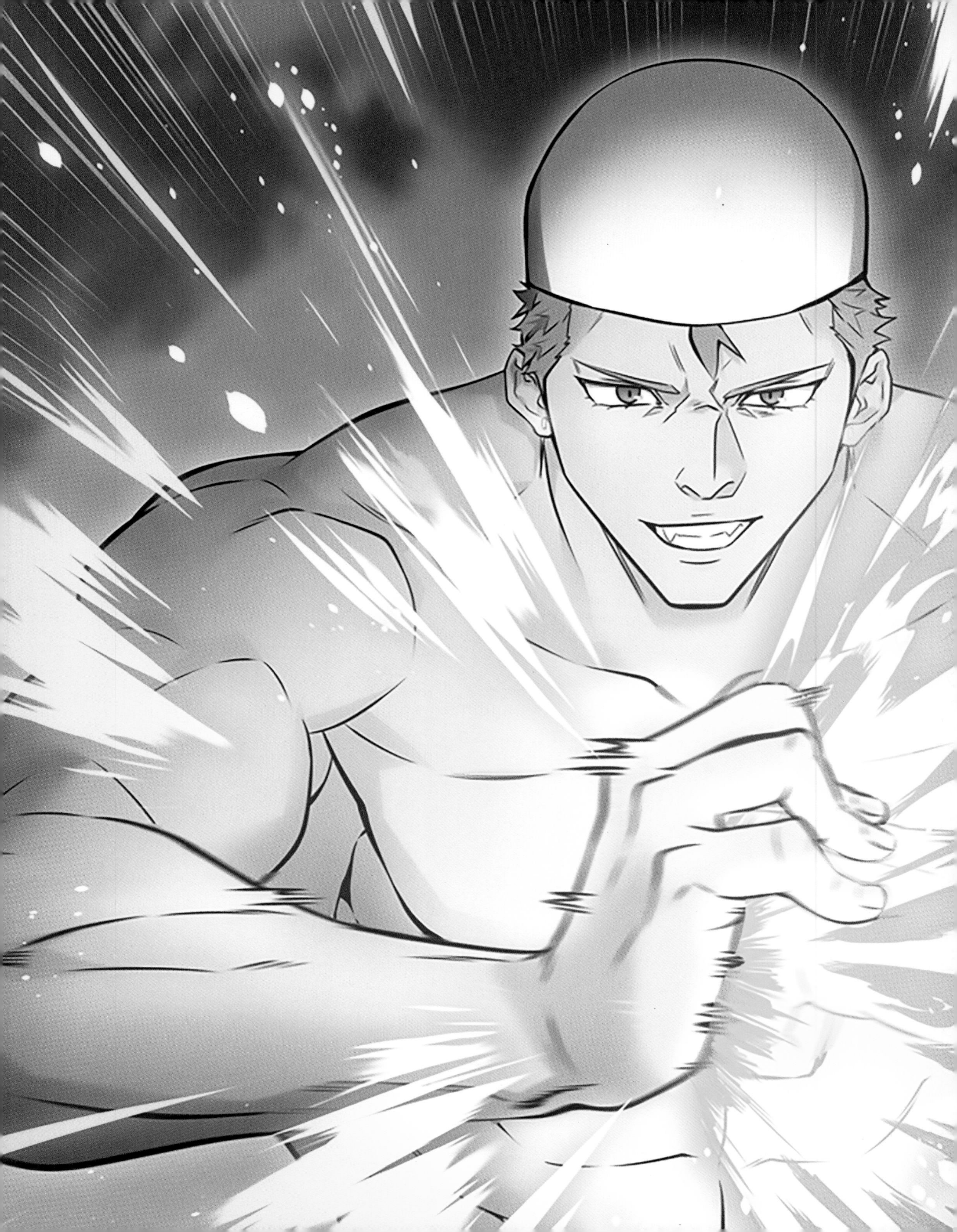

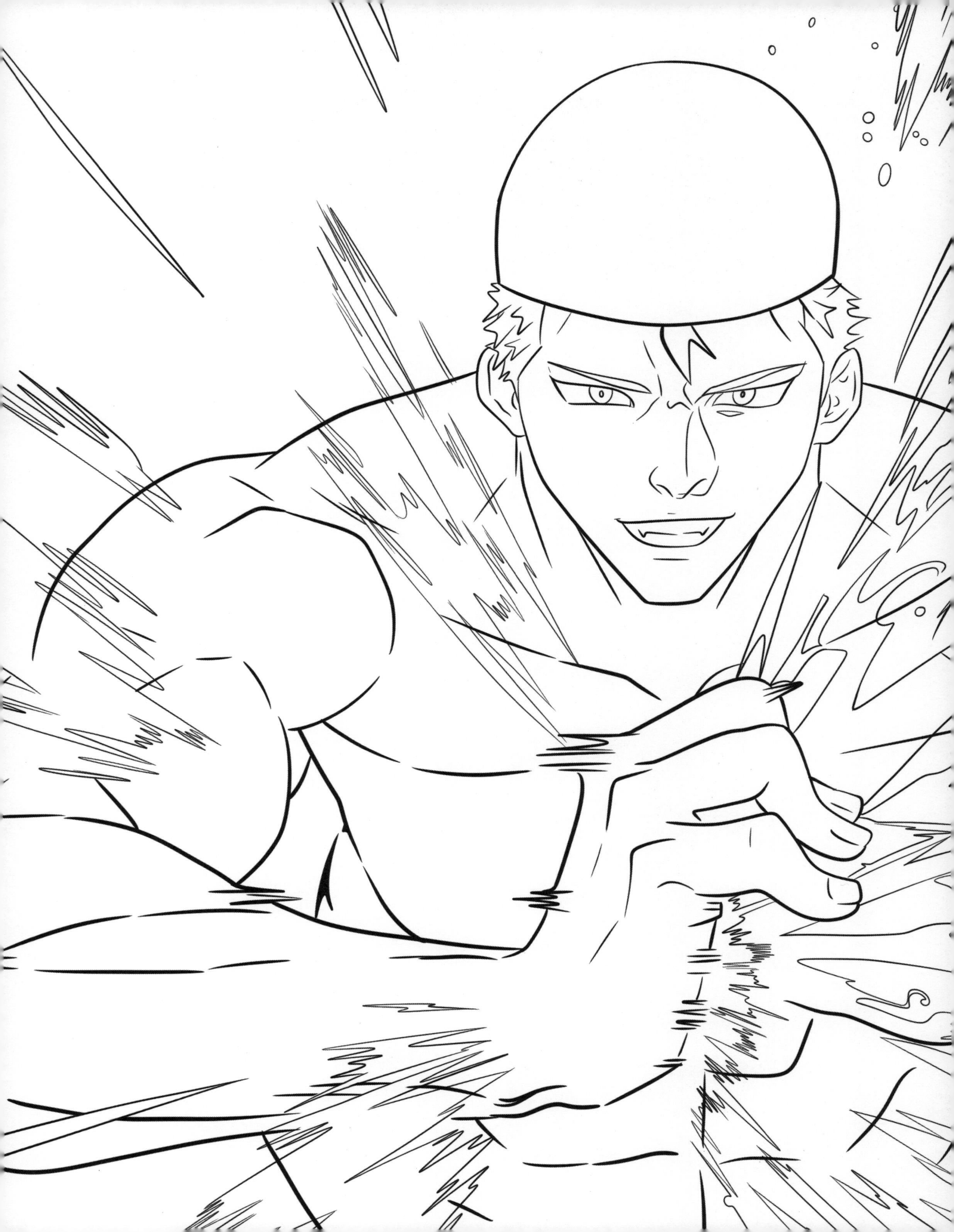

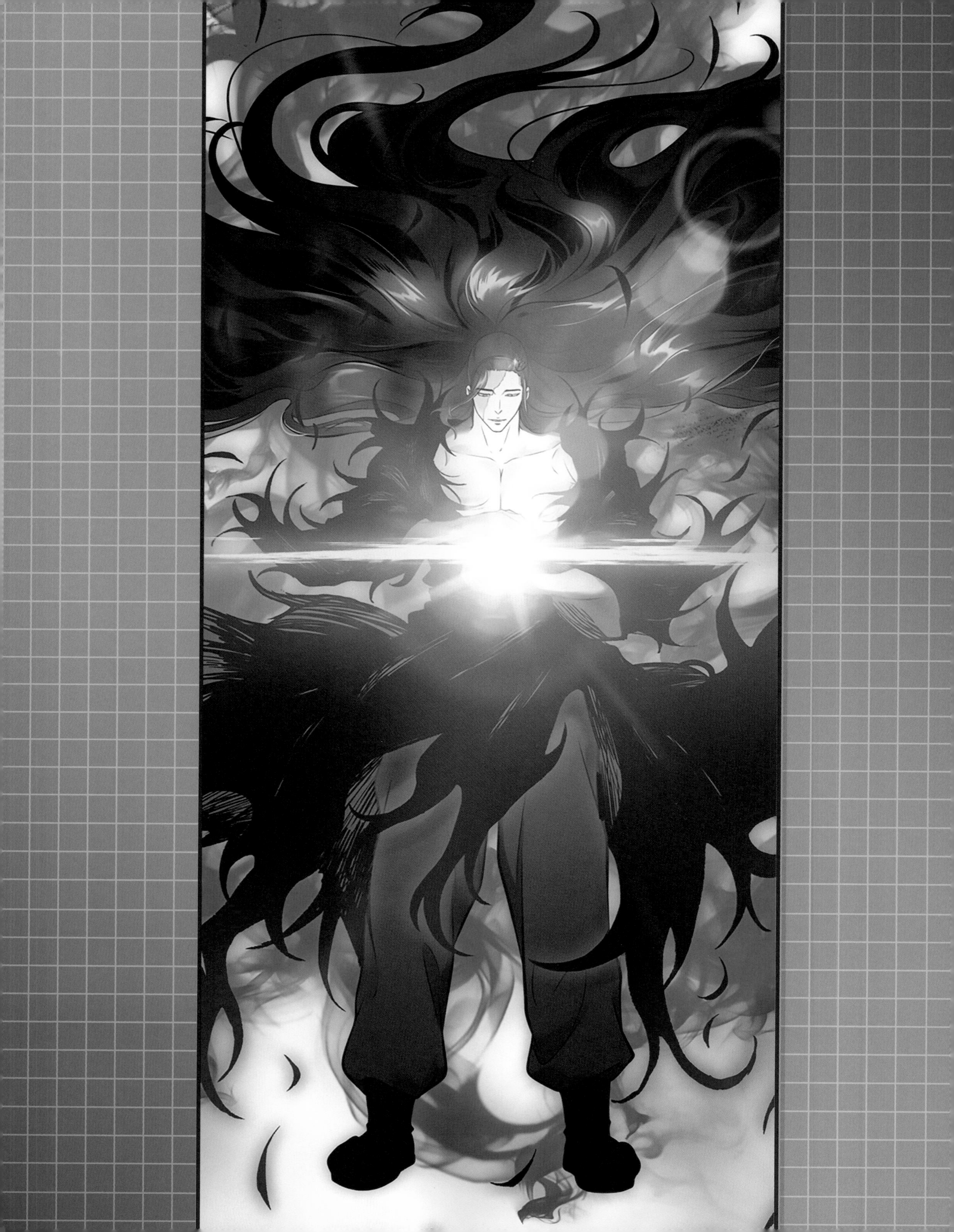

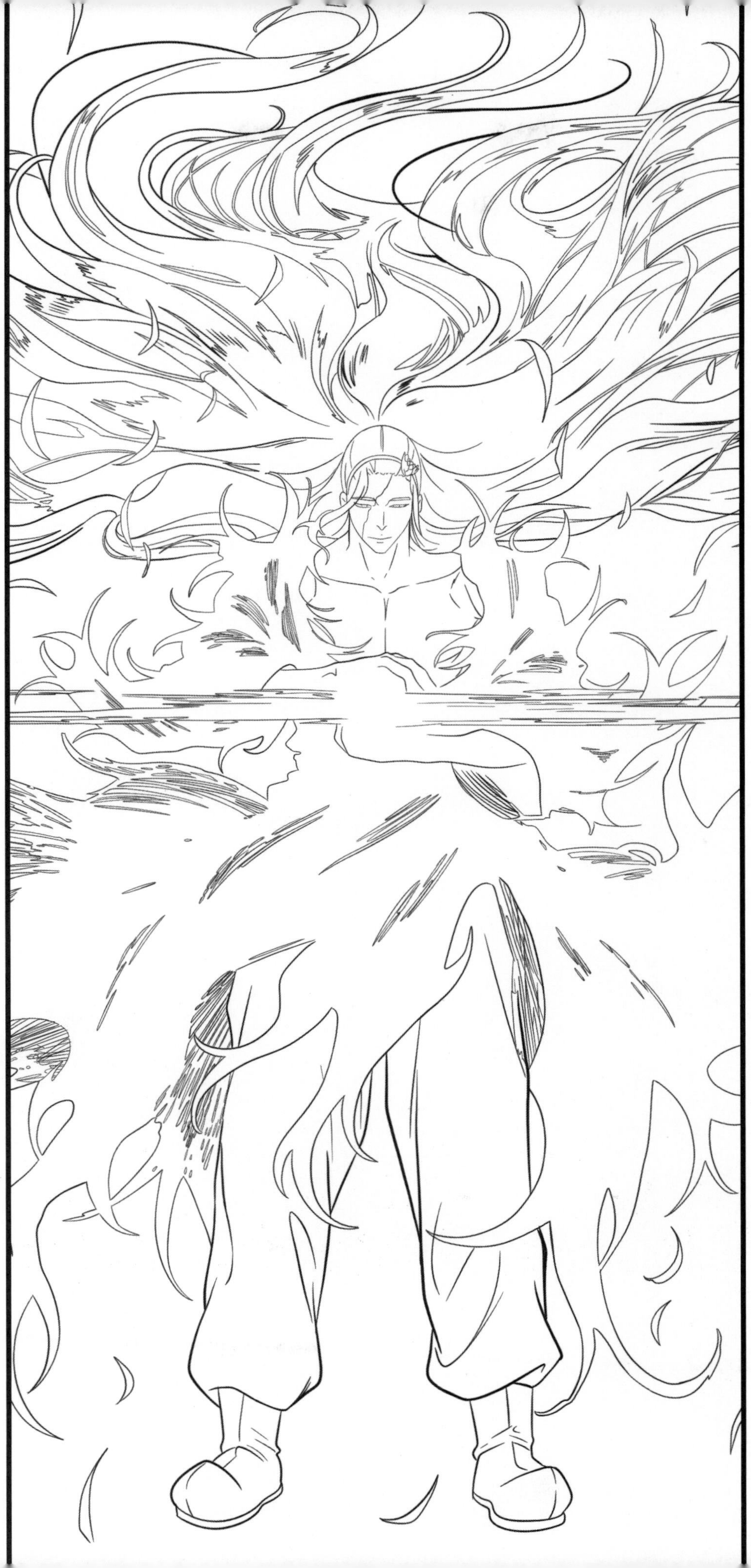

Quarto.com | WalterFoster.com

First Published in 2025 by Walter Foster Publishing, an imprint of The Quarto Group,
100 Cummings Center, Suite 265-D, Beverly, MA 01915, USA.
T (978) 282-9590 F (978) 283-2742

Walter Foster Publishing titles are also available at discount for retail, wholesale, promotional, and bulk purchase. For details, contact the Special Sales Manager by email at specialsales@quarto.com or by mail at The Quarto Group, Attn: Special Sales Manager, 100 Cummings Center, Suite 265-D, Beverly, MA 01915, USA.

10 9 8 7 6 5 4 3 2 1

ISBN: 978-0-7603-8972-0

Line art: Ryan Axxel
Design, layout, and editorial: Christopher Bohn and Coffee Cup Creative LLC
WEBTOON Rights and Licensing Manager: Amanda Chen

Printed in China

ABOUT THE CREATOR

Tower of God writer and illustrator Lee Jong-hui, who publishes Tower of God under the pen name **S.I.U.** (Slave. In. Utero.), majored in visual arts education at the university level before being conscripted into the military. Under the suggestion of a senior army official, **S.I.U.** started drawing cartoons. During this period, **S.I.U.** drew ten "books" worth of practice cartoons, which formed the backbone for the Tower of God comic he later created for the internet. He loves soccer and the sea. Many of his characters' names are inspired by soccer players, and he integrates aquatic themes into his stories.

For more from S.I.U., check out:
refrainbow.com
Instagram @official.tower.of.god